BY
ALEXANDER GORDON SMITH

THE DEVIL'S ENGINE

HELLFIGHTERS

THE
DEVIL'S
ENGINE

HELLF

FARRAR STRAUS GIROUX
NEW YORK

GHTERS

ALEXANDER GORDON SMITH

Farrar Straus Giroux Books for Young Readers
An imprint of Macmillan Publishing Group, LLC
175 Fifth Avenue, New York 10010

1 3 5 7 9 10 8 6 4 2

fiercereads.com

Library of Congress Cataloging-in-Publication Data

Names: Smith, Alexander Gordon, 1979– author.
Title: The Devil's Engine : Hellfighters / Alexander Gordon Smith.
Other titles: Hellfighters
Description: First edition. | New York : Farrar Straus Giroux, 2016. |
    Series: The Devil's Engine : 2 | Summary: "Fifteen-year-old Marlow
    understands that their former leader must be stopped from using the
    two Devil's Engines in his control to open the gates of hell—something
    he cannot do until he discovers the location of a mythical third machine.
    Marlow and Pan must take up this deadly duel with an all-powerful
    enemy that seems utterly impossible to win"—Provided by publisher.
Identifiers: LCCN 2016006938 (print) | LCCN 2016032243 (ebook) |
    ISBN 9780374301729 (hardcover) | ISBN 9780374301736 (ebook)
Subjects: | CYAC: Science fiction. | Demonology—Fiction. | Monsters—
    Fiction. | Horror stories.
Classification: LCC PZ7.S6423 Df 2016 (print) | LCC PZ7.S6423
    (ebook) | DDC [Fic]—dc23
LC record available at https://lccn.loc.gov/2016006938

Our books may be purchased in bulk for promotional, educational, or
business use. Please contact your local bookseller or Macmillan Corporate
and Premium Sales Department at (800) 221-7945, ext. 5442, or by e-mail
at MacmillanSpecialMarkets@macmillan.com.

*To Elspeth
(we know your name now).
Welcome to the family!*

PART I

INSTIGATION

KEEP GOING

Her foster mom had always said that hell was a place you walked to on your own two feet.

It wasn't a lake of fire; it wasn't some fairy-tale land where sinners broiled in their own remorse, poked at by devils. No, it was just where you ended up when you went too far in the wrong direction, when you were too stubborn or too stupid to turn back, to admit you were wrong.

Hell was *right here*, and she was about to walk in through the front door.

Amelia stepped into the road, into the flashing neon lights reflected in the rain-slicked asphalt. The reflections blazed orange and yellow, like flames, but she was shivering as she bolted to the far sidewalk, to the building that sat there. It was a run-down walk-up, hunched against the night like a sleeping beast. The door was red. Bright red. It didn't belong here, the way that nothing belonged here, the way that *she* didn't belong here. She reached out for it and paused, the rain a cold mist that played with her fingers. From somewhere above her came a noise, something that was half shout and half scream. It was cut off with a dull thud, then silence again, like the building was trying to lure her in.

She swallowed and glanced back over her shoulder at the

street, at the lights of Astoria behind her. It was nearly eleven. Her mom wouldn't even know she was missing until the morning. She could sneak back home, curl up under her blankets. Sure, home wasn't heaven or anything, but at least her mom cared.

But *he* was here.

Sniffing against the cold, Amelia turned back to that big red door and pushed gently. It swung open like a crocodile's jaw, too easy, too eager. Inside was a lobby drenched in sulfurous yellow light, mailboxes to one side, a fire extinguisher to the other. A narrow hallway led into darkness, stairs visible at the end of it.

Something detonated with a soft thump, like a distant explosion, and the whole building swayed. Amelia rocked back and forth, and for a moment she understood that she wasn't really here, that she was somewhere else. The lights flickered, the building settled, and suddenly she wasn't alone.

"I knew you'd come."

He stood in the lobby, his eyes gleaming shards of obsidian.

Her stomach lurched like a startled animal, like it meant to bolt right out through her skin. He smoothed his hair back and smiled, holding out his hand. A gold ring glinted in the artificial light, winking at her.

Hell was a place you could get to only on your own two feet, and she used them now, walking toward him as confidently as she could. He opened his arms, slowly, and she thought of a bear trap being set up to spring. The building rocked again, swaying from side to side as if the world was trying to shake her from its back. Then the floor seemed to tilt downward and she slipped, sliding into him. His hands snapped shut around her neck, crushing, choking, and she screamed.

"You're mine now," he said, his lips against her ear. And the rush of panic that roared through her was like standing in the path of a subway train. She fought him, slapping her hands against his shoulders, but he was an engine of stone and steel, his arms ratcheting tight around her throat.

You're not here, she heard herself say, but the fear was as real as it had ever been. He was going to kill her. Why had she listened to him? Why had she agreed to meet him? Nobody even knew where she was. Nobody would know where to look for her.

She opened her mouth, sought the flesh of his chest, clamped her teeth down. This time he was the one who screamed, and he pushed her away, his face warped by fury. She staggered back, spitting out the wet taste of copper. She wasn't in the lobby anymore, she was inside his apartment. Candles burned, the air was thick with cigarette smoke and something sweeter. Then he was on her, charging like a bull, blood spilling from the open mouth she'd left in his chest.

Hell was a place you walked to on your own two feet. She ducked beneath his sweeping arms, pushed through the ugly smell of him. There was a lamp beside his bed, big and gray. It didn't have a shade, just a dead bulb. She reached for it without thinking, knowing that there was nothing she could do to stop herself, knowing that this had already happened. She might as well try to stop the sun from rising.

"Get—"

It was all he had time to say before she turned, swinging the lamp like a bat. It was almost too heavy for her to lift, but once it was moving she didn't have to do anything, she let momentum work for her. He was running too fast to stop, so blinded by rage that he didn't even see it. They met like colliding trains—

thunk

5

—the base of the lamp a wrecking ball that stopped him in his tracks—

thunk

—and dropped him to the floor as if he had never truly been alive—

thunkthud

—as if he were a puppet stuffed with sand and sawdust, strings snapped.

Thunkthud

—she watched the lamp hit and she watched him fall, again and again and again—

thunkthud, thunkthud, thunkthud, thunkthud

—she would be watching it forever—

thunkthud, thunkthud, thunkthud, thunkthud.

This was hell, after all. She'd walked here on her own two feet.

Thunkthud, thunkthud, thunkthud, thunkthud.

"Hey."

The room disintegrated, rocked into rubble and dust. Pan rose from it so fast that she couldn't even scream, burning into darkness like a rocket ship. She sat up, her heart rattling like a tired old motor, trying to open eyes that felt as if they'd been glued shut. Something impossibly hot but icy cold tingled at the ends of her fingers, the air full of the smell of electrical charge.

"Whoa! Pan!"

The world tumbled back into place and she blinked at it, her mouth gaping. Truck was right in front of her, the big guy's bald head gleaming in the light from the train car. He was holding her shoulders with the strength of a bear. She tried to speak, found that she couldn't, like that part of her brain had been left behind in the dream. Instead she lifted a hand, seeing brilliant blue sparks run back and forth between her blackened fingers like snakes of light, slithering into nothing.

"It's okay, kiddo," Truck said, holding on to her for a moment more before letting go. "Just a nightmare." The whole train seemed to rock as he sat back against the seat. He uttered a soft, almost subsonic laugh. "For a second there I thought you were gonna fry us all."

Pan flexed her fingers, shaking loose another handful of sparks. They drifted away, sputtering out on the floor. Truck was right to be afraid. If she'd lost control in her dream then she might have taken out the entire railcar.

It was the risk you took when you had the power of the devil inside you.

Just like that it came rushing back—everything, every scrap of her life, every single footstep on the road to hell. She saw the guy she'd killed when she was thirteen, back when her name had been Amelia, not Pan. She saw the cops, the cell, the promise that she'd be locked up for life. She saw Herc, the shambling old dude who'd padded through the door. He'd told her all about an army known as the Fist, all about the secretive guy in charge, Sheppel Ostheim. And he'd offered her a choice.

"Come fight for us," he'd said. "You're tough, you've got a good heart, you're a soldier, and right now we need people who can fight. Ostheim has given me permission to recruit, and I want you. Because there is a war raging as we speak. A war you'll never hear about on the news, you'll never read about in the papers. But this war, it will change the world. Change the world, or destroy it. Door number one, I leave you here and you take your chances in lockup on Rikers Island while you await your trial, and then a prison upstate once you're convicted. Door number two, come with me and save the world."

Door number two had led straight to the Engine.

She saw it now, that madness of moving parts buried deep beneath the streets of Europe. A machine that could not have been built by human hands, a machine that could rewrite the code of the universe and give you anything you asked for. Literally *anything*. She saw herself make her first deal—incredible strength and impossible speed—and felt the joy of it, the knowledge that she was more than human. And the terror that after 666 hours the deal would come to an end, and the Engine would send its demons to collect her soul.

Only the Lawyers kept her safe, the quantum mathematicians who broke into the Engine and cracked the code of the contract. Not that their success was guaranteed, of course. When you used the Engine, there was always a chance you would end up being dragged kicking and screaming into the flames.

Because that's where her foster mom had been wrong. Hell *was* real. Hell *was* a world of fire. And once they took you there, you'd be screaming for the rest of time.

"Pan?" Truck said, pulling her back. She glanced at him, tried to find a smile. When she couldn't, she turned her attention to the window. It was pitch black outside and her reflection stared back at her like a ghost. The train thumped forward on the tracks—*thunkthud, thunkthud, thunkthud*—carving through the night. The big guy sniffed, cleared his throat. "You sure you're okay?"

She snorted at the absurdity of the question. She had never been so far from okay. Her group, the Fist, had been all but wiped out. Their Engine—the only thing that gave them power—had been taken. Their Lawyers had been butchered, their other Engineers assassinated. Now the dark side in this war—a bunch of world-murdering bastards known as the Circulus Inferni—possessed not one but two Engines. Their leader, Mammon, was practically unstoppable. His goal wasn't just to win the war. He wanted to use the Engines to open up the gates to whoever created them. He wanted to bring the Devil back to Earth. It was only a matter of time before he worked out how to do it.

And now that the Circulus Inferni had both Engines they would be gunning for the Fist's last four Engineers—her, Marlow, Truck, and Night. And when they found them, there would be hell to pay.

"Where are we?" she said. Truck shrugged, staring at the black canvas of the window.

"No idea. Germany maybe. Europe is bigger than I thought it was."

He stretched, then turned to the shape curled up beside him. Night was fast asleep, almost lost in the folds of Truck's jacket. There was no sign of Marlow.

"I sent him to the café car," Truck said, patting his enormous stomach. "Haven't eaten in like forever."

"You ate five baguettes and all that disgusting liver spread back in Paris," Pan said. "That was a few hours ago. I don't think you're going to starve."

Truck grumbled something back but she ignored it, checking her watch. There was no time there, just a countdown. The sight of it made her blood swim cold, as if the night had leaked into her veins. *586:12:13:58*. Twenty-four days and change until her contract ran out and the demons came for her. Usually she wouldn't be concerned. Twenty-four days was enough time to crack half a dozen contracts. But with no Lawyers, and no Engine, she was powerless to escape. These could be her last twenty-four days on Earth, and what would come after was so, *so* much worse than death.

"How much longer till we hit Prague?" she asked.

"Few hours yet," Truck replied. "You might wanna grab some more shuteye."

Drop down into the past again, into that apartment, into the blood. *Thunkthud. Yeah, no thanks.*

"Nothing from Herc?"

Herc had been inside the Engine when the Circle had breached the door. He'd been the only one to make it out, but they hadn't heard from him since. *Please be alive.* She willed the thought out into the dark, hoping it would find him. *Please be okay.* Truck shook his head, a glimmer of worry passing across his poker face.

"Man, I wish Marlow would get a move on," he said. "I'm gonna waste away over here. You'll have to stop calling me Truck and start calling me, I don't know, Smart car. Or Scooter."

Despite everything, Pan almost smiled.

"Shut up, Scooter," she said.

She stood, stretching, hearing her joints pop like Bubble Wrap. The car was pretty empty, a handful of men and women in suits and a bunch of guys at the far end who'd been drunk and merry when they'd joined the train but who were now all fast asleep and snoring. A young guy two booths over looked up at her, smiling, and she threw a scowl back at him until he turned away.

"I'm gonna go stretch my legs," she said. "Going mad sitting here."

"Well, if you reach the food car grab me a Coke and a Snickers, yeah?" said Truck, shifting his weight. "Big one. Keep me going until Marlow gets back."

She threw him a tired smile. Her entire body ached—partly

from the battle in New York, partly because it's what the Engine did, drained you of everything other than what you had dealt for.

"You ever think maybe it's not the Engine you need to worry about, it's the cholesterol that will kill you?"

"We all got our demons," he said.

"Amen to that," she said, holding on to the back of her seat as the train rocked.

"Hey, kid," Truck called out. "You be careful out there. Don't go far. Never know what you might find."

Only she *did* know.

"Hell," she said.

"Huh?" said Truck.

"Nothing." She pushed away from the chair, set off for the car door.

Hell was out there.

And once again she was walking into it on her own two feet.

DEAD MAN WALKING

Marlow wasn't sure how it was possible to get lost on a train, but somehow he'd managed it.

He reached the end of yet another car, the door sliding open automatically. The train felt like it was going at three hundred miles an hour, bucking so hard that twice now he'd almost spilled into the laps of other passengers. He pushed through into the next car, scanning the handful of people there. Nobody looked familiar.

He was positive he'd set off against the direction of travel. But he'd reached the end of the train with no sign of a café car, and now that he'd doubled back it felt like he'd come too far. But he would have noticed if he'd passed the others, wouldn't he?

Bracing himself against the restroom cubicle, he scrunched his eyes closed and rubbed them with his fingers. *Christ*, he was tired. Everything still ached from the battle in New York. His body felt like it had gone through a meat grinder then been fed to a pack of dogs. Not to mention the fact that the Engine was still sapping every ounce of energy that wasn't being used to fuel his powers.

He opened the restroom door and stepped inside, the over-zealous air freshener punching him in the nostrils. The face that stared back at him from the graffiti-etched mirror was a corpse's—too gaunt, too bruised. It was like he'd been buried for a month before clawing up from his grave.

Dead man walking.

Which wasn't too far from the truth, was it?

He didn't even know how he'd ended up here, a soldier in a secret war. It didn't make any sense. His brother had been the hero—blown up while serving his country in the Marines. Danny had always been the brave one, the one who walked fearlessly toward chaos. Their mom had always made it clear that Marlow was nothing like his brother, that he didn't deserve to live under the same roof. And that was true, wasn't it? After all, here he was, hiding in the restroom and wishing he never had to leave.

He perched on the toilet, reaching for the metal sink and grasping it. He took a breath and then squeezed. The metal buckled like it was tinfoil, and when he pulled his hand away the imprint of his fingers was left, a sculpture in steel. He still had the powers the Engine had given him—the strength of ten men, the ability to run faster than sound—but for how much longer? The Circle would break his contract as soon as they could, then he'd have nothing. Mammon and his soldiers could crush him and the other Engineers as easily as a kid stamping on ants.

Not Pan, though. Pan had been promised a different fate. Her contract would be left to expire, and once that happened the demons would come for her.

That's the price you paid when you pissed off the bad guys.

The train lurched from side to side hard enough to crack his head off the wall. He grunted, bracing himself until the rocking calmed. A storm was brewing in his gut, but it wasn't as if there was anything left in there. He'd emptied himself out on the plane journey over. Plane *journeys*. They'd chartered a ride out of Pennsylvania, a tiny propeller plane that kicked like a rodeo bull and didn't have a restroom. They'd had to fork out another hundred bucks when they landed in Kentucky just for the cleanup. From there they'd taken another jet-prop to Chicago, then bought their way onto a cargo plane heading to Paris. Somewhere in those fourteen hours in the air Marlow was pretty sure he'd chucked up every major organ in his body.

The train wasn't much better, but at least they were on solid ground.

He stood up, took a leak while he was here, then washed his hands in the buckled sink. When he opened the door there was an old man waiting, tutting impatiently, and Marlow muttered an apology as he edged past him. He carried on walking the way he'd been going, wondering if he was going to hit the tail end of the train, if somehow his friends had just vanished. The thought of it, of being alone as he tore his way toward the dark heart of Europe, was enough to make him want to collapse into a seat and curl up tight.

He passed a young couple watching a TV show on an iPad, then a table with a family of three kids, all fast asleep. The next door slid open to let him through and he crossed between the cars. A woman was walking toward him and he stepped into an empty seat to let her pass, staring at the window. All it revealed was the reflection of the train interior, and his own miserable expression, but the bone-yellow face of the moon hung overhead, watching. He thought he could make out mountains there, too, lined up against the horizon. Their jagged mass made him think of the hulking wrecks of ruined ships.

"*Danke,*" the woman said.

"No problem," Marlow said. "I think."

He stepped through the next door. Up ahead was a group

of young men, maybe half a dozen of them sprawled over twice as many seats. They were drunk, and they were loud, and they were all wearing Bayern Munich soccer shirts. One of the guys, lying across a bank of seats, stuck his foot out to block the aisle. He fixed Marlow with dark, red-flecked eyes.

"Was ist das Passwort, Arschgesicht?"

Marlow kept his head down, sighing. He was too tired for this. He pushed against the guy's leg but his tormentor held firm. Another of the men hopped down from the table he'd been sitting on, swigging from a bottle. The whole car stank of alcohol.

"Passwort," the first man said.

"Look," said Marlow. "It's late, I'm tired. I—"

"Er ist ein Amerikan Dummkopf!" shouted another of the men, obviously delighted. They were all getting up now, crowding the aisle. Marlow flexed his fists, knowing that one blow could knock them clear through the wall of the train. So why was his heart machine-gunning in his chest?

The train rocked hard and Marlow lost his balance, lunging to the side and almost falling into the foot well. The men howled with laughter and one of them threw a bottle at him. It bounced off his hip and rolled on the floor, the last dregs of vodka glugging into the carpet.

"Hey, just leave it, yeah?" Marlow said. He looked back, wondering if he should just walk away. *Run* away. It was what he did best, after all. He'd spent his whole life running. If he took flight now he'd move faster than sound, he'd be at the other end of the car in less than the blink of an eye. He'd done enough fighting this week to last a lifetime, a hundred lifetimes, and with creatures infinitely worse than this group of drunken douche bags.

"Hosenscheisser," said one of the guys.

Marlow turned to them. The first guy was on his feet now and close, close enough that Marlow could smell his breath. The reek of it made his eyes water but there was something else there, something worse than the sting of alcohol. It smelled like bad eggs, like something rotting. His stomach rolled into a cramp and he pressed a hand to it, grimacing.

"You really don't want to do this," Marlow said. "You have no idea."

He wondered if they would understand him, then the first guy smiled, smoothing back long, greasy hair.

"Poor little American boy, lost in the woods," he said in a heavy accent. His hands snapped out and caught Marlow in the chest, driving him back. One of the other guys was scrabbling over the back of the chairs, leaping to the floor behind Marlow, penning him in.

"*Mach es*," the guy said.

"*Ja!*" said another guy. "*Er hat es verdient, die Arschgeige.*"

"Ass violin?" came a voice from behind the group, one that was beautifully familiar. "Did you seriously just call him an *ass violin?*"

The men twisted around, and in the gap between them Marlow caught sight of Pan. She was leaning against a seat, so exhausted she could have been a hundred years old. But the relief of seeing her still made him feel like a kid whose mom has shown up just as he's about to get his head dunked in the can.

She said something else but it was drowned out by a serenade of wolf whistles from the other members of the group. They were shuffling toward her like the walking dead. Pan rolled her eyes and looked at Marlow.

"You really know how to make friends," she said.

"Hey," he replied, shrugging. "What can I say? I'm a popular guy."

"Die Klappe halten!" said the first guy, jabbing a finger at Marlow. "You shut it right up if you know what is good for you."

There it was again, that stench of moldering food, of burning. It was enough to make him gag, and Pan must have smelled it, too, because she put a hand to her mouth.

"Jesus," he heard her say. "What the hell is that?"

The first guy lunged at Pan, grabbing her free hand.

Bad idea.

"Hey, baby—" was all he had time to say before Pan let loose a short blast of electrostatic energy from her fingers. An explosion of light and a pistol shot rocked the train, and the guy thumped into the roof like he'd stuck a fork into a power outlet. He landed on the back of a seat, then flopped onto the floor, his whole body spasming. He farted loudly, the smell filling the car and making Marlow's eyes water.

"Now that's what I call an ass violin," Pan said. "Anyone else?"

The guys were spilling back into their seats, gibbering like idiots. Pan just yawned, shaking the last of the charge from her fingers. Every light in the car was in a tizz, sparks raining down.

"Schwein!" yelled one of the men. He looked like he was about to charge at Pan, so Marlow placed a hand on his shoulder and flicked gently, like he was swiping his fingers over an iPad. The man slammed into the window hard enough to crack it, falling to the floor with a groan.

The four remaining guys were panicking, caught between him and Pan. The lights flickered off, the world outside etched in moonlight, perfectly visible. A second later they burned on again, trapping the car inside its own reflection. Marlow ducked into a seat, held out his hand.

"Go on," he said. "Just leave it, yeah? Just go."

The train rocked on, oblivious, and the window cracked

further. A jagged scar splintered it from corner to corner, and the car filled with the deafening whistle of the wind. Marlow looked at it, studying the reflection of the men in the dark glass. Five of them, huddled in a group like frightened dogs.

Five of them?

That stench again, rolling through the car like the train had just plowed into a garbage dump. Marlow clutched at his mouth, pinching his nose. He looked at the men, holding up their hands in surrender. Four of them, standing right there in front of him. Then he turned to the window to see that fifth face, as faint as a phantom's until the lights cut out.

Not a reflection. It was somebody on the other side of the glass.

Somebody clinging to the side of the train.

Somebody grinning right at him.

The world flipped in a sickening twist of vertigo and he screamed Pan's name, pointing. The lights strobed, turning the world into chaos, a mirror maze gone mad. Pan followed his finger, and he saw the moment she understood, saw the expression on her face morph from tiredness to uncertainty to panic to full-blown terror—all in the space of a single heartbeat. She opened her mouth, but only a groan spilled out, low and awful. She didn't need to speak, though. He knew exactly what she was thinking.

They've found us.

UNDERSTATEMENT OF THE CENTURY

It had happened.

The Circle had found them.

Pan barely had time to acknowledge the grinning face at the window before it moved, *fast*. She saw a hand draw back, something glinting against the distant mountains. The same hand jabbed forward like a snake, puncturing the broken window.

She didn't understand what happened next, because what happened next was impossible.

The window stretched into the car, the glass bending like it was molten. Where the tip of the knife was it began to change shape, the point morphing into a snout, the glass beneath fracturing into a mouth, edged with gleaming teeth. It was as if a bear were pushing itself through the window. The translucent face uttered a bestial howl and Pan fell back against the seat, her legs no longer strong enough to hold her.

Whatever it was, it kept coming, a hand shattering free, swiping through the air and turning one chair to splinters and foam. It grabbed at another seat, trying to haul itself into the train. The glass formed shoulders, then a torso, ripping itself from the frame and filling the car with wind and thunder.

The drunken men were screaming, falling over themselves as they tried to escape. They weren't quick enough: the creature—*no, say its name, Pan, it's a demon, how could it be anything else?*—opened its jaws impossibly wide and lunged, clamping them shut around one guy's head. It sounded like somebody crunching an ice cube, and through the glass she saw his skull crushed like porcelain, an explosion of brain and bone. His body fell to the floor, twitching, gushing like a fountain.

"Pan!" It was Marlow, pushing against the tide of men as he tried to get to her. The demon glanced at him, dismissed him with a snort, then twisted its head to her. It had no eyes, and yet she could feel it studying her, trying to work out who she was. But it couldn't be here, it couldn't have come for her. She checked her watch. She had time, *she still had time.*

She lifted her other hand, feeling the electrostatic charge build up in every fiber of her body. The demon screeched, the sound primeval, and it threw itself at her, as big as a tiger, its glass body making it almost invisible as it shredded through chairs and tables.

She braced herself, forced the charge up her arm. Before she had a chance to fire, though, the demon exploded, detonating like it was packed with C-4. Shrapnel tore through the car and she threw up a hand to protect her face, crying out as glass embedded itself in her skin. When she looked again the demon was gone but a teenage girl was vaulting in through the missing window. The wind turned her short, red hair into a tornado, one that half concealed her face. But Pan still knew her.

The girl who'd been in Budapest with Patrick Rebarre, the enemy Engineer. The Circle had kidnapped Charlie, Marlow's friend, and dragged him to Europe, tried to use him as leverage to get Marlow to talk. And this girl had shot him in cold blood. It had been the beginning of the end—because Charlie had been working with the Circle all along.

The girl grinned.

"Thought you could hide from u—"

Pan opened her fist, the electrostatic charge like an unleashed dog. A fork of lightning crossed the car in a booming flash, hard enough to blow out another two windows. The girl was fast, though, twisting behind a chair. The charge blistered past her and caught the retreating men, lifting them up and tossing them down the car like they were rag dolls. Had Marlow been there, too?

No time to check. The redhead was back on her feet, a blade in one hand, that crap-eating grin plastered over her face.

"That all you got?" she said, then drove the knife into the top of the nearest table.

As soon as she pulled the blade free the table came to life, the surface folding like origami, one section splitting into a gaping maw while the legs wrenched themselves from the wall. It was another demon, made up of the table and a section of the train floor. It shook itself like a wet dog, its noseless face sniffing at the air. The train groaned in protest, the raging tracks visible through the hole the demon had left.

What the hell?

Pan fell back through the sliding door into the darkness between cars. The creature was there in a heartbeat, too big to fit, its snapping jaws loud enough to make her ears ring. Then, just like the last one, it blew apart in a hail of lethal pieces that threw Pan along the floor and into the door of the next car.

She groaned, shaking the blotches of light from her vision. She could hear screams behind her as the rest of the train caught on that something was wrong. The redheaded girl was marching leisurely down the aisle, using the tip of the blade to pick at a fingernail. She looked at Pan and shook her head.

"Finding you was too easy," she shouted over the howling wind. "Mammon knew exactly where you would be. He wants—"

The girl's head snapped forward and she dropped to her knees. Marlow was right behind her and he hit her again, driving her into the floor. He scooped her up and tossed her out the window like she was a bag of trash, dusting his hands off. Pan picked herself up, her flesh glinting with flecks of broken glass and steel.

"She won't be dead," she said as Marlow reached her. "And she won't be alone."

"How'd they find us?" he said, following her through the sliding door. The car was full of frightened faces, and the sight of Pan with her injuries didn't do much to calm them. She ignored the stares. They needed to get to Truck and Night, needed to get the hell off this train.

"Had to happen eventually," she said. "It's the Engine. Can't have it inside you without kicking out a homing beacon. Mammon probably didn't even have to look for us. As soon as we landed in Europe it would have been like a siren going off in his skull."

"So what do we do?"

She thumped past an old guy gesticulating at her and spouting French, walked through the next set of doors to see Truck right ahead. The big guy did the perfect double take when he saw her, hauling his massive bulk up from the seat.

"Ah, crap," he said. "Already?"

"Already," she replied. "Night, wake up."

Truck reached down and shook the girl gently until her head emerged from the coat, dark eyes blinking.

"Already?" she said in her Spanish accent.

"Yeah," said Pan. "That bitch from Budapest."

"Any others?" Night said as she hopped off the chair, as graceful as ever.

"Yeah," Pan said.

"What are we going to do?" Marlow asked, looking back, then out the window, then at her. "We've beaten them before, we can do it again."

Maybe, but something told her that Mammon wouldn't underestimate them twice.

"We crush ass," said Truck, slamming a fist into his palm with a dull slap. He frowned, stared at his hands. "Oh," he said.

"What?" Pan asked, but she already knew. Now that she was paying attention she saw that Truck looked different. Smaller, somehow. His skin looked healthier, more color in his eyes. "No, Truck. Don't you dare."

He thumped the window with his fist, grunting in pain. Then he looked down at Pan with an expression that belonged to a lost child.

"Circle cracked my contract," he said.

So he was the first. They could crack only one contract at a time, and each one might take days. It made sense to take Truck out of the game. His strength was legendary, and he was an experienced soldier, too. Pan swore beneath her breath. This was bad. Without his powers, Truck was about as useful against the Circle as a baby hippo against armed poachers. He'd be as vulnerable as any of the normals on the train.

"No," said Night, throwing herself on him, her arms not even making it halfway around his gut.

"Hide," Pan said. "They'll be coming for you, Truck. They'll know you won't be able to fight back."

"No way," he said. "I'm not leaving you guys, I'm not running. Can still knock some teeth out."

"Truck," said Night, letting go of him. "Don't argue. You can't win this one."

"Listen to her," Pan said.

"Screw you both," he said. "You're forgetting my other powers."

He lifted both hands and proceeded to extend his middle fingers, waggling them in front of Pan's face.

"Boom. Now what's the plan? We fight?"

She shook her head and opened her mouth to speak, only to be cut off as the sliding door opened and a crowd of people appeared in a surge of panic.

"Come on," she said. She didn't want to find out what they were running from. She squeezed a burst of crackling electricity up to the ceiling, holding the crowd by the door, then led the way down the aisle and into the next car. It was the restaurant car, half a dozen people eating a late dinner.

"You have to be kidding me," said Truck, aiming a scowl at Marlow. "You couldn't find the goddamned café in *the next car down?*"

"I went the wrong way!" Marlow protested.

"Not the time," Pan said. She spotted what she was looking for, pulling the emergency brake lever on the wall.

Nothing.

She tried again. Whatever happened next, it would be safer for everyone if the train wasn't moving. But the lever was useless. If anything, she thought, they seemed to be going even faster, plates and glasses juddering across tables and spilling to the floor. The diners were growing concerned, standing, crying out. Pan cursed again, pushing through the car until she reached the next emergency alarm. She pulled it hard enough to snap it free. Still nothing.

"They've got control of the train," she said.

"You serious?" asked Truck. He reached down and grabbed a handful of fries from an old man's plate. "It's an emergency," he spat as an explanation.

"Why?" asked Marlow, looking at her. He answered his own question. "They're going to crash it."

"What better way to kill a handful of Engineers?" she replied, setting off again. "We need to get to the driver."

She shouldered her way past the diners, all of whom were on their feet. One of them grabbed at her arm and she turned to see a middle-aged guy in an expensive suit. A younger woman—who could have been a *Sports Illustrated* swimsuit model—stood beside him, looking just about as sick with fear as anyone Pan had ever seen.

"*Qu'est-ce qui se passe?*" the man asked, his fingers gouging trenches in her flesh. She tugged loose, practically hissing at him.

The woman by his side doubled over, gagging, and the man turned his attention to her. All Pan wanted to do was keep walking but something about the woman rooted her to the spot. She sounded like she was choking, and when she straightened up again there was a baseball-sized lump in her throat.

"Peekaboo."

The voice came from the woman, but not from her mouth. It sounded like it was being spoken from deep inside her throat, like a ventriloquist. She made a noise like a cat trying to cough up a hair ball. Her whole face was bulging, like something was

25

pushing against it from inside. Beads of blood were forming on her ballooning lips. The man in the suit staggered away, falling on his ass, and the woman lurched from the booth. More muffled words came from her ballooning throat: "I found you."

"Ah, jeez," said Pan, feeling the pins and needles in her arm as she prepared to unleash another charge. "This is gonna be bad."

Understatement of the century.

ONE FOR SORROW

The woman grabbed a handful of her own face and ripped it away, tossing the bloody mess onto her dinner plate, where it sat like a glistening steak.

Beneath was another face, a man's face, his grinning teeth the brightest thing in the world.

What the—

He lunged across the table, wrapping red-painted nails around Marlow's throat and squeezing. It was like being suddenly underwater, Marlow's lungs spasming so hard he thought his ribs were going to snap. The woman's skin was sloughing off as if the man were wearing a suit, the flesh beneath smeared with blood and dotted with tattoos. Panic drove Marlow's fist out before he even knew it, his knuckles ripping off another chunk of loose flesh. One of the woman's dead eyeballs rolled out and there was another beneath, burning with fury.

"Marlow," the thing mumbled, teeth pattering onto the table as new ones pushed through. "Mammon sends his—"

Something smashed into the creature's face with a sound like a cathedral bell. The pressure on Marlow's throat vanished and he clawed in a breath, reaching instinctively for the asthma inhaler he didn't have.

"Move!" yelled Truck, barging past Marlow, a fire extinguisher gripped in his hands. He drove it into the man's face, knocking him against the window, then again, and again, the sound of it making Marlow's stomach shrivel. When he pulled it free there was nothing left of the creature but a cowl of loose skin, drenched in blood.

"What was that?" Marlow said, still gasping for air.

"A Magpie," said Pan, pushing through the screaming crowd. She was trying not to show it but Marlow could see the fear there, in every movement. "The power to put yourself in some-body else's body. I don't know who first thought of it but it's just about the worst thing you can do."

"Good way to travel long distances, though," said Night, hopping along beside. "You can leapfrog continents, so long as there's somebody to leap into."

"So he's—" Marlow didn't even have time to finish the ques-tion before a man at the back of the restaurant car started choking, putting a hand to his bulging throat.

"Nope," said Pan. "They're really, *really* hard to kill. Come on."

She jogged through the door and Marlow followed, swallow-ing the fear down into his churning stomach. The whole train was in an uproar now, the aisles blocked with terrified passen-gers. Pan swore, grasping at her hair.

"This isn't going to work," she said. "Night, you think you can get up top?"

"Of the train?" she said, one eyebrow just about launching itself into orbit. "Sure, *de nada*."

"Get to the front, try to stop the train. We'll fight our way through and meet you there."

"I'll go with her," said Marlow before he could even think about it. "I can keep up."

Pan nodded, wiping a shaking hand over her mouth.

"Watch out for that redhead," she said. "I don't know what

kind of powers she traded for but I've never seen anyone be able to conjure demons like that. Never. Not even the Pentarchy."

Something roared in the railcar behind them, unleashing a current of screams. Pan glanced over Marlow's shoulder and he could see it in her eyes—not just fear but something else, something that sent a bolt of panic up Marlow's spine.

Resignation.

He reached out and grabbed her shoulders, careful not to squeeze too hard.

"Pan, we can do this," he said. "We *will* do this."

She offered him a weak smile, one that quickly took flight. She pushed him away, turning and plowing down the aisle.

"Just get to the front," she shouted back. "And if you can kill that bitch on the way then nobody is going to complain. Come on, Truck."

"Good luck," the big guy said, rolling after her with the gore-smeared fire extinguisher still gripped in his fingers.

"*Yo y tú, amigo,*" said Night, standing to one side and gesturing at a window. Marlow took one last look at Pan then jumped onto the seat, placing both hands on the glass and pushing gently. The pane exploded from its panel and the sudden rush and roar grabbed Marlow by the stomach and threatened to pull him out with it. He choked back a scream and grabbed the top of the window, his fingers squeezing the metal like it was dough. The world flashed past in shades of black and gray, too fast.

"I'm not sure if I can do this," he yelled, his words swallowed whole by the wind.

"It's easy," said Night, appearing by his side. She stretched, grabbing the side of the train and pulling herself up, vanishing in a flash. "Just don't look down."

He looked down.

Beneath him the ground seemed to thrash and churn as if it were an ocean. Even with the power of the Engine inside him he wasn't sure if he'd survive that fall. Maybe it would be better if he stayed inside the train? Yeah, Pan and Truck would need his help, he should *definitely* head back inside.

He heard the sound of the sliding door, looked down to see the Magpie stride into the car, peeling scraps of a stranger's face from his own. The man scanned the crowd then found Marlow, spitting out a slab of pink tongue before grinning.

Screw this.

Marlow braced his foot on the edge of the window and reached up, gouging a handhold in the roof of the train. Then Night's slender hands were wrapped around his, pulling him up. It was like being caught by a tornado, the strength of the wind unbelievable, making him slide along the smooth roof. He ducked down and rooted himself in place, tears turning Night into a blur.

"Come on," he thought she said, his ears full of thunder. "It's not far."

He blinked, staring past her to where the head of the train coiled into the mountains, everything painted silver by the light of the moon. How many cars? Four? Night turned and vanished as she broke into full speed.

It's not far.

Marlow lowered himself into a sprinter's start, took a deep breath of freezing air, then started to run. Instantly the world slowed into blissful stillness, the wind dropping to a breeze, the world sliding past like a lazy river. Night shuddered back into view, leaping onto the next car. Marlow followed, careful not to trip on the vents. He propelled himself over the gap, the rush of it almost enough to make him smile.

He landed, sliding on the smooth metal, and for a second he thought he was going off the side. He collapsed onto one knee and time snapped back on, full of fury, the wind so powerful it actually lifted him off the roof for a second. He punched downward with enough force to put a hole in the metal, clinging on until the vertigo had passed.

A voice behind him, whisper thin. He turned to see *her*, the redhead, two cars back. She wasn't holding a knife this time, she was holding a gun. A *big* gun.

Marlow pushed himself up, hearing the *crack crack crack* as she fired. He started to run again, the wind snatching the breath from his lungs. One bullet passed him, as slow as a paper plane, red hot. Then something caught him in the shoulder, not fast but relentless, burrowing into his skin.

He fell back into real time, landing hard, his shoulder on fire. The wind tried again to snatch him, dragging him toward the edge of the train, and he only just managed to stop himself tumbling over into death. He steadied himself, grabbed at his shoulder, and saw blood on his fingers.

I've been shot.

And even as the horror of it was sinking in he looked back, saw the girl leap over the gap between cars, saw her aim her gun and fire.

He rolled, trying to get back to the middle of the train. The bullet pinged off the roof, another searing just over his head. The coldness in his shoulder was fast becoming pain, the fingers of his right hand numbing—*ohcrapohcrapohcrap*—and she was still advancing, her hair a blazing pyre, her grin brighter than the moon. She leveled the gun again.

"Hey, *puta!*"

Night fizzed into view beside Marlow, waving her arms. Then she was gone again, the girl firing one more round into nothing. She chucked the gun, pulled out a knife, then lurched to one side like she'd been hit by an invisible sledgehammer.

Marlow clambered to his feet, tested his shoulder again. It was bleeding, but there was no entry wound. It had grazed him. He started running, back the way he'd come, gritting his teeth against the agony. The world slowed and he saw Night skid to a halt, spin around, then start back. The redhead was moving impossibly slowly, twisting the blade earthward, stabbing it toward the roof. Marlow saw that it was made of old metal. It reminded him of the bolts Pan had used in her crossbows.

He leaped the gap onto the next train car, running at the redhead from one direction while Night converged from the other. Night got there first, shoving the girl with everything she had. The redhead teetered back in slow motion and almost fell, managing to get one foot behind her to brace herself.

Then Marlow was there, skidding to a halt, the roar of the wind like a building had just exploded next to him. He punched, the redhead weaving out of the way with expert grace. She ducked under his arm and deflected Night's kick, twisting her body and planting a big black boot in Marlow's gut. He staggered back, wheezing. The redhead crunched an elbow into Night's neck then started to drive her toward the side of the train.

"No!" Marlow yelled, throwing himself at the redhead, unleashing a punch. She saw it coming, jabbing out her other elbow so that Marlow's fingers crunched into it. He cried out, feeling like he'd plunged his knuckles into broken glass. Then that same elbow connected with his nose, once, twice, in an explosion of light and agony, another kick lifting him off the roof. The wind got under him, tossing him down the train car like he was made of paper.

He didn't stop for long enough to let the pain in, running

back the way he'd come, fast, fast enough to slow time again. Night was teetering on the edge now, almost over, and Marlow lashed out with everything he had, feeling the whole force of time as it crunched back to normal, all that power clenched inside his fist. It struck the side of the girl's head like a cannonball and she dropped, rolling into the wind. Marlow used his momentum, stamping hard. She wormed back, his foot leaving a crater in the roof where her head had been. Then she flipped, landing on her haunches, the blade still gripped in her fingers.

"You guys just don't get it, do you?" she said, shaking blood from her nose, from her mouth. She looked groggy, but she was still smiling. The Engine was already starting to heal her. "It's over."

Then she plunged the knife into the roof, and all hell broke loose.

ABOMINATION

There really was no accounting for how goddamned *stupid* people could be.

Pan had given up trying to push the other passengers out of the way and now Truck was taking the lead, crunching down the aisle like an icebreaker. People were scrambling to avoid him, but there was still a crowd up ahead as the passengers stampeded away from danger. The train was going faster than ever, each curve in the track making the car snap back and forth like a toy shaken by a kid.

"Move!" roared Truck, brandishing his fire extinguisher. He was right, he didn't need his powers to be intimidating, he was the toughest guy she knew even outside of the Engine—a lifetime of bareknuckle boxing would do that. But he was flagging already, one trembling hand resting on the top of each seat, the other struggling with the weight of his makeshift weapon. He looked so *human*.

She glanced back, two dozen more people crammed right up against her, the whites of their eyes like the crests of waves. In the shifting gaps between them she thought she saw the Magpie at the far end of the car but she couldn't be sure. Truck had stopped and the tide was crushing her, the stink of fear and body odor making her feel like she was drowning in flesh.

"Goddammit, Truck, go!" she yelled.

"Go where?" he replied. "There's a bottleneck."

Above the screams she could hear another voice, somebody calling her name. She looked back again, that bloodied face even closer than before, staring at her. She lifted her hand, ripples of light darting between her fingers.

She shunted the person behind her to the side, another couple of people jumping out of the aisle to avoid her. He was right there, a guy a little older than her, every inch of his body tattooed, dressed in the scraps of skin and cloth that was all that remained of whoever he'd leaped into. He flicked his fingers, spraying blood and fingernails, then charged.

Pan opened her hands, both of them, lightning burning out of her with such power that she felt like she was being turned inside out. She had to close her eyes against it, worried that it would burn out her retinas. When she opened them again the aisle was empty, the chairs reduced to sculptures of molten metal and smoldering cloth. The smell of cooked flesh hung in the air and she gagged at what it meant.

Lose a life to save a million, she quoted Herc, blinking away tears. *It's the only way.*

And even as she thought it she saw the Magpie appear behind a mangled chair, his skin pocked with burns—that dead man's grin still there, like he was a painted doll. She tried to will another burst of charge but she'd burned herself out, there was nothing left inside. She clenched her fists, her jaw. Let him come. That was the thing about wishing to travel into somebody else's body, the contract was so complicated that you couldn't wish for anything else alongside it. She could take him.

He took a step toward her, the train rocking so hard that for a moment she thought it had come off the tracks. His eyes never left hers. The exhaustion was a chain around her ankles, a noose around her neck. She could barely even raise her finger to goad him on.

"Come on, then," she said. "What are you waiting for?"

"Uh-uh," said Truck, planting a massive hand on her shoulder and pulling her out of the way. He stepped past, resting the fire extinguisher on a chair. "I got this. You find a way to stop the train."

"Truck—"

"Go!"

Pan paused for a moment more, long enough to rest a hand on his back. His skin was so hot, like he had burning coals beneath his shirt. She wasn't sure if she was trying to collect some of his strength, or just put the last of hers into him. Either way, she couldn't face the thought of letting go. He glanced at her, winked.

"I got this, kiddo," he said again. "Go."

She snatched her hand away and turned, gritting her teeth to keep a scream inside. She could barely see the people in front of her, they were just obstacles to be moved, and she punched and pushed her way through them until she got to the door, squeezing through into the next car. The tide here seemed to have turned, people pushing back the way they'd come.

Great.

It was easy to see why. Or . . . not *see* so much as *feel*. There was something wrong in here, something *bad*. It hit Pan right in the gut, like somebody had plunged cold, dead fingers into the squirming mass of her intestines and was scratching her spine with dirty nails. Pan gasped for breath, pushing farther into the sickness, into the evil, godforsaken *wrongness* of the car.

Then she was free of the crowd and the aisle lay ahead of her, suddenly quiet. The last person scampered out of the door and the screams became muted, like they belonged in another world. The car bucked to the side—nothing to do with its speed, everything to do with her failing equilibrium—and she sat on the edge of a seat to catch her breath.

It seemed like forever before she remembered how to stand. She started walking, feeling the air around her grow thick and hot, heavy with the stink of sulfur. Whatever was up there, it smelled like it had crawled right out of hell's backside.

Turn around, said her head. *Find another way out.*

But the train had to be going at 150 miles an hour, maybe more. She might survive, Marlow and Night, too—*might*—but Truck would be reduced to paste. She had to find the engine, had to find the brakes.

Just keep walking.

She did, reaching the end of the car just as the train plunged into a tunnel. Her ears popped with the change in pressure and she flexed her jaws until her hearing returned. Something was different about the train here. Parts of the walls had crumbled away, and in the gaps she thought she could see something pink. She ducked down, taking a closer look.

Bricks.

There was no doubt about it. There were bricks inside the train walls.

The connecting corridor was pitch black, the lights burned out, and she pushed through it into the next car. If the last one had been weird, this one was off the charts. Most of it was made up of bricks, the kind you'd find in a house. The window frames were half metal, half painted wood. Even as she watched, the floor seemed to alter its shape, carpet sinking away into asphalt. The seats were juddering like they didn't know what to do with themselves, like they wanted to run. The train was shaking even harder, every tremor making her bones ache.

She wanted to stop. Because if hell was a place you could get to only on your own two feet then why on earth would she keep walking?

Her body wasn't listening, carrying her down the aisle. A strange light seeped in through the next door, yellow and orange and red, and she walked toward it like a fish approaching a lure. Plaster dust was raining down from the ceiling, great cracks appearing there with wooden boards visible behind. Pan had the impression that she was walking through a theatrical set, that the whole thing was about to be pulled down around her.

She wiped the back of her hand over her nose, pressed on. The door wasn't a sliding one anymore—or at least half of it wasn't. The rest was wooden, and painted. She grabbed the handle, pushing until it opened fully. Beyond was something that simply couldn't be, but was. A street, the width of the train. The train car's ceiling had crumbled away in places, and through it fell a fine mist of rain. At the far end, where the door should be, was the bottom story of a building.

His building.

And Pan actually laughed with the relief of it. It was the building from her dream, the building in Queens where she had killed Christoph, the man who'd tried to take her as his own when she was thirteen. Which meant she was still asleep. Which meant that they hadn't been found.

She opened her mouth and laughed until tears streamed down her cheeks. She laughed even when she saw a man through the red door of the building, even when he opened it and stepped into the car. It wasn't Christoph this time.

It was Mammon.

The sight of him, even in this thing that had to be a dream, made her want to scream, made her want to throw herself into the night, into death. But it couldn't be. Not even *he* could warp reality like this, could he?

This isn't a dream, he said without opening his mouth. His eyes were closed, too, like he was sleepwalking.

"Sure," she said. "The train just turned into a building. Just like that."

So what was that worm of discomfort that had burrowed into her stomach? The train was still moving fast but it sounded like it was struggling. Through the sash windows she could see sparks flying up from every wheel, like there was a fireworks show out there. And she realized that it was the weight of the building, the train couldn't cope with it.

"This isn't real," she said.

You're wrong, was his answer, spoken right into the middle of her skull. *You are wrong about so much.*

"No," she replied, putting her hands to her ears. Above him, the building was growing. Bricks splintering out of nothing, stretching into the sky like plants. A neon sign was sprouting from the luggage rack, flickering wildly. The noise the train was making was like an erupting volcano. How long before the car crumpled under its own momentum, before they were all crushed?

Things could have been so different. They still can.

"No!" she said again. "You bastard, you've got what you wanted. You have both the Engines. Why are you here? Just leave us, the world's gonna end soon enough, right? Just leave us be."

No. Not until you see the truth.

She shook her head, the sobs hauling themselves out of her

so hard that her whole body was shaking. It was going to end here, she knew that much. Right here, on a New York City street that had appeared on a train in the middle of Europe. She didn't even know which country she was in. It was all going to end, every second of her life leading up to this point.

And then what? Then *they* would come for her. She was under contract and the demons would come, they would open up the ground beneath her feet and drag her into the fire. That would be her home until the end of time.

"Just do it," she said, or didn't say, her voice so faint it might have just been a breath.

You could have joined me.

"Why?" she said, wiping the tears away, furious with herself for crumbling. "Why would I do that? Why would anyone do that?"

Because things would be so much easier, he said. *So much better. You're wrong about everything.*

"Wrong about you breaking through the Red Door, about you killing everyone?" She spat out a bitter laugh. "How did that feel? Huh? Seth, he was an old man. How did it feel to kill him?"

Take one life to save a million, he said, like he had pulled the thought right out of her head. *They were wrong and they would not listen.*

"Not to you," she said. "Not in a million years. And I won't either."

She jabbed a finger at the man who couldn't really be there. Fear burned in every single cell of her being—so much of it that it had seared a hole right through her, had left her hollow. She was too frightened to feel afraid.

"Just do your worst, Mammon," she said, almost choking on his name. "Just do it. You know what? I don't care. Open the doors, let them in, watch the world burn. Make the most of it, because you know what? You know what, you son of a bitch? Someone will find a way. Not now, maybe not for a hundred years, but sooner or later somebody will kick your scrawny ass right back to where it came from, right back to hell. And I'll be there, Mammon. I'll be there waiting for you."

She laughed, a sound that belonged inside a madhouse, a sound that scared her. She felt like her body was a grenade, pin pulled, that any second now it would blast into a million parts. Only her anger was holding her together and she clung to it, clenched every muscle and just clung to it.

"I'll be waiting."

Mammon smiled. A soft, gentle smile, like somebody dreaming. Then his eyes opened, and it was as if a spotlight was shining through them, light pouring into the car like liquid, pooling on the floor. The sudden, shocking force of it made her stagger back, a hand to her face.

I see you, said Mammon.

The light burned brighter, hotter, louder. It was too much, *too much.*

I see the truth of you, came that voice again, like he was whispering into her ear. *So lost. So wrong. It isn't too late, Amelia.*

"No," she managed.

It isn't too late to change your mind, to come with me.

"No."

They are lying to you. It isn't too late to see how wrong you were, Amelia.

"Never."

Look at me, Amelia.

She shook her head, the light carving its way into her brain even through her closed eyelids, even through the flesh of her arm.

Amelia.

"Don't call me that!" She wasn't that girl anymore. She wasn't frightened little Amelia anymore.

Amelia.

So bright, so loud. She wasn't even sure that she still had a body. The force of him might have disintegrated her altogether, might have reduced her to dust and ash, scattered her to every corner of the Earth. He'd killed her, he'd ended her, he'd taken everything that she was.

Just like Christoph had, all those years ago.

"No," she said again. She reached deep down inside, into that sudden emptiness, and found a spark.

Amelia, all you have to do is listen to me, and trust me. It is not too late.

"I'm not Amelia, you asshole," she said.

She pulled her arm away from her face, opened her fingers, stared right at the abomination that stood before her.

"My name is Pan."

I know, Mammon said. *And I came here to help you.*

WHY IS THERE A HOUSE GROWING OUT OF THIS TRAIN?

The demon hauled itself into the world, shredding reality as it came.

It was like somebody had cut its shape from the train roof, the metal shearing loose into a structure of teeth and claws. Sparks detonated into the night as it tugged its bulk free—something halfway between a spider and a dog. It slipped on the metal, its back end falling into the car below, its huge claws gouging the roof for purchase. It had no eyes, but it didn't need them. Its elongated snout sniffed at the air, turned toward Marlow, and peeled open like a crocodile's. Then the demon lunged, faster than it looked, those jaws snapping shut so hard that they punched out a shock wave of air.

Marlow staggered back, colliding with Night. She grabbed hold of his arm, both of them trying to stay upright on the trembling train. The demon threw itself at them, scuttling on eight or nine legs. It had moved only a few feet, though, before it exploded with the force of a car bomb.

Behind it, the redhead was already plunging her blade into the next section of roof. Another demon was forming there, its birthing scream louder even than the roar of the wind. This one dropped inside the hole it crawled out of and Marlow could hear the cries from inside the train, could smell the slaughterhouse stench as it carved its way through whoever was down there.

"I got a million more," the redhead yelled, retreating toward the front of the train. "This knife opens a hole between worlds."

She ducked down and jammed the blade into the roof again. Inside the car there was a muffled detonation, the windows shattering as the second demon exploded. The next one was on the move, long and stick-insect thin, struggling on three needle-shaped legs. It lost purchase, slipping off the side of the train, its flailing limbs almost decapitating Marlow as it spun past into the darkness.

"How the hell is she doing that?" asked Night, her hand still on Marlow.

He shook his head. It was the wrong question. The right one was how were they supposed to get close enough to stop her?

The redhead spun the knife in her fingers. Past her, the engine barreled onward, visible a couple of cars ahead as it arced around a wide bend in the track. Marlow smudged the tears from his eyes, hunkered down closer to the roof. It had to be an illusion, but it looked like something was *growing* out of it. The car was changing, getting taller, sash windows appearing in its bulk. So many sparks were shooting from the wheels that it looked almost as if the train were a speedboat traveling on a lake of fire.

"Marlow," said Night, leaning in to him. "Why is there a house growing out of the front of this train?"

Not an illusion, then.

There was something else up there, too. Something beyond the impossible train. It looked like a darker patch of night, almost solid. Then he understood that it *was* solid. They were hurtling toward a mountain.

Right into a *tunnel*.

"Hey!" he called, waving his hands at the redhead. "You . . . uh. Nice wig, my mom has one just like it."

"What?" said Night. "A *wig*?"

The redhead was frowning but he wasn't sure if it was because she hadn't heard or hadn't understood. Either way, it was working. The pitch-black bulk of the mountain grew behind her, the mouth of the tunnel somehow even darker, like it had been cut right out of time and space.

Just a few seconds more.

"How do you keep it on in this wind?" he yelled. "Glue? Duct tape?"

The redhead yelled back, but her words were snatched away by the wind. She lifted the knife over her head, ready to plunge it down again. Behind her the tunnel mouth opened wide, the top surely low enough to rip her head clean off. Marlow grabbed the roof, sinking his fingers into the metal, bracing himself. Night must have seen it, too, because she swore, throwing herself onto her stomach.

The front of the train punched into the tunnel hard enough to demolish the top of the building that was growing there. It was enough of a warning, the redhead dropping without even looking back. Then they were sucked into the tunnel so hard and fast that Marlow's lungs locked, his whole body tight with panic. He couldn't even scream, just clenched his jaw so hard he thought his teeth might shatter. A few feet above his head the ceiling ripped by, light fixtures whumping past his ears like bullets.

Ahead, bathed in weak orange light, the redhead fumbled with the knife and thrust it up into the ceiling. She screamed, the speed of the train ripping the blade from her fingers. Not before another demon had crawled loose from the wound in the tunnel roof, though, this one as big as Truck and almost as ugly. It shook itself like a bear, its face made up of a chunk of concrete and rock and half of a light fixture—the yellow plastic cover looking almost like an eye.

It roared, pushing itself up, strong enough to tear pieces from the tunnel walls. Then they were sucked out into the night again, the pressure change like daggers in his ears. The bear demon charged at him on all fours.

Come on, Marlow thought, bracing himself. *Explode.*

It didn't. It bouldered over the gap between cars and then it was too late. Marlow started to run toward it, an instant of slow motion where he could see the demon's immense torso—made of rubble and concrete but as flexible as dough—and the way the ugly mess of its head seemed to open like it was hinged, the gaping darkness of its throat visible beyond. Then they collided, a tackle that shook every single bone in his body to dust.

The momentum of the demon spun Marlow around but he managed to keep his feet on the roof, his hands gripping fistfuls of stony flesh. He punched it once, not caring where, shrapnel exploding from his knuckles. It howled again, blasting Marlow with the stench of sulfur. He ducked under its jaws, felt a claw peel open the skin of his back. The pain was so intense it didn't feel real, and he launched an uppercut into the demon's chest, following it with a punch to the head. It teetered back, found its balance, started forward again, then blew itself into chunks.

Night hopped over the debris, reached his side, and together they looked toward the front of the train. The redhead stood there, glaring back at them. Then she glanced to the side, took a deep breath, and hurled herself into the darkness. Behind her the engine car was more distorted than ever—that same brick building seeming to grow up into the night. Even as he watched, Marlow saw a neon light flicker into life.

"This is really weird," he yelled above the roar of the wind.

"You *think?*" said Night. "Come on."

She set off, taking her time so as not to slip on the remains of the demons. The train seemed to be traveling faster than ever, tearing around another bend in the track. Marlow was leaping between cars when the wall of mountains to both sides gave way and the world opened up onto a vista of silver. There was an immense canyon right ahead, bathed in moonlight. Crossing it was a bridge that could have been the remains of a dragon—skeletal ribs and arches that must have stretched five hundred feet to the other side.

Speeding train. Bridge. Demons. Canyon.

Not a good combination.

He dug deep, broke into a sprint—everything but him slowing to a crawl. The locomotive was actually morphing, pieces of metal splintering into spinning fractal shapes before reassembling themselves into bricks and guttering. It was back to the height it had been when they'd entered the tunnel, and growing fast. Marlow could make out drywall, pipes, even a toilet in the shifting mass of its interior.

He was halfway down the penultimate car when a different force hit him—like a sledgehammer in the stomach. He faltered, skidding onto his knees and clutching himself. It felt like everything that made him *him* had suddenly festered inside, turned to rot. Night had stopped right next to him and the expression on her face said it all. He knew this feeling. He'd experienced it once before.

Back at his school.

Back when it had been destroyed.

"Mammon," he whispered. Night clenched her fists and kept moving, her body leaning into the wind. She reached the gap between the car and the engine—the *building*—and stopped.

Marlow growled against his terror, forced one foot forward, then another, until he was standing next to her. The building was close enough to touch. *Definitely* not an illusion. Those were real bricks, covered with real grime, daubed with real graffiti. The flickering neon light looked like it had been cut in half, reading *otel*.

"Hey, anytime you're ready."

Marlow glanced at Night, then nodded. He reached down and grabbed the edge of the roof, peeling it back like he was opening a sardine can. The car below was drenched in darkness, the only light coming from the sparking wheels. He thought he heard a voice down there.

Night hopped in, making no sound as she landed. He leaped after her, landing on a floor that had to be asphalt, wet with a rain that wasn't falling outside. Right ahead of them was the door to the next car, leading into the darkness of the connecting corridor. The squirming in Marlow's guts was worse than ever, and there was definitely somebody speaking.

Pan.

He pushed through the door, slipping on the wet asphalt. Through the final door the world was alight, bathed in illumination so bright that it might have burned right through his skull. He could make out a silhouette in the cold fire, one that looked Pan-shaped.

"That you guys?" somebody said behind him and he almost screamed. It was Truck, scrambling in from the car, that fire extinguisher still gripped in his hands. "This is really weird."

"Yeah, we got that," said Marlow, blinking spots of light from his vision.

"I think it's . . . I think she's in there with Mammon," Truck said.

"Yeah, we got that, too," Night said.

"We should probably go help," said Marlow.

"Yeah," Night replied. But nobody moved. Marlow glanced at her, then at Truck.

"Hey," the big guy said, shrugging. "I'm powerless, unless she's on fire."

"Mind if I borrow it?"

"Be my guest," said Truck, holding the extinguisher out.

Marlow took it. It was a poor weapon, especially against something like Mammon. But what else could he do? Taking a breath, he pushed through the door.

HANG ON

I came here to help you, Mammon said again.

"What?" Pan said, struggling to process the words. "Help who?"

And she would have said more except she felt the gust of wind as something passed her, something fast. Marlow fizzed into view next to Mammon, screaming, a fire extinguisher clenched in his fists.

"Wait!" she yelled, but before the word was out of her mouth Marlow drove himself into Mammon. They rolled up the car's aisle together, slamming into the front of the building that had grown there. Marlow ended up on top, fumbling with the weapon, somehow managing to thump it down onto Mammon's head. It sounded like a watermelon being crushed.

Another gust of wind, then Night was there, too, with a savage kick. The light that poured from Mammon's eyes snapped off, plunging the car into darkness. Then it blazed back on again in an explosion of fire, so powerful that Marlow and Night were thrown back, their sprawling bodies rolling up the car.

Mammon was showing no sign of getting up. He lay there on the floor of the hurtling car, those headlamps blazing at the ceiling. The train was shaking hard, pieces of the building ripped away by the wind. Something cold dropped onto Pan's neck, squirming down the back of her shirt, and she grabbed for it—a maggot. More were falling now, a rain of them.

So be it, Mammon said.

"Wait!" she said again. The building up ahead was decomposing, fast, the bricks crumbling into writhing white larvae. Mammon himself was putrefying, like a slow-motion video of decay. His body puffed up, mold blossoming on his skin, erupting into maggot flesh.

So be it, he said again, and then the voice was gone.

Pan swore, tried to take a step toward Marlow only to find that her foot was sinking. The floor of the car was changing again, softening into rot. The poisonous smell of it was overwhelming, making her gag. Up ahead the top two floors of the building gave in, a mound of maggots—millions of them—spilling out into the night. The car was suddenly full of wind, kicking the rot into a tornado. Somehow the train was still moving, barreling into the darkness.

Right toward a bridge.

"We need to go," Truck said, wheezing up beside her.

"Marlow, Night," she yelled, "get up!"

They were trying, both of them swimming in the decaying remains of the car. She struggled to Night first, offering her a hand. By the time she was free Marlow was out, too, and they retreated together, into the next car back. Pieces of who-knew-what were thumping over the roof, the train shaking like a carnival ride. They had to be going at two hundred miles an hour—and with no actual engine. It was impossible.

More impossible than Mammon making a building grow from nothing?

"What did he want?" said Truck.

To help, she thought, but said, "Nothing, the asshole was just distracting us."

"Any ideas?" said Marlow. The train thundered its way onto the bridge and Pan's stomach almost erupted from her mouth. The floor was vibrating so much now she could barely stand. Sparks were still flying from the wheels, the world tearing past outside so fast that she couldn't even look at it without screaming.

Any ideas?

The car bucked as something ripped under the wheels, hard enough to jolt them all off the floor.

"Yeah," she said, gripping the nearest chair with everything she had. "Hang on."

The train kicked again, the whole vehicle screaming. The struts of the bridge ripped past outside, too fast, and Pan had to screw her eyes shut against a crippling wave of vertigo. Then they lurched to the side and she was thrown across the aisle. Suddenly the car was tilting like a capsizing boat.

Hang on!

The train came off the rails, juddering as it punched through the side of the bridge. For an instant they were suspended in midair, Pan's stomach turning inside out, then they were falling. She tumbled down the aisle, bouncing off the tops of the seats. Somebody grabbed her wrist and she felt something pop deep inside her shoulder, so painful that a grenade might have exploded there. Her body crunched to a halt and she blinked past the tears to see Marlow, clutching a chair with one hand and holding her with the other. She was almost grateful until she remembered that the car was still falling, plummeting toward whatever lay beneath the bridge, everything inside about to be crushed to a—

They snapped to a halt, the force almost pulling her free of Marlow's grip. The car lurched a couple more times then swung gently, creaking like a church bell. Debris rained down from above, a corpse thudding down between the chairs. Pan watched it drop into the rotted remains of the engine. It ripped a hole right through it, falling into the night, toward the moonlit sheen of a river.

Maybe a hundred feet beneath them.

Pan swore beneath her breath, the waves of agony from her dislocated shoulder threatening to pull her into another kind of darkness.

"Hang on," Marlow said, tightening his grip on the chair. He tried to yank her up and the scream burned from her lungs before she could stop it.

It was echoed by another one, somebody crying out as they fell from the car above. They spun down the aisle, snatching wildly at Pan before dropping into oblivion. The train trembled, then slid another few feet toward the river. How long before the car snapped free altogether?

Marlow pulled again, gently, guiding her onto the back of a seat. She scooted away from the edge, clutching her arm. Then he was there next to her, his face the color of ash.

"Where are the others?" she said.

"Here," came Truck's reply from somewhere overhead. "We're good. Gonna try to make it into the next car."

"Your arm?" said Marlow.

"Dislocated," she said. She stretched herself out on the chair as best she could, grimacing as she held out her hand to Marlow. "Need you to pull it. Gently."

Marlow made a face, but he took her hand and did as she asked. The world went white, every muscle in her shoulder crying out. The car juddered again, slipping further, but Marlow kept pulling, so hard she thought her arm would rip off like a chicken wing. Then, just like that, the joint slotted back into its socket. The relief of it was so great that she could have laughed. She shook free of his grip, sitting up. Every time the car swung she could see the route up, toward the door. It looked like a mountain.

But what choice did they have? It was either up or down.

Marlow was already on the move, grabbing the seat like a ladder.

"You need a hand?" he asked her.

"You need a black eye?" she replied, scowling. He rolled his eyes and swung himself up to the next seat. Pan ignored the niggling pain in her arm and followed him. Above her she could see Truck struggling, his face etched with concern and drenched with sweat. Night was already close to the door, climbing as gracefully as an acrobat.

The train dropped again without warning, the sound of shearing metal making her think there was a demon in the car. It snapped to a halt and the lights exploded into sparks, plunging them into darkness. Suddenly the outside world was there, drenched in moonlight. She could make out one of the immense columns, the bridge just overhead.

She pushed on, hauling herself up using the chairs and tables until she'd reached the top of the car. Marlow was there, one foot on either side of the door, and this time she accepted his hand, letting him pull her up beside him. She stood there for a moment, catching her breath and feeling his against her neck. She realized he was still holding her hand and she pulled it free.

"Perv," she said, using the luggage rack to clamber into the next car. This one was at a forty-five-degree angle, making it easier to climb. Through the windows at the far end she could make out the bridge, illuminated by firelight. A haze of smoke hung in the air, layered with distant screams. Night and Truck had stopped to catch their breath, both of them wedged against a table.

"No hurry or anything," said Truck, checking his watch. "Not like we're on a train that's about to drop us to our deaths."

"I couldn't go any faster," she said, surprised by how much effort it took to get the words out. "Your fat ass was in the way."

He laughed, holding out a hand the size of a bear's paw. She batted it away, grabbing a fistful of his shirt and using it to haul herself past them.

"Don't mind me," he grumbled.

"I never do," she said, putting a foot on his shoulder and pushing up. Not far now, another twenty yards or so. And her attention was so fixed on the exit that she didn't see the person next to her until a weak hand wrapped itself around her arm. She choked back a scream and snatched her arm free, staring at a girl who couldn't have been older than seventeen. She was curled up on a chair, her face a mask of terror.

"Help," she said, reaching for Pan again.

"I . . ." Pan swallowed, looking up. She shook her head. "I can't."

She kept climbing. There was more at stake here than one girl—*sacrifice one life to save a million*—and besides, what was stopping her from following them? She pushed on, one foot in front of the other.

"Please!" screamed the girl. "I'm scared!"

Join the club.

"It's okay," she heard Marlow say beneath her, and she didn't have to look back to know what his big bleeding heart was doing.

"Thank you," the girl said. "Oh God, thank you."

Pan scaled the last couple of seats and reached the door. The glass had blackened, and when she grabbed the handle it was hot enough to make the flesh of her palm sizzle.

Dammit.

She shuffled across to the window, craning her neck to see that the next car along was a barbecue, flames erupting from the windows. Half of it jutted out from the bridge, the other half clamped in a dragon's claw of broken railings and struts.

So close.

"We're going to have to go out," she said.

"Out?" replied Truck as he squashed in beside her. She pressed herself back against the seat so that he could punch the window, throwing himself at it until it popped out of its frame.

"Not having powers *blows,*" he said, sucking the blood from his knuckles. "I'm a three-hundred-pound weakling."

Pan helped him push the glass free, watching as it dropped into the canyon below. Then she reached up and grabbed the top of the train, easing herself out. The drop beneath her felt Grand Canyon–deep, and she felt like somebody had reached into her stomach and was trying to tug it loose. She sucked it up, clambering frantically onto the sloping roof of the car. The wind whipped at her, screamed at her. Her sneakers slipped and for a moment she thought she was going, but she wedged one foot against an air vent to keep herself in place.

Truck's face appeared and she moved out of the way to let him up. The next car was thankfully almost horizontal. The only problem was that parts of the metal roof ahead were glowing red hot, the air above it shimmering. It was a straight shot to the bridge, though, if they didn't burn up before they got there.

"Any more ideas?" Truck asked from her side.

"Yeah, don't stop," she said. Truck's sarcastic whistle was carried off by the wind.

"Man, you're a fountain of good advice today, Pan," he said.

Pan glanced over, found a scrap of smile to offer him. Past

Truck, Marlow was doing his best to climb onto the roof with the teenage girl on his back. Her arms were so tight around his neck that he was struggling to breathe. He wheezed his way up, staying on his hands and knees. Night followed, hopping over him and standing there with her hands on her hips as if she hadn't noticed they were on a burning train above a hundred-foot drop.

"You guys hear that?" Truck asked, shouting over the wind, over the roar of the fire, over the screams from the other cars. "Pan's tip for the day, don't stop."

"Wow," croaked Marlow, getting to his feet, trying to pull the girl's hands free and only making her hang on even more tightly. "You should write a self-help book."

Pan turned back toward the bridge. "Go scr—"

The train rumbled, seemed to shriek like a living thing. Beneath them the bottom car surrendered, tearing free and dropping earthward. A ripple of motion passed up the train, everything bouncing like a diving board. Pan watched it fall, counting to five before she saw it hit. She tried not to think about how those five long, lonely seconds would feel if she messed up now.

She took a deep breath of cold mountain air, then ran for the gap, hurling herself over it. She landed hard, touched her fingers down for a moment to steady herself. The metal beneath her was hot enough to cook burgers on. She kept going, feeling the soles of her sneakers melting on the roof, trying to trip her up.

There was a crunch as somebody landed behind her but she didn't look back. The bridge was thirty yards away now, people visible on the tracks, climbing from the doors, ghosts in the smoke.

Another thump, a scream from the girl on Marlow's back.

Pan kept running, twenty yards, close enough now that some of the people on the bridge were pointing at her, shouting. Her sneakers weren't sticking anymore, there was no fire on this side of the car. She slowed, gasping for air that was thick with smoke, that stank of burning flesh.

That scream again. Pan glanced back, past Truck. Marlow was on the roof of the car, the girl still clamped to his back. He looked like he was *dancing*, staggering from side to side, perilously close to the edge. He was groping for the girl, slapping at her.

The girl's face was changing, like she'd eaten something that was expanding inside her. Her cheeks bulged, splitting, her eyes rolling back in their sockets. She was trying to scream again but she was just gargling blood. With a sound like a gunshot her skull cracked in two, opening up to reveal another one beneath.

No.

Pan doubled back, the electric charge a cold heat in her fingers. She was too far away, though; she stood a good chance of frying Marlow alongside the Magpie if she shot from here. Marlow was down on his knees, the Magpie choking him, his grin blazing through a sticky layer of the girl's blood and hair. In the shimmering heat haze they didn't look real, they looked like a piece of burning film.

Truck was already running back, but Night was there first, blurring out of sight for a second then reappearing. Her fist connected with the side of the Magpie's head and ripped away half of the girl's skull like a coconut. She hit him again but he didn't even seem to notice, his arms locked tight around Marlow's throat. Marlow was blue now, his eyes bulging like pickled eggs. With a soft *whumph* his trousers erupted into flames from the heat of the roof.

Screw this.

Pan stretched out her fingers and unleashed a charge, a small one. A fork of lightning burned through the air, snapping into the Magpie's side with a deep, bone-rattling peal of thunder. He cried out and let go, falling onto his back and shuddering like he'd been Tasered. Marlow limped up, slapping at the flames and doing his best to breathe.

"Get out of the way!" Pan yelled at him, feeling the electro-static energy build up inside her again. Marlow staggered to one side but Night was there, dashing in. She kicked the Magpie in the stomach, driving him toward the edge of the car.

"Go to hell," she screamed, kicking out again. *"Hijo de—"*

The Magpie grabbed her foot, used it to pull himself up. Then he clenched her throat in one hand. Night punched him in the head, ripping away more of the girl's face, but the Magpie held firm. He wrapped his other hand around Night, smothering her. His grin was wider than ever, looking right at Pan.

"And then there were three!" he yelled.

He clutched Night's squirming body to his chest, then he threw himself from the roof of the train.

NIGHTFALL

Just like that, she was gone.

Marlow staggered up the train until the heat was bearable. He collapsed to his knees and craned over the edge. Night and the Magpie were two silhouettes shrinking into the tinfoil glow of the river, falling, fading. Somebody skidded down next to him—Truck, struggling to pull in a breath before howling Night's name into the darkness. He was holding his own face with those big hands, his eyes wider and brighter than the moon.

It's okay, he thought. *They'll land in the water, she'll be okay.*

Below, they hit the river, a silent splash that looked no bigger than a dime. Truck howled again, a sound so full of rage that it took Marlow's breath away. Pan had staggered to his other side, and he looked up, saw her standing there with her hands in her hair, her face a phantom's. She met his eyes and he knew instantly. He knew there was no hope.

"Oh God," said Truck, sobbing now. "Oh God, no. No. *Night!* We have to . . . We have to . . ."

It was too late. Far below, the silver heart of the river was starting to foam. It was as if the sun were rising down there, a soft glow pulsing out of the water, bringing it to a hissing boil that Marlow could hear above the roar of the fire. The earth split, revealing a molten core that burned a pocket of day into the darkness. And Marlow knew what it meant, he knew the horror of it.

Night was dead.

She had died under contract with the Engine.

They were coming for her right now, pulling themselves out of the soil, out of the rock, out of the water. The demons were coming for her, and they would drag her down through the melting rock, through that suppurating hole in reality. They would drag her straight into the depths of hell.

And even now, even above the fire, above the hiss, above the shouts from the bridge, above Truck's gasping, heartbreaking cries—even though Night was dead—he could hear her.

He could hear her *scream*.

He turned away, blinking fire from his vision, as if everywhere he looked, the world was burning. That's when he felt it, felt it like somebody had rammed a knife right into the heart of him, had drawn that blade from his sternum to his gut. He opened his mouth and groaned, then he turned and wrapped his arms around Truck—just to anchor himself, to stop himself from slipping away into oblivion—felt the big guy's whole body tremble with the force of his cries. He pushed his face into him and let it out, because there was simply nothing else he could do.

A hand on his arm, gentle but insistent. Pan was there, her face set in stone, her teeth clenched so tight that her jaw bulged Magpie-big. Her eyes were red raw and filled with something that Marlow couldn't identify—something he didn't *want* to identify.

"Let's go," she said quietly. Her hand hovered in front of him, and after another eternity he managed to take it, letting her lift him to his feet. They each took one of Truck's hands and he rose like a child, his body sagging, his head tucked into his chest. His cries were silent now, but no better because of it. Only when they were sure he wasn't going to topple off the edge did Marlow let go, Pan leading Truck up the train toward the bridge.

Goodbye, Night, Marlow said without looking down. His fists were clenched so hard, his nails had gouged trenches in his palms. *I'm sorry. I'm so sorry.*

He followed Pan and Truck up the train, squeezing between the severed railings and dropping down onto the tracks. There had to be a hundred people here, *two* hundred, all of them sobbing and crying and holding one another. Marlow pushed through them, seeing wounds, missing limbs, seeing children howling for parents and parents crying for their children, seeing men and women so covered in blood that they might have been skinned alive. They were still pouring from the cars, some of them carrying the wounded and others carrying worse. The train was a dead thing that lay half on, half off its tracks, snaking into shadow, its head hanging limply over the side of the bridge. The fire was spreading, too, cremating it and everything that remained inside.

Marlow walked, not caring where he was going, just another shell-shocked, blood-soaked victim. The wounded snatched at him, pleaded with him, but he didn't meet their eyes. He just walked, stepping past the injured, stepping over the dead, until the crowd began to thin. He spotted Pan and Truck, two mismatched lumps of shadow standing farther down the line. It took everything he had just to make it to them, and when he did, he found he was capable of nothing more. He turned back to the train and just watched, watched as the fire spread, as it tore its way out the windows.

From over the side of the bridge came a roar as another car

snapped free, plunging into the canyon. Passengers were scattering, some of them on their cell phones. It wouldn't be long before the place was crawling with ambulances, police, and other first responders, asking questions to which they would never accept the answers. Pan saw it, too, because she wiped a filthy hand over her bloodied face and turned, walking down the bridge. When nobody followed, she looked back.

"We can't stay," she said.

"We can't leave her," said Truck. He was no longer crying but there was nothing left in him, his face a badly fitted mask, his eyes big and unblinking. "She might have made it, the demons might have come for the Magpie. She might be down there . . ."

"She's dead," said Pan. "She's gone. We have to move."

The look that Truck shot her could have blown the top of her head off.

"She's dead," Pan said again. "You want to stay here and mourn her then you go for it, but that redhead is still out there somewhere. You stay here, Truck, you let them know how upset you are with them while they're pulling you to pieces. Okay?"

He seemed to expand with rage, then just as quickly he deflated, nodding once. Pan looked at Marlow, shrugging her shoulders to say, *Come, or don't.* Then she spun away, stumbling over the tracks. Truck followed, sniffing. Marlow paused, wondering what would happen if he went the other way, if he blended into the crowd or vanished into the night. What would happen if he just turned and ran? Would the Circle still cancel his contract? Or would he wake up in a few weeks to the smell of sulfur, to the feeling of a demon sinking its teeth into his flesh?

And what about everyone else? The chorus of sobs and screams and cries echoed off the mountains, like it was coming from all around him. It was as if the whole world was mourning, and it would be, wouldn't it? Once Mammon worked out how to unite the Engines, once he found out how to open the gate into hell. Everyone on the planet would be carrying their dead into the night.

But what could they do? Him, Pan, a powerless Truck?

And then there were three.

They still had to find Mammon, had to defeat him, had to kill the redhead and every other Engineer he had on his books. Not to mention whatever else he threw their way. The sheer, staggering impossibility of it almost knocked him to the floor.

Just run, he told himself. *Just keep running.*

Because that would be easier, surely. At least then he wouldn't have to push on, he wouldn't have to fight anymore, wouldn't have to make any more goddamned decisions.

He'd just keep running until the day hell caught up with him.

And it was the fear of it that drove him forward, that drove him toward Pan. Because one thought scared him more than anything—that he would burn, and it would all be for nothing.

He jogged after her, casting one more nervous look over the side of the bridge. The ground below glowed as softly as a dying pyre, embers throbbing as the night took control once more. Then nothing. Only the river remembered, its course forever altered by the ruptured ground—now a lake full of moonlight.

I'm sorry, Night, he said again as he went. *I promise it won't be for nothing.*

He had no idea if it was a promise he could keep.

PRAGUE

Pan wasn't sure how much later it was that they drove over the city limits into Prague.

She wasn't even sure she knew how they'd gotten here.

She could remember walking, stumbling along the tracks in the dark, seeing the helicopters appear overhead like flies. It had been almost dawn by the time they reached a level crossing, scuffing their way onto the road, shuffling along until the sun was peeking over the horizon and they found their first car. The driver hadn't been too keen on taking them anywhere—and Pan didn't blame her, because all three of them were crusted with blood and gore—but a quick burst of lightning from her fingers and a scowl from Truck had given the woman a sudden charitable streak. She'd handed them the car and the keys and half a dozen paper bags filled with groceries and waved them on their way.

Truck had taken the wheel, even though he didn't seem like he was capable of driving. The big guy wasn't talking, and that was fine with her because talking was just too painful. She'd curled up in the passenger seat and tried to switch off, only the memories wouldn't let her. They were too powerful, flooding her head just as the big silver river had flooded the canyon.

She had watched them against the dark like they were being played on a projector—Night arriving at the Pigeon's Nest, so frightened that for all the time Herc was introducing her she hid behind him, her face pressed into his back; Night emerging from the pool after making her first contract, a grin on her face that seemed bright enough to reach the surface.

Only when the memories became too loud against the silence of the road had they started to talk. It was Truck who kicked off, the words exploding from him like he was a can of soda shaken to the point of detonation, like he just couldn't keep it in.

"You remember the story about how Herc found her? How she rolled him over?"

Night had been fifteen and sleeping rough in Hell's Kitchen, her days spent pickpocketing tourists while they were on Daredevil tours run by her partner in crime. She'd mistaken Herc for a mark as he was leaving a safe house and tried to snatch his wallet. Herc had always claimed he'd sensed her, that he was too sharp to ever be robbed. But Pan knew differently.

"Only reason he caught her was because of that stupid squeezy toy he keeps in there." Incredibly Pan had giggled as she said it, a sound that she could barely recognize. "The one that used to belong to his dog. Started squeaking as she was running down the road."

And the stories had spilled out of them, riding on a wave of laughter. Night had died, but right there—speeding across Europe in a battered Volvo with a big plastic grinning Jesus mounted on the dash—they had brought her back to life. It was as if she were riding along with them, sitting in the back with Marlow, staring intently out the window with those big brown eyes the way she always did, chewing her nails and jiggling her leg, unable to stay still. Pan could almost feel Night's grin like a ray of sunshine on the back of her neck, one that made her hair stand on end.

Yeah, somewhere down the line they had made her immortal.

"Weird being here without her, though," said Truck. The Volvo rattled as he pulled them off the motorway, heading into the center of the city. There were cars everywhere and none of them seemed to be following any rules—everyone serenading one another with honks and curses. Truck jabbed a finger at the driver of a delivery truck, swearing at him out the window. "Sorry," he said to the plastic Jesus. "But yeah, weird."

"Weird without all of them," said Pan. "Seth, the Lawyers, Betty, even Hanson."

The Pigeon's Nest was gone, almost everyone had been killed. This city just didn't feel whole without them, didn't feel real. The anxiety crunched her insides in a fist of steel and she pulled her legs up to her chest like she could just fold herself into nothing, fold herself up and out of the world.

"What are we doing here anyway?" said Marlow from the backseat. "The Engine is gone."

"*Really?*" she said. "Marlow, I had no idea. Thanks for the news bulletin. Next you'll be telling me it's your fault, that you led Charlie inside so that he could hand it over to Mammon. Oh, wait, I knew that, too."

Silence, until Truck whistled softly. "Awkward," he muttered.

"I was just saying," said Marlow. "The Circle will be expecting us, won't they? They'll know we're coming."

Pan took a deep, juddering breath then blew it calmly between her lips.

"The Red Door was connected to a dozen different cities," she said. "Prague, Budapest, Rome, places all over Europe. I don't think the Circle would have known every destination.

They might be watching, but I don't think there will be Engineers here, not unless they followed us from the train."

"So . . ." said Marlow.

"So Herc got spat out somewhere in Europe, right? This is the place we used more than any other, this was *home*. If he's . . ." She swallowed hard. "If he's still alive then he'd know to meet us here. He *would*."

Believe it enough and maybe it will come true.

"You remember where it was?" Pan asked, turning her attention to Truck. He nodded, honking at a jeep as they rumbled over the Vltava River. Pan closed her eyes—she'd be happy if she never saw a bridge again. He swung right at the far end and for a while they bumped and ground their way through traffic, Truck doing his best not to run over the swarms of tourists who spilled out into the streets. Gradually the city grew quieter and the crowds thinned, the grand old buildings of central Prague giving way to cobbled streets and tightly packed apartment buildings.

"This one?" Truck asked, craning over the wheel to stare at a junction.

"Next," she replied, nodding down the street. He turned off when they reached it, the Volvo rattling over the uneven surface, past a handful of abandoned buildings, until they saw the crumbling spire of the old church. Truck pulled up in front of the gates and Pan almost screamed for him to keep going. She didn't want to be here, didn't want to see what Mammon and his freaks had done to the place. Instead she clamped her mouth shut and gripped her seat as Truck cut the engine.

They fell into a silence that was ocean-deep. She coughed quietly, swallowing hard to try to settle whatever was crawling around in her stomach. She felt properly sick, her guts roiling like something was attempting to turn her inside out. The sensation spread, crawling along the underside of her skin, tickling her bones and making the cavern of her skull seem to ring. She half expected to see Mammon stride around the corner again. But this was a different kind of horror, one that she knew well.

"The Red Door," Truck said, scratching at his arm hard enough to leave great big welts there. He was right—that same madness of screams and sighs, insect clicks and whispered tongues. It was fainter now, no doubt about it. The door had gone, but there was a stink in the air like an animal had marked its scent. It didn't seem possible that just a few days ago walking into this church had carried you through space right into the heart of the Engine.

"We should probably circle the block awhile," said Marlow. "Make sure we're not being watched. Right?"

"Sure," she said, popping her door. "You can never be too safe, Marlow."

She stepped out into the sweltering heat of Prague, instantly breaking into a sweat. Out here the sensation was worse than ever, like a clutch of wasp eggs had hatched inside her and were burrowing their way out. She doubled over and retched, a string of acidic drool hanging from her lips. When was the last time she had eaten? A day? Two, maybe?

"Marly's right, Pan," said Truck as he followed her out, one hand rubbing his enormous stomach. "Got to be careful, after . . . you know."

She'd almost managed to forget the train for the moment, and his reminder sent a bolt of fury through her. Let them come. Let them try again. She'd murder them for what they did to Night. She'd decorate the streets of this ancient city with the filth that flowed through their veins. A burst of static sparked from her fingertips without her permission.

She shook loose a handful of sparks and tried to will some strength into her trembling legs. Ahead of her the gates were half open and she pushed through them, fingers splayed and full of charge just in case Marlow and Truck were right. The small courtyard beyond was empty of people but full of stuff—crates and Dumpsters, big halogen spotlights on metal poles, plus the cars. One of Hanson's ridiculous blue BMW Hurricanes sat facing her, waxed and polished and ready to go.

He'll never drive it again, she thought, wondering if there had ever been a time when she could have felt sorry for him.

She finally turned her attention to the Red Door. Or at least the space where it should have been. The church was still there, the tower a stunted thumb with the top joint missing, its roof a collection of rafters jutting up like a dead man's ribs. There was a perfect rectangle of darkness in the wall, still kicking out that bowel-loosening sensation of pure evil.

The gates creaked behind her as Truck rolled in, Marlow peeking out from behind him with big, frightened eyes.

"Doesn't exactly look like a war zone," said Truck.

"Why would it?" she said, not taking her eyes from Marlow. "Our side didn't even get a chance to fight."

She could picture it, Mammon and his Engineers walking through the courtyard—maybe this one, maybe one of the others—knowing that all they had to do was knock. Charlie would have been waiting for them, would have opened the Red Door from inside and ushered them through. It would have been quick. Bullwinkle and Hope were under contract but neither of them would have been able to stand up to Mammon. Not even Hanson, although he would have put up one hell of a fight. No, it would have been a massacre, pure and simple.

A sound from the church, then an explosion of wings as a couple of doves took flight. Her heart almost leaped up with them and she had to swallow it back. She watched them rise into the big blue sky then blinked away the sting of the sun. When she looked back at the church all she could see was fire.

"Come on," said Truck, walking past her and cupping his hands against the window of one of the Land Rovers. He checked them all then made his way slowly to the church, his fists clenching and unclenching by his sides. "Herc? Yo, Herc, you in there?"

The sensation in her stomach knotted even tighter. Something was screaming for her to run, to turn tail and get the hell out of here. Truck was hovering by the doorless door and somehow, even though the entry was only a couple of inches taller than him, it seemed to dwarf him, made him look insect-small. The darkness inside was more than just dark, she was sure of it. It was the kind of darkness you got when somebody cut a hole in reality; the kind of darkness you could fall inside and never come out of.

"Truck," she said, her voice crackling.

He braced one hand on the frame and leaned in, his head and shoulders vanishing into the gloom.

"Truck," she said again. The itch inside her skull was worse, crawling above her eye socket. Was there a voice there, too? A manic whisper that seemed to come from deep inside her but also from far, far away. She pressed a fist to her forehead, squinting at Truck. He looked as if he had frozen, his top half held in a fist of darkness.

Marlow walked past her, heading for the church, and she reached out and stopped him.

Truck was moving, but there was something wrong. His hand was dropping to his side but it was like watching a slow-motion replay. His body was twisting, too, impossibly slowly.

It took almost thirty seconds for his shoulder to appear from the darkness of the doorway, the same again for his head.

"What's wrong with him?" said Marlow.

Truck's face was flickering like a video game glitch, his body seeming to move at different speeds as if he were a collection of parts that had come undone. Then the last of his face peeled free and he snapped back, his words racing out of his mouth.

". . . nooooothiiiing, buuut caan't see much in there." He frowned at Pan, shrugged his big shoulders.

"What?"

The tickling sensation in the front of her skull shifted to her eye. Something was actually crawling in there, something big. She scratched at it, felt movement beneath her fingers—a fat, egg-bloated bluebottle, peeling its way from her eyelid. Pan's scream was too big to fit up her throat, reduced to a groan of horror as she pinched the insect between her fingers. Its hairy body resisted for an instant and then popped into mush that she smeared down her pants.

"Jesus," she said, the word almost shaken to pieces by her thrashing heart. "We should go."

"Yeah," said Marlow, nodding furiously. "Yeah, that's the best idea you've had all day."

"Truck," Pan said again. "Come on, this is—"

The darkness behind Truck was changing, the doorway rippling like spilled ink. A long, thin shape was pushing itself free of it, stretching out of the church, snaking right toward Truck's shoulder. Pan swore, calling out a warning.

He heard her too late, the shape branching into a hand, fingers landing on Truck's shoulder, clenching his shirt. He yelped, throwing his bulk away from the door and wrenching free. Pan was on the move, the charge just about burning a hole in her hand. Whoever was in there, they were about to get fried.

A voice came oozing from the shadows, starting slowly then catching up with itself. "Easy does it, Pan."

The face that spoke was taking shape, pushing itself from the dark—a grizzled chin, a broken nose, more scars than a cage fighter, then two gray eyes that radiated so much warmth, Pan couldn't help herself. She ran right at him, stumbling over the cobbled ground.

"Herc!" she cried, and he was barely out the door before she thumped into him, hard enough to knock the breath from her lungs. She held him like he was a life raft and she was about to tumble over a waterfall. She sobbed into his shirt, breathing in the smoky, Old Spice smell of him. And she felt the hitch of his chest as he cried, too, his face pressing into the top of her head, his tears falling into her hair. Time had broken again. She just held him, and for those seconds—those infinite, endless seconds—everything was okay.

It was a lifetime later that Herc coughed, easing her away. She peeled herself from him, everything trembling. She'd left a wet patch on his shirt but at least the sobs had stopped.

"Hey," he said, smudging away his own tears. His eyes were red-rimmed, like he hadn't slept since this all began. He scanned the courtyard and nodded to Truck, then to Marlow. She saw the moment his face fell, almost sliding right off the bone.

"Night on lookout?" he asked, and when Pan shook her head he choked on another sob, turning away for a moment to study the church wall. When he looked back there was an anger that Pan had never seen before. "Those assholes," he muttered. "But you, you're fine?"

"Oh sure, Herc," she said. "Never been better."

"Glad to see your sarcasm bone wasn't broken," Herc said. "Truck?"

"Circle canceled my contract," he said, staring at his hands like they'd betrayed him. "But I'm still breathing."

"What about you, Marlow?" Herc said, and the look he threw across the courtyard wasn't exactly friendly. Marlow must have seen it, because he stared at the ground, tracing patterns in the dirt with his sneaker.

"It wasn't my fault," he said. "I didn't know Charlie was going to do that."

Herc opened his mouth, then snapped it shut again. He chewed something over then said, "It doesn't matter now. It's happened. Important thing is you're here." He glanced at the gates, then up into the empty sky. "Come on, we're too exposed out here."

Pan nodded, turning away from the church.

"This way," Herc said from behind her, gesturing into that block of darkness. Pan shook her head. Her tears had washed away some of the Red Door's taint but it was back now and stronger than ever, her head packed tight with whispers and moans that couldn't come from anything human. Herc ushered her forward. "It's safe," he said. "They won't find us here."

"Herc, a fly just crawled out of my eye," she said. "A freaking *fly*. Out of my *eye*. There's no way I'm going through that door."

Herc sighed.

"I know," he said. "It sucks. But I promise you, you're going to want to see what's in there. *Who* is in there."

"Who *is* in there?" Pan asked. Herc looked up at the sky again, searching for something.

"I can't say, not out here." He offered her his hand. "But come on, there's someone I want you to meet."

WHAT'S NEW?

Herc went first, stepping into the ruined church. He didn't quite vanish, not the way people did when they went through the Red Door. This close, she could still see the outline of his broad shoulders against the darkness, as slow and black as pitch. She reached tentatively after him, seeing the shadows creep up her fingers, the sensation like reaching into a freezer. When she pulled her hand out again tendrils of darkness stuck to it, dissipating like smoke.

"Anytime you're ready, Pan," said Truck. "I gotta take a dump in the next ten seconds or I'm gonna pop."

"Nice," she said, still not moving.

"Who do you think's in there?" said Marlow. "You think it's a trap? You sure that was Herc?"

"Yeah, it was him," she said, and she had no doubt. Every iota of him was just the way she remembered it. It was him, Herman Cole, in the flesh. Her hair was still damp from his tears.

The thought gave her courage and she pushed her hand back into that cold, silent darkness. Then she walked into the door. There was an instant where her body felt as if it were quietly being pulled apart—like the gossamer-thin bonds between each cell were expanding. Then, just as quick, the sensation was gone.

"Not so bad, right?" asked Herc. He stood in front of her, and behind him was the mangled body of the church. Honey-colored light dripped in from the ceiling, pooling on a tiled floor that was thick with rubble and rot. The pews were in disarray, scattered like bones. The windows were boarded tight, the altar stripped bare of everything but an overturned table. There was a wooden cross on the wall but all that remained of the figure it had once held was a puddle of bronze on the floor, like it had melted.

"Better than walking through the Red Door," she said, shuddering at the memory. She'd walked into this church a hundred times or more, but she'd never seen the inside before—the Red Door had always carried her someplace else.

"Got that right," Herc said. "Door's gone but it's left its mark. Look."

He pointed over her shoulder and she turned to see the courtyard, Truck and Marlow standing there and looking right at her. They were moving like puppets, fast and jerky, everything speeded up. She was smiling before she even knew it.

"Last time I saw Truck move that fast was when I told him the Lawyers had started serving bacon doughnuts for lunch," Herc said as the big guy pushed his way inside, slowing down to real time. Truck shivered, then pulled a pained expression.

"Bastard cramps," he grunted. "I think I'm crowning. You got a john in here?"

"Nice to see you, too, Truck," said Herc. "Past the altar, down the stairs. No can anymore but there's a sink and a floor, take your pick."

"Gross," said Pan.

"Hey, when you gotta go, you gotta go," said Truck, scooting down the aisle. It sounded like somebody was playing the trumpet in his pants. "Sorry!"

Marlow was the last, almost falling through the door. He staggered, nobody there to catch him, dropping onto one knee and gagging. Pan felt a sudden rush of sympathy for him. He'd been duped just like the rest of them, and he had that added burden of guilt on his shoulders. All of this on top of the fact that he'd been an Engineer for less than a week. The poor kid's mind must be on the verge of shattering.

But still, if it hadn't been for him insisting that Charlie was safe, pleading with them to help him, convincing Herc and Hanson to let his friend into the Engine, then she'd be standing inside the Pigeon's Nest right now—their headquarters, named for the disgusting Nazi decor left over from the war, and the legions of dead pigeons—popping the tab on a Diet Coke and watching TV with Night.

She turned away, left him to get up by himself. The corners of the church were still crowded with darkness, impenetrable even though her eyes had adjusted. She couldn't see anyone else here, though.

"Who did you want us to meet, Herc?" she asked him. He looked over his shoulder, into a pocket of nothing beside the altar.

"You won't believe me if I tell you," he said. "Hey, Shep, they're here."

Shep?

Pan felt something shift inside her, thought that any minute now she was going to have to scamper after Truck and make use of whichever receptacle he wasn't occupying. Herc couldn't mean . . . There was no way . . .

From the shadows came a nervous cough, then a sniff, followed by a voice that was choked by its thick European accent.

"Are you sure it is them?"

It had lost its ring of authority, but she still stood to attention as soon as she heard it, fast enough to give herself a head rush.

Holy sh—

"It's them," said Herc. "No doubt. Pan, Marlow, let me introduce you guys to Sheppel Ostheim."

Pan panicked, not sure whether to bow or salute or curtsy. She did a combination of all three, feeling like an idiot. Sheppel Ostheim, the general who ran the Fist, the guy who had overseen every single operation for as long as she'd been here, the man she'd only ever spoken to on the phone, whom nobody had met. Of whom nobody had ever seen so much as a photo.

Until now.

Another nervous cough, then the sound of scuffing footsteps. The silhouette of a man appeared in the dark, low and stooped, an old-fashioned fedora hat, the glint of glasses. Then he stepped into the light, and Pan had to do a double take because this guy didn't match the image she'd had in her head, not one bit. She'd always pictured Ostheim as one of those movie stars that were aged, but not past their prime. One of the ones that looked like they could take a break from their bridge game and still kick your ass. A Tommy Lee Jones, or a Harrison Ford, or a Morgan Freeman.

The man who stood in front of her looked more like Toby Jones—short and slightly plump, drowning in a cheap brown suit and tie. He took off his glasses and wiped them on his jacket, pushing them back onto his nose and blinking through them like a frightened dormouse. He cleared his throat, took another step forward, then took off his hat. Beneath was a comb-over of epic proportions, one that drooped over his face. He smoothed it away, then seemed to finally find the courage to walk to Herc's side. Even when he straightened he only came up to Herc's shoulder.

"I am sorry for my manners," he said. "It has been a difficult few days. It is a pleasure to finally meet you, Pan. And Marlow, yes?"

Marlow had made it back onto his feet and he stood next to Pan, offering his hand.

"Marlow," he confirmed. Ostheim stared at his outstretched palm for a while, making no attempt to greet it. Eventually Marlow let his arm drop to his side, sharing a look with Pan that said, *Seriously?*

"I am sorry, again," Ostheim said. "It has been a long time since I was among people. Please forgive my rudeness, but I am not a well man." He laughed apologetically. "Germs are everywhere, *ja?*"

"No worries," said Marlow. "It's cool."

"You are fine?" Ostheim said. "Both of you, yes? You are not injured?"

"We took a beating," said Marlow. "My knees got grilled. Nothing we can't handle."

"What happened to Night?" Herc asked. "How did she—"

"She went out fighting," said Pan. "It was a Magpie. Marlow tried to rescue a girl and the son of a bitch stole her body. Grabbed Night and threw himself off a bridge. She didn't stand a chance."

"You sure she's—"

"I'm sure," spat Pan. "She was under contract, they came for her."

Herc's head fell. Ostheim gently placed his hat on the nearest pew so that he could clean his glasses again. This time he didn't put them back, just stared at them as if they might hold all the answers.

"I am sorry," he said again, a broken record. "She was a brave Engineer, one of the best. A soldier. She did not deserve to be murdered like that."

"No, she didn't," said Pan, and she would have gone on except another rolling wave of sickness rippled outward from her stomach, drenching her in cold sweat. "Herc, can we just get the hell out of here?"

"It is unfortunate," said Ostheim. "But necessary. Herc suggested that we meet here. He never gave up hope, and I see now that he had no reason to. He said that you would make your way to Prague, sooner or later. Even if he had not, I would have suggested it. The Red Door was a knife wound in the fabric of reality, one that has been here for centuries. Even though the door has gone, you cannot rend time and space in that way without leaving a permanent wound. That sickness you feel, it is the Engine in your blood, it is crying out for the other side."

Great.

"But it also serves to mask us. Mammon will be searching. He located you once by sniffing out the Engine inside you, he will do so again. But here, in the scar of the Red Door, we are hard to find." He finally replaced his glasses, patting the seat of a pew. "Please, sit. We have much to discuss."

Sitting down was the last thing Pan wanted to do, but what choice did she have? She scuffed her way through the rubble and dirt, lowering herself onto the uncomfortable bench.

"You, too, Mr. Green," said Ostheim.

Marlow sighed, slumping down next to her. Ostheim sat on the pew opposite, running a hand over his thinning hair again. She noticed that his fingers were trembling, until he clamped them between his legs. He blinked at the floor a couple of times, placing his hand on a leather briefcase beside him as if to check that it was still there. "I do not need to tell you how bad this situation is in which we find ourselves. How serious it is."

"You're not kidding," said Truck as he appeared from the stairs. He wafted his hand in front of his face. "I think I just opened the gates of hell down there all by myself."

"*Truck*," growled Herc. Truck spotted Ostheim, frowning.

"Who's the old dude?" he asked.

Pan almost slapped a hand over her face.

"Truck, this is Ostheim," she said.

The big guy stopped dead, his mouth hanging open. To Pan's surprise, Ostheim laughed.

"There is no need to be startled, Truck. It is a pleasure to meet you. Please, join us."

Truck did as he was told, the bench bowing as he lowered himself onto it.

"Damn," he said again. "I'm glad you're here."

Pan was, too. Glad to see Herc and Ostheim. For the first time since New York she felt like she could switch off, like she wasn't the one who had to make the decisions. The relief of it made the weight of darkness inside the church twice as heavy, made her feel as if she could close her eyes right now and sleep for a week. Only the sickness that boiled in her stomach, and the poisonous Red Door whispers that hissed at her from inside her skull, kept her awake.

"It was my grandfather's grandfather who first found the Engine, you know," said Ostheim. "A long, long time ago. Long before the Nazis invaded Prague and took it for themselves. It was he who first found the Red Door of *Praha*, and who learned how to open it. Of course he was one of the first to be taken, when he tried to use the Engine. But his son, my great-grandfather, spent his life there, learning everything there was to know about this . . . this infernal creation. It was he who learned about the two groups who had once waged war—the Circle and the Fist. He searched for the facts of it, the truth that was buried inside the lie of history. And he vowed that he would do everything he could to prevent the Engine from falling into the wrong hands."

Ostheim cleared his throat, staring into nothing, into the past.

"It is a burden that we have all taken upon ourselves to carry, generation after generation. Ours is not a happy story, it is one of constant struggle, and plagued with many deaths. But I like to think that without it, the world would be a very different place. If we had not fought so hard, then the Engines might have already been reunited."

"And now they have been," said Pan.

"Not quite," Ostheim said. "Mammon will not know how to join the Engines, he will not know how to open the gates."

"That's good, right?" said Truck.

"But," said Ostheim, raising a finger, "the Engines them-selves will know. It is all they dream of, it is the purpose they serve. They were designed to be united, they were created for that one reason—to open a door into hell."

Pan shuddered so hard the pew creaked. She wrapped her hands around herself straitjacket-tight, leaning forward.

"They were designed to make bargains, weren't they?" Truck said. "To get souls."

"Yes, yes, they were. But this is—" He threw his hands up. "I don't know, this is just fluff. Filler. It is like saying that the purpose of a car is to keep you dry during a storm. It will, but it is designed for so much more. As far as we are aware the Engines were built this way so that men would never lose them. An old machine, buried beneath the ground, can be easily dismissed. *Ja?* But a machine that can grant any wish, not so easy to forget."

"But who?" Pan asked. "Who could have built them? I mean . . . I mean not *that*."

"The Devil?" Ostheim fixed his small, blinking eyes on her. "We do not know, child. Who can say? Not even in all the books we have found, in all the histories of all the world, have we discovered the answer to that question. But ask yourself this: With everything that you have seen, everything that you have experienced, everything you have fought, and everything you have lost, who do *you* think built these things?"

This time it was Ostheim who shuddered, a spasm passing through him hard enough to knock loose those lonely strands of hair from his oily scalp.

"I have said this to all of you before, the divide between our world and theirs is paper thin." He waved a hand through the air. "The demons are here right now, teeming on the other side of the void. Old magic keeps them there, the first rules of the universe. But all it takes is one tear, one rip, and they will flood the world in an ocean of blood."

"Hey," said Marlow. "Like that girl's knife, the redhead. She was jabbing it in stuff and demons were coming out."

Ostheim's eyebrows nearly launched themselves off the top of his head. "This is true? I did not think it was possible. A knife, made from the Engine, yes?"

Pan shrugged, saying, "Yeah, I think so."

"Then the Engines are indeed growing more powerful. If a piece of them can open a rift to hell—even a small one such as that—then it means the mechanism is orienting itself to open the gates. You see, the Engines were created to be the blade that makes such a tear, to let the demons through. And they will not come alone."

Pan closed her eyes and saw it, the creature inside the Engine—never up close, never in detail, just a mountain of madness on the edge of her vision, one that studied her with a clutch of eyes that looked like festering holes in meat, who asked her in a million voices what she wanted to trade her soul for, and whose laugh was the sound of a million bones breaking at once. She'd always known it, past the exhilaration of getting a new contract, past the adrenaline of each mission. Mammon and the enemy Engineers were just pawns. This thing was the king.

"Mammon will be working hard, he will be locked away, focused on discovering how to bring the Engines together. But—"

"Mammon was there," said Pan. "On the train."

Ostheim frowned, swiping his hair back into place. "What?" he said when he had recovered.

"He was there," Pan said again. "I don't know if it was him, or if he was just . . . just projecting himself or something. But there was no doubt about it."

"He made a house grow out of the front of the train," said Marlow.

"He spoke to me," Pan went on.

"And what did he say?" asked Ostheim, his glare burrowing into her.

"I don't know. I don't remember." Pan pushed her mind back but it was reluctant to go there. *I'm here to help.* "He said something about helping us, I don't know."

"Mammon is a master of deception," Ostheim said. "He has learned from the best. He is himself a father of lies. He was there to distract you, or to kill you. You only have to look at the noble Night to see his intentions."

"But if all he wants to do is unite the Engines," said

Marlow, "then why chase us halfway across Europe? It's not like we're in a position to stop him."

"No?" said Ostheim, and for the first time since they had met his eyes lit up. "But that is where you are wrong, my young friend. Mammon may have the Engines, and he may have Engineers. But he is not invulnerable. Far from it. He knows that you are still a threat, that you will be coming after him."

"You're saying we can find him?" said Marlow.

"Yes."

"And we can crush his ass?" asked Truck.

"Oh yes."

"And what's the *but*?" asked Pan, sensing one hanging in the air between them. Ostheim smiled, revealing a row of small, neat teeth.

"Ah yes, the *but*. A simple one. But it will not be easy, Pan. Not easy at all. And if we fail, then you will not just lose your physical body. Your soul will be torn apart, for an eternity."

"And the world will end," added Herc matter-of-factly.

Pan laughed. *Soul shredded, world ended.*

"What's new?"

HE WOULD HAVE SAID YES

"It may be hard to believe now," said Ostheim. "But we have a number of things in our favor."

The old guy opened his leather briefcase and Marlow took the opportunity to study him. Admittedly he'd spoken to Ostheim only once, by phone, but this wasn't who he'd pictured on the other end of the line. The voice he'd heard then had been little more than a whisper, but it had radiated power. This guy was a joke. If Marlow had seen him walking through the streets of Mariners Harbor he probably would have started calling him names and lobbing beer cans at him.

Ostheim found what he was looking for, setting a sheaf of coffee-colored papers down on the pew next to him.

"One, we still have powers." He glanced at Truck. "Not you, I am afraid." Then at Marlow. "And you, friend, I imagine they will turn to your contract next. You are strength and speed, yes?"

Marlow nodded. "The good looks are all mine."

Nobody laughed.

"An easy contract to break, which is a pity, but they will still require a day at least, hopefully more. Pan, am I right in thinking that Patrick Rebarre told you your contract would be left to expire?"

"Yeah," Pan said. "He said it. Right before the demons dragged his sorry ass down to hell. Him and his wormbag sister."

"I heard. No mean feat, defeating a resurrected soul like Brianna. The fact that you won that battle is what gives me hope." He smiled again, but it was short-lived. "It would be cruel of them to let you die like that, Pan, but I would not take Patrick's word for it. Mammon knows that you are more dangerous with powers than without, and I would not be at all surprised if he set about stripping you of your contract."

Pan blew out a long, unsteady breath and Marlow could almost feel the relief ebbing from her, could almost hear her reciting *please, please, please.* She must have sensed him watching because she shot a scowl his way. He twisted his head back to Ostheim so hard that his neck spasmed.

"So yes, we have powers."

"Don't forget about these babies," said Truck, flexing his biceps. The flab of his arms grew firm, like two melons hiding beneath a blanket.

"Of course," said Ostheim. "And, Herman, I know that you have . . . resources."

"Damn right I do," he grunted.

"Good. We have our army. It is small, but it is not without merit. It is enough."

If you say so, Marlow thought.

"You said a number of things," said Pan. "What else?"

"I am afraid that by a number I really meant two," Ostheim said. He turned to the papers, lifting the top one and unfolding it. It was the size of a bedsheet and he struggled to lay it out on the church floor. Marlow craned in, seeing that it was a map, an old one. "This is Paris, circa 1400."

"Paris?" said Truck, nodding. "City of Love."

"Indeed," said Ostheim. "Although not in this case."

"You think this is where the Engine is?" asked Marlow.

Ostheim sighed. "Perhaps if you all let me speak, you will find out. What you must remember is that the Engine itself has not moved. It cannot move, it is simply too big, and too complex. Whoever designed the Engines created them so that each would have a single entrance, and a single exit."

"The Red Door," said Pan.

Even hearing her say it seemed to make Marlow's head pound the same way it had the first time he'd been here, just before Pan had led him into the Nest.

"The Red Door," said the old man. "Each of the Engines has one. A wound in the world, a scalpel taken to the flesh of our universe. The Engines' creator cut a hole right through space and time, then sealed it tight with something right out of hell, something conjured with old magic. When Mammon breached our Red Door and entered the Nest, he did not seek to move the Engine. He only wanted to hide the entrance. He reprogrammed the Red Door so that it would be hidden, so that it would no longer open."

"But how?" asked Pan.

"Because he is powerful," said Ostheim. "He is the most powerful entity I know. He has used the Engine so many times that it is permanently in his blood. He is not yet a devil, but he is well on his way."

"One of the Pentarchy," said Marlow, remembering what Pan had told him. "One of the Five."

"A quaint title. But meaningless. There have only ever been two foolish enough, or wicked enough, to push the Engine to its limits. Mammon, and a woman called Meridiana." Here Ostheim hawked up a ball of phlegm and spat it across the church. It sat on the stone floor, glistening. "She paid the price for her greed. Her suffering will . . ."

He seemed to remember himself, smoothing down the map.

"It matters not. If we had kept the Engines apart then eventually Mammon would have gone the same way as *her*. Make too many contracts and the very fabric of your being changes, it corrupts. When you reach the point of no return then even a canceled contract leaves its mark. It makes you powerful, yes, but it takes much more. It possesses you."

Marlow squeezed his fists, felt the strength there, and suddenly hated it.

"Now, though, with both Engines at his command, Mammon's powers are immense. He was able to cut the Red Door off from every one of its locations."

"But he can still get out," said Marlow. "I mean there must still be a door."

"Clever boy," said Ostheim. "There *is* still a door. The Red Door exists, but only in one location—its *original* one."

"Where the Engine was built," said Pan.

Ostheim nodded. "That door simply cannot be moved. It can be concealed. It can be bricked over, but it cannot be moved."

"And it's in Paris?" asked Marlow.

"That I cannot say for sure," Ostheim went on. "But it is my best guess."

Marlow heard Pan sigh.

"So it might just be in Paris," she said. "Which happens to be one of the biggest cities in Europe, and home to a few hundred thousand buildings and a few million people. No problem."

"Hey," said Herc. "Don't forget who you're talking to, kid."

Ostheim held up a hand to calm him.

"It is not their fault, Herman. Please. As I was saying, we have another thing in our favor. Mammon is seeking to unite the two Engines, and this will cause him problems. Two machines of this magnitude, of this *power*, cannot exist even close to each other without producing a signal. Think of it like . . . like two transmitters positioned next to each other, emitting feedback."

The comparison didn't exactly help, and Ostheim must have seen the look on Marlow's face.

"You do not need to know the science, just know this: for as long as the Engines are in Mammon's possession, until the moment he unites them, we stand our best chance of finding them."

"And destroying them," said Marlow.

"Yes," Ostheim said. "Once and for all."

"So we're heading to Paris," said Herc. "Now."

Nobody seemed to respond, other than an exhausted yawn from Truck.

"*Now,*" Herc said. "Come on. Who are we?"

"Hellraisers," said Truck.

"I said who are we?" Herc tried again.

This time everyone joined in. "Hellraisers!"

"That's right," he said. He walked off, disappearing down the stairs, wafting his hand in front of his face. "Hell's bells, Truck, what have you been eating?"

"What *hasn't* he been eating?" Pan said, jumping to her feet.

Marlow was about to follow her when Ostheim called his name. The little guy was pushing himself up, those renegade strands of hair falling over his face again. Marlow had a sudden urge to grab a pair of scissors and snip them off. Ostheim walked stiffly to the far corner of the church and beckoned with his fingers. Marlow hesitated, looking to Pan for help and getting nothing but her cold shoulder.

"Come, Marlow," said Ostheim. "I will not bite."

Marlow popped his lips, then made his way over the rough ground, through the pool of sunshine, back into shadow. Ostheim was cleaning his glasses again, and he replaced them on his nose to study Marlow intently.

"I know this has been hard for you," he said after a moment. "You were betrayed by somebody you called a friend. Charlie took you for a fool, he took us all for fools. His actions have brought this world closer to ruin than anything in history."

Marlow hung his head, wishing that the floor would open up beneath him, a demon's mouth swallow him whole. Better that than to stand here being reminded of his own mistakes. Because that's what Ostheim was really saying, wasn't it? *Your actions, Marlow, your actions have brought the world closer to ruin than ever before.*

"No," said Ostheim, those small eyes like chips of obsidian, gleaming in the dark. "No, Marlow. I do not blame you, and neither should you pour blame upon yourself. This is what Mammon wants, to divide us, to make us weak. Tell me, honestly, did you know what Charlie's intentions were?"

Marlow spluttered out the ghost of a laugh. He couldn't even believe it now, despite everything he'd seen, everything that had happened. Not Charlie—his best friend, his *only* friend. They'd known each other for so many years, inseparable, until this.

"No," he said, locking eyes with Ostheim. "I had no idea."

Ostheim studied him for a moment, then nodded.

"Why do you think he did it?"

"I don't know," said Marlow. "I guess he was pissed at me

for leaving him when all this kicked off. But I didn't want him to get hurt, didn't want anything to happen to him."

"Some of the greatest tragedies in history were born from good intentions," said Ostheim.

"They must have gotten to him, Mammon and the others. They must have taken control of him somehow."

"No," said Ostheim. "No, if they had poisoned Charlie's mind, his personality, then Hanson would have sensed it before bringing him into the Nest—even if he was unconscious. No, this was Charlie's doing, pure and simple. It was his choice."

"I don't know, they must have convinced him, then. But it doesn't make sense. I mean he was a good guy, he got pretty worked up sometimes, threw a few punches, but he always did the right thing. I don't get why he would have joined *him*."

"It's like I said. Mammon is a father of lies, a master deceiver. Charlie may not even know that he is fighting for the wrong side."

"Yeah," said Marlow, nodding. That thought hadn't even occurred to him. "Yeah, that makes sense."

"Can you tell me anything about him, anything that might help us?"

Marlow chewed his lip, staring into the shadows of the church.

"Family he may try to contact? Brothers and sisters? Other friends he could reach out to?"

"No," said Marlow. "He was in foster care most of his life, no brothers, a sister somewhere but they haven't been in touch for years. He didn't really . . . I mean he wasn't the kind of guy you warmed to easily, y'know? Kept the walls high, kept the door locked, until he trusted you."

"And your school, would he have tried to make contact?"

"School?" Marlow shook his head. "Hell, no. He was doing good there, but he hated it just as much as I did."

"Very well," said Ostheim. "One more question, Marlow, and this is the most important. If we find the Engine, if we find Charlie, will you be able to convince him of the truth? Will you be able to win him back to our side?"

Marlow closed his eyes, thought back. The first time he'd met Charlie, the kid had been about to beat two high school football players into the ground. He'd talked him down then, even though he'd almost lost some teeth for his trouble. And how many times since had they held each other back, stopped each other doing something really, really stupid? More than he could count.

"Yeah," he said. "I can talk him around."

Ostheim smiled.

"That is good news. Very good news indeed. We may stand a chance here, Marlow. We may yet pull this world back from the brink."

He smiled again, then began to walk away.

"Mr. Ostheim," said Marlow, but when the old man turned around he couldn't find the strength to carry on. What was he supposed to say? *I'm too scared, I can't do this.* How would that sound? But it was the truth. His brother, Danny, had been the soldier. He'd been the one to charge into gunfire, to put himself on the line for his country, for his friends. Danny had been the hero, and look where it had gotten him—blown to pieces by a roadside bomb, scattered over the Afghan country-side, his coffin empty.

Ostheim scrutinized him, and once again he seemed to pluck the thoughts right out of Marlow's head.

"Can I tell you something, Marlow? Can I tell you a secret?

I never wanted to do this. When I was a child, growing up in Vienna, all I ever wanted was to be a musician. The piano was my thing." He played an invisible one, his eyes twinkling at the memory. "I had three brothers born before me, and a sister, too. And every single one of them wanted to follow my father's art, wanted to carry on our family's duty to the Fist. Their only ambition was to study the Engine, to work out what it was and how it could wield so much power. Their only dream in life was to locate its twin, to find the other Engine, so that they could destroy any chance the Circle had of opening the gates. They were the jewels of my father's eye, the pride and joy of my grandfather."

"What happened to them?" Marlow asked when Ostheim didn't go on.

"They died, of course. All of them. These were the days before the Lawyers, you understand. Our contracts, even the easiest of them, were unbreakable. One by one my father needed them, and one by one they sacrificed themselves to his command. Until only I remained."

There was a shout from across the church, Herc yelling that it was time to go.

"I tell you this because I, too, was scared. I cannot convey to you the extent of the fear I felt, and how crippling it became. I wanted no part of this, no part at all in my father's work. I just wanted a chance to live my life like every other soul in this world."

"But you're here," said Marlow.

"I am here. Yes. I am here. Because I understood that fear is simply *imagining* the worst that might happen. It's your mind's way of keeping you from harm, a preventive measure. Back then, as a child only slightly younger than you, I thought the worst that could happen was my own passing, my own sad little fate."

"And that isn't the worst thing that can happen?"

"Tell me, if you could ask your brother one question, what would it be?"

Marlow frowned. The truth was he couldn't even remember Danny, he'd been so young when he'd heard he wasn't coming home. All he had to go on was that fading photo on his kitchen wall, Danny in his combat gear, his smile the brightest thing in the desert sun. It made him think of his mom, sitting at home slowly drowning in Bacardi. It felt like somebody had crushed his heart in their fist, and his face twisted with the pain of it.

"I'd ask him . . ." *What? Why he'd signed up? Why he'd wanted to fight?* The answers to those questions were too easy. He'd fought for freedom, he'd fought for what was right, he'd fought for Mom, for his kid brother, and for Marcy, the girl he'd always liked. Marlow stared into the shadows and for an instant he thought he saw him there, a tall, well-built figure wearing sand-blown desert camo and Oakley shades. Danny, shaking his head and smiling. Marlow blinked and the figure was gone. He turned back to Ostheim. "I'd ask him if he thought it was worth it. Dying, I mean. I'd ask him if he thought he had made a difference."

"And what would his answer be?"

This time Marlow smiled.

"Yes," he said, and some of the fear had floated away, had left him like a cloud passing out from in front of the sun. "He would have said yes."

"There you have it, Marlow," said Ostheim, walking away. "Now, come. We have a war of our own to fight."

PART II
RETALIATION

BIENVENUE

"Herc, we got a problem."

The helicopter banked hard, the ground lurching up in the port windows and the sun burning through everything starboard. Pan could feel the pulse of the blades inside every cell of her body, a roar in her blood that might have been the Engine itself. She gripped the edge of her seat until her stomach had stopped doing somersaults. Truck was sitting on the seat opposite her and he leaned over his shoulder, yelling to Herc.

"Herc, I mean it, a *big* problem. We've got ten seconds, maybe less. It's gonna blow."

"I'm doing the best I can." Herc's reply was fed into her ears through a giant pair of headphones. The chopper leveled and through the window Pan could make out the Eiffel Tower, a single finger rising toward the heavens, like Paris was flipping them the bird, saying, *Go away, you're not welcome here.* "We can't land for another five. Can you hold it off?"

"I ain't holding nothing," Truck said.

"Pan?" Herc pleaded.

Pan turned to the seat next to her. She didn't think it was possible for anyone to actually turn green, but Marlow was doing his best Grinch impression right now. He was gagging like a cat about to cough up a hair ball.

"Sorry, Herc," she said. "Detonation imminent."

"Goddammit!"

Marlow doubled up and sprayed the contents of his stomach across the chopper floor and over Truck's shoes. Truck screamed in an impressive falsetto, pulling his legs up like a cartoon elephant that's seen a mouse. Marlow hurled again, just a dribble this time.

"Marlow!" yelled Herc. "You're cleaning that up before we go."

Marlow crunched back against the seat, his face slick with puke and sweat. He looked at Pan with an expression that said, *Just kill me now*, and she almost felt sorry for him.

Almost.

Her own guts squirmed again as the helicopter descended, the streets and trees and houses and people zooming into focus below. Herc steered them over a wide gray river, all the while speaking to somebody on the radio. There was a gold-and-black skyscraper up ahead, standing alone in a sea of smaller buildings.

"Man, these were my favorite sneakers," said Truck, doing his best to scrape off the sick against the edge of the seat. He opened his mouth, turning to the seat next to him, whatever he was about to say dying in his throat.

Pan could see it, the moment he remembered Night wasn't sitting there.

Truck glanced over at Pan, then turned to the window, jaw clenched. Pan had to swallow something huge down her throat. Night would have loved this. Yeah, they were on a mission, yeah, they would probably all be dead in a couple of days. But Night loved the traveling, loved the adventure. Seeing a new city was the thing she got most excited about—she'd have had her hand on the door already, jiggling impatiently, ready to spring out and breathe in a big lungful of *somewhere new*.

And instead she was burning up in hell, a demon's plaything.

"Hold on to your hats," said Herc as the apartment tower vanished beneath them. The chopper dropped, rotating slowly. "And, Marlow, if one more thing comes out of your mouth before we land then I'm going to eject you into the Fifteenth Arrondissement, okay?"

"Got it," croaked Marlow, swiping the back of his hand over his lips.

The helo bumped as it landed, the thrum in Pan's body fading as the rotors slowed. She breathed in deeply, the stench of vomit overpowering. Grabbing the handle, she wrestled the door open, stepping into the heat and the wind of a Paris afternoon. She ducked beneath the rotors, walking as close to the edge of the building as she dared. The vast city sprawled out before her, sparkling in the sun and shimmering in the haze that rose from the roof. It didn't look real. Her insides still hummed, and it was nothing to do with the helicopter. Her Engine was out there, somewhere. *Both* the Engines.

And they were calling.

"Whoa," said Marlow as he joined her. He had some of his color back but she still didn't trust him not to simply wilt over the side. "Nice view."

She didn't reply, turning to see Herc and Truck clamber out of the helicopter. Ostheim wasn't with them. The old guy had gone to speak to some friends in high places in order to get them into Paris unseen. Pan still couldn't get over how ordinary he had seemed—the guy who turned up at the door to sell you replacement windows, or who did your dad's taxes. The sight of him in the flesh hadn't exactly boosted her confidence, but then this was *Ostheim*, he was legendary. Whatever his secret was, he kept it well hidden.

Herc was on the edge of the landing pad, talking to someone in a suit. They shook hands—a heavy white envelope passing from Herc to the man—and the other guy walked off with a big smile. He shot them a glance as he went and she wondered what he was thinking—three kids and an old guy rocking into Paris on the sly. He probably thought they were pop stars.

Pop stars that had just been in a bar fight with a herd of rhinos.

"You ready?" Herc bellowed over the whine of the chopper.

She nodded, skipping between the air-conditioning units and joining Herc by the stairs. He held the door open for her and she jogged down a couple of flights into the main body of the building. There was an elevator dead ahead and she jammed her thumb on the button. Behind her, the others stepped out of the stairwell.

"So, we're here," said Truck. "What now?"

"Now we hunt," said Herc. "Like Shep said, the fact that the Engines are closer than ever means they'll be louder than ever. You guys feel anything?"

"Nope," said Truck. "Got diddly."

"You won't," said Herc. "Your contract's popped, the Engine isn't in you anymore. Pan, Marlow, how about you guys?"

"Feeling pretty sick," said Marlow as the elevator doors opened. "Does that count?"

"No, that's just you being the whiniest landlubber in history," said Herc. The elevator car wobbled as they stepped inside, the doors sliding shut. Herc pressed the button for the lobby. "Pan?"

Her body answered for her, a shudder passing up her spine. The electrostatic energy was boiling up her veins, making the inside of her skin itch. One wrong move, one twitch or sneeze, and she might just bring down the whole tower. But she felt strangely vulnerable, too, like she was made of glass—that infinitesimal hum she felt inside her at just the right pitch and frequency to shatter her into a million pieces. Being under contract had made her feel a million different things, but she'd never felt this before. This was new.

"Yeah," she said. "I got something."

"Good," said Herc. "Good. You just keep focusing on whatever that something is and we stand a good chance of finding wherever it is we need to go."

"Wow, specifics, I like it," muttered Pan. The elevator counted down the last few floors then eased to a halt, opening up at the end of a large lobby. It was packed with a muddle of office staff and what looked like tourists lining up behind a red rope. The rush of voices and movement was overwhelming and the anxiety of it hit Pan like a physical blow. She shrank away, backing into Marlow, felt his hand on her shoulder—and the weight of it anchored her, held her still for long enough to draw a shaky breath.

You can do this.

She followed her thoughts out into the lobby, heading into the crowd. Somebody in the queue shouted something in a New Jersey twang and she looked to see a family there, all four of them wearing baseball caps, the perfect cliché. And God, didn't it make her feel homesick? She wanted to run over and join them, go see the sights of Paris, eat frog legs and snails and Royales with cheese or whatever it was they served here. She didn't want to have to go find an Engine, fight a bunch of Engineers and Mammon and demons and *worse*. It felt like the whole weight of the tower was pushing down on her and she had to gulp at the air again, everything underwater.

Then they were out, pushing into the muggy heat of the city.

It hit her like New York did, that rush of traffic and people and noise, *so much* noise—the air swam with sirens and a ceaseless crescendo of horns from the cars; shouts and barks and the thump of their departing helicopter as it soared away overhead. She bit her lip, hard, following Herc as he strode across a wide stone plaza toward the road.

"First things first," he said over his shoulder, and she lost the rest because a couple of men on the far side of the square suddenly started swinging punches at each other, great big haymakers that hit nothing but air. They were both yelling in French, their eyes wide with rage. A fist connected, a nose exploded, then a couple of security guards from the tower were there, blocking her view.

Nice, she thought, and would have said more except the world started to tilt, a rush of vertigo like she'd just stepped off a roller coaster. It lasted only a second but it was enough to send her staggering to the side. She blinked and everything was normal again, all except Truck, who was staring at her.

"Hey, I didn't see the minibar on the chopper," he said with a soft smile. "You could have shared."

There were more shouts coming from the street, a couple of taxi drivers slinging insults at each other from their vehicles.

"I thought you said this was the City of Love," Marlow said as they walked toward the cabs.

They reached the sidewalk and Herc rapped on the window of one of the taxis, the driver spinning in his seat and grunting something at them.

"Rue Saint-Paul," Herc said. *"Tout de suite, oui?"*

The driver looked at them like they'd just spat on his windshield, then he reluctantly waved them in. It was a tight squeeze, Truck taking up most of the backseat, Marlow almost perched on his lap, but soon they were moving. The traffic crawled, made worse by the fact that at least three other fights broke out on the way—one between a couple of teenage guys, one among a group of girls, and one between an old man and what looked like a nun.

"Did you guys see that?" Pan said as they tore past.

"Never pick a fight with a nun," said Truck, one hand rubbing his temples. "Those gals got magic powers. Hey, Marly, you wanna move up maybe?"

The big guy shot Marlow a .44-caliber scowl and Marlow tried to shuffle to the side, his elbow hitting Pan in the ribs. Again that rush of panic flooded her, like she was an empty bucket held in a cold river.

"Get off, Marlow," she said, elbowing him back. She felt like putting her hand to his face and unleashing a blast of lightning, see how much he shuffled then.

"You kids stop fighting back there," Herc roared. "I swear I'll rip your . . ."

He paused, massaging his head.

"Jesus," he said. "Anyone else feel that?"

Pan swallowed down a mouthful of bile and the city lurched again, barely noticeable but definitely there—the subtlest of buzzes, like a fly trapped in your fist. She looked out the window and the street shimmered, the lines blurring for a fraction of a second. And she could almost see it, everyone's faces changing—smiles and chatter suddenly all angry eyes and gnashing teeth—and changing back in a heartbeat.

"They're here," Pan said.

The Engines. This had to be them, didn't it? Kicking out their putrid signal, corrupting everything around them. It meant they were close. That was the good news. But the flip side was that Mammon was close, too, and his Engineers could be anywhere—the redhead and whoever else he had working for him. More Magpies, maybe. Pan glanced at the driver, wondering when he'd start pulling off his own face. But the man was just steering through traffic, barking out what sounded like French swearwords at anything in his path. They were going over a wide, tree-lined river, the spire of Notre Dame visible to the left. There were half a dozen police boats in the water, lights flashing, but she couldn't see what they were doing.

"Hey," said Herc, and she saw that he was on his cell. "Five minutes. I want to be in and out, okay? Taupe there? Yeah, good. And make sure the big girl is out, I want her."

Big girl?

Herc hung up, turned to the window.

"Jesus," he said again. The Right Bank of the Seine was worse, flashes of violence wherever she looked. A car lay crumpled around a lamppost, a sunburst of blood on the windshield. An ambulance was struggling up the street, too many vehicles and people in the way.

Herc looked over his shoulder, met Pan's eye. She could read his thoughts like they were carved on his forehead.

If it's like this now, then how bad is it going to get when the gates are opened?

It took them ten minutes, in the end, to navigate a handful of narrow streets. The taxi pulled to a halt outside a bakery, brakes squealing. The driver just about had his hand in Herc's face, demanding the money. Pan left him to it as she clambered out into the street, which was almost empty, although she could hear angry shouts from nearby.

"Well, here we are," said Herc as he joined her.

"A bakery?" said Marlow as he hopped up onto the curb. "Wow, Herc, you're really bringing out the big guns. What are we going to do? Beat Mammon to death with a baguette?"

"Lob croissants at him?" added Truck. He frowned. "Man, I want a croissant."

"No," said Pan, ignoring the way the city seemed to flicker and shift, another wave of anxiety snatching at her guts. "We're going to buy a batch of cookies and convince him to change his ways, right?"

Herc turned and smiled at them, all scarred lips and missing teeth.

"You have no idea how right you are," he said, leading them through the door.

HERC'S BIG GIRL

The aroma of baking bread grabbed Marlow like a hug, pulling him into the store. He'd never experienced anything quite like it—this was the smell of home. At least he imagined it would be, if his mom had ever baked bread. The closest she'd ever really come to cooking was burning frozen pizzas in the oven or adding an accidental flambé to her martini while drinking and smoking at the same time.

The shop was busy, three men behind the counter and three times as many customers lining up. The display stands were full of things Marlow had never seen in his life, breads in all shapes and sizes and colors. Cakes, too, in a case to the side that Truck was already drooling over. He turned to Herc with an expression that belonged to a hungry puppy.

"Aw, man. Herc, you know I love you, right? Just one, okay? Just that cream bun there. And an éclair to keep it company."

Herc ignored him, nodding to one of the servers, a hulking guy whose shiny bald spot was compensated for by a shaggy beard that stretched to his sternum. He looked more like a biker than a baker. He handed a customer some change then walked out from behind the counter, cleaning his flour-covered hands on his apron.

"*'Errrrman,*" the big guy said in a heavy French accent. It took

Marlow a moment to notice he'd spoken Herc's full name. "I would say it was good to see you, but we both know you wouldn't be here if things were good, *non?*"

Herc grunted a reply and shook the man's hand.

"Come, *mon ami*, Taupe is waiting for you."

He led them past the counter and through a door in the back of the shop. Beyond was a short corridor that led into the heart of the bakery itself. The heat back here was intense, like they'd walked into a furnace, and Marlow had to wipe the sweat from his forehead. There were two industrial-sized ovens against the far wall and the man walked to the farthest. He grabbed the handle, opening the large door. Inside was not an oven but a corridor that stretched into darkness.

"I am sorry to hear what happened, 'Erman," the man said, clapping a big hairy hand on Herc's shoulder. "We never thought we would see the day that Mammon took the Engine. Our city, it is eating itself. Be quick, friend. Find him."

Herc nodded curtly, then walked into the oven. Pan followed, then Truck. Marlow hurried after them, finding himself walking down a set of steep stone steps. They doubled back on themselves into a cellar, small and softly lit. There was one room, and one man in it. He was in his twenties and looked like he'd just walked off a movie set—Gallic good looks, perfect dark hair, and a smile that seemed spotlight-bright, especially when he turned it toward Pan.

Five seconds in and Marlow already hated him.

"Taupe," said Herc.

"Herc," the guy replied as they shook hands. His accent was more subtle, his English better. He was standing in front of a table that had been draped with a dustcover. Marlow couldn't make sense of any of the shapes beneath. "Ostheim said you would come, and he said you would need help."

"He was right on both counts," Herc said. "You got what I need?"

"As always."

The guy grabbed the dustcover and pulled it away, revealing an assortment of weapons that would keep a Special Forces unit in business. Marlow counted half a dozen machine guns, twice as many pistols, a box of grenades, a couple of crossbows, and something that he thought existed only in action movies.

"Is that a *bazooka*?" he asked before he could stop himself. Everyone turned to look at him, and the French guy smiled even harder.

"You will have to fight Herc for it," he said. "This is his *big girl*."

"Shut up, Taupe," said Herc. "Got rounds?"

"Three," said Taupe. "Enough?"

"It'll have to be. You got the other thing, right?"

Taupe shuffled uncomfortably, wiping a hand over his mouth.

"Taupe, tell me you got it."

"I did," he said after a moment. "I do not like it, Herc. It is fighting fire with fire. It could do more damage than Mammon."

"No," said Herc. "It couldn't."

Taupe considered it, then nodded. He reached under the table and wrestled out a large green rucksack that looked like standard army issue. He dragged it across the floor and straightened, a sheen of sweat on his face.

"Use it wisely," he said. Herc grunted, a noise that could have been a thanks or a laugh.

"What about intel?" Herc said. "You found anything?"

Taupe shrugged.

"Maybe, maybe not. We have been monitoring activity, there are some leads. Coding machines have been going nuts. Our people are out there. Herc, you met Ostheim. What is he like?"

Herc snorted, shaking his head. "You wouldn't believe me if I told you. Hell, you wouldn't believe me if I showed you a photo. Guy's . . . Well, he's not . . ." Herc swore, looked to Pan.

"Looks like he couldn't win a fight with a blindfolded, one-legged kitten," she said.

Taupe frowned.

"All these years fighting for somebody, who'd have figured?"

"Hey, he's still Ostheim," said Herc, nervously scanning the walls, the ceiling. "Don't judge a book by its cover, and all that. He's still Ostheim."

Taupe swallowed hard, nodding. Then he broke into a smile again.

"New recruits, I see," he said. "They seem to get younger every time." He glanced at Marlow. "Younger and rougher around the edges."

"Yeah?" Marlow said, trying and failing to think of a come-back. "And who the hell are you? The baker?"

Herc sighed.

"Marlow, Pan, Truck, this is Taupe. Ex-Engineer turned . . . I don't know, what's the kind word for it? Mercenary? Profi-teer?"

"Please," said Taupe. "*Businessman* is just fine. It is good to meet you, Marlow, Truck. And Pan, what an honor. I did not think it was possible to make a deal with the Engine for such beauty."

Are you serious?

Marlow bit back a laugh, then almost choked on it when he saw Pan blush. She smiled, holding out her hand for Taupe to shake. He grabbed it and kissed it, holding it for a fraction too long. Not that Pan made an effort to pull it away.

Marlow shuffled uncomfortably, realizing that his own cheeks were heating up. For a cellar, this place was *hot*.

"You were an Engineer?" asked Pan when the French guy finally let her go. "I thought Engineers just, you know, stayed or died. I didn't think anyone had actually left."

"Not many," said Taupe. "Just a handful. I made more than thirty contracts, back when I was a teenager. More missions than I could count."

"Eighty-four," said Herc.

"But age is not an Engineer's friend. Eventually the contracts became too complex even for . . . even for Saul, God rest his soul. So I left."

"Been working with us ever since," said Herc. "Logistics, weapons, recon. Makes a damn fine sourdough, too. You heard about Saul, then?"

Taupe nodded. "Yeah, I heard. That bastard Mammon. I did not think it was possible, Herc. I did not think anyone could breach the Red Door." He glanced at Marlow and the room heated up another ten degrees. "But we will find him. He is here, somewhere. The Engines are here. After all these years of looking, now is our chance. The blood on the streets does not lie."

"Only good thing about the Engines being reunited," said Herc. "Hopefully they'll lead us right to them."

"They know that," said Taupe. "They'll be waiting. And Mammon will be throwing out Engineers as quickly as he can. Finding the Engine is one thing, getting to it alive is something else."

"Which is where my big girl will come in," said Herc, walking to the table and hefting the bazooka onto his shoulder. "You can make a deal for anything you like, but a high-explosive antitank warhead to the face is gonna end you, contract or no contract."

"Amen to that," said Truck, walking to the table and picking up a shotgun. "Dibs."

He took a crossbow in his other hand and gave it to Pan. She took it, investigating its weight and sights.

"We have only three bolts," said Taupe. "All we had left after Morocco. They're old magic, though, straight from the Engine, and they'll put a hole in a demon."

"Cool," said Pan, and Marlow wasn't sure if her smile was for the crossbow or for the Frenchman.

"Marlow," said Herc. "Grab something."

"I'm fine," he said, flexing his damp hands. "Got powers."

"They might not last," said Herc. "Mammon could end them any minute now. Go, take a weapon."

Marlow swallowed, wondering how his throat could have gotten so dry. Herc was right. His contract could be canceled at any time. It wasn't the loss of his strength and speed that scared him, it was the fact that his asthma would come back—and it would come back *hard*. The monster around his throat would be pissed, and he didn't even have an inhaler. He coughed at the thought of it, rubbed his chest. Then, when he realized that everyone was waiting for him, he walked to the table. The guns looked big, and mean, and ready to put a hole in him the moment he laid his hand on them.

"They won't bite," said Taupe with a high-pitched chuckle. Marlow wanted to throw a punch at him, see if he was still laughing then. He reached out and grabbed the biggest machine gun, lifting it awkwardly to his chest. It stank of metal and grease.

"Bloody hell, Marlow," said Herc. "Put that down. Taupe, give him a forty-five, would you?"

Taupe laughed again, pulling the assault rifle from Marlow's grip. He laid it on the table then picked up a small black pistol, handing it over. With every pair of eyes in the room on him, Marlow didn't have any choice but to take it. He studied it. It looked like it fired Pez candy.

"It'll give you time and space if you need it," said Herc. "Remember, unless they've traded for invulnerability then you can still kill them."

"The perfect little gun for *le petit garçon*," said Taupe, and he had the nerve to fire a wink at Pan.

She stifled a smile and Marlow's blood pressure rose so high he thought the top of his head was going to pop off. He tucked the gun into the waistband of his pants before he would crush it into a paperweight.

"It's not about the size, *Toupée*," he muttered. "It's about how well you can use it."

"And do you know how to use it?" the guy replied without missing a beat.

Once again Marlow's brain gave him nothing to come back with and suddenly the whole room was laughing. His hackles rippled up and for a moment the world burned so bright that he wasn't sure he could control himself. Then he felt a hand on his arm.

"Ignore him, kiddo," Herc said, hefting the rucksack onto his back. It looked heavy. "We got more important things to worry about. Taupe, ain't no point us sitting here staring at the walls. Where's the best lead, where can we start?"

"Where to start?" The French guy mulled it over, his eyes scrolling the dirt floor. "In this city, where else could it be? We start with the dead."

NOPE

Paris was losing itself.

Pan watched it coming apart at the seams, the threads that made this great city being pulled by the Engines that surely lay somewhere beneath it. Through the filthy window she saw people running down the streets, teeth bared; she saw dogs savaging their owners; she saw broken windows and a burning car and at least two dozen emergency vehicles fighting to get through the chaos. As they pulled back onto the road that ran parallel to the river she thought she saw people jumping from the bridges, a line of them, like synchronized divers.

"Hang on," yelled Taupe from the driver's seat. He had loaded them into an old Russian army bus that looked like it hadn't been driven—or cleaned—since World War II. The windows were smeared with orange dirt, and what must have been half a sand dune formed drifts around their feet every time the bus turned a corner. He changed gears and the vehicle bellowed, shuddering so hard she had to grab the seat in front to stop from sliding onto the floor. The crossbow dug into her back and she shifted it to the side.

"It is not far," he said.

"Thank God," muttered Marlow from across the aisle. "He needs a driving lesson."

She ignored him, sneaking a glance at Taupe's reflection in the rearview mirror. The guy was cute. Ridiculously cute. Even amid the chaos, even though he was driving them to war, there was no denying it. More than that, though, she'd heard about him. Betty, the woman who'd patched them up after each mission, who'd done her best to stitch the pieces back together, had always spoken about "the Frenchman." She'd been a little obsessed with him, which was kind of weird given that she'd been in her fifties and Taupe had been a teenager.

Less weird, though, now that Pan had met him.

Pull yourself together, she thought, turning to the window. They passed a fire truck that was actually on fire. That had to be one of the signs of the apocalypse, right?

She looked at the mirror again, studying Taupe's eyes, the furrow of his brow. He must have sensed her because he looked up, his reflection winking. She turned away sharply, the heat burrowing into her face. Marlow was looking at her, too, and he was wearing the expression of a kid whose favorite toy has been snatched away.

"What?" she demanded.

"He's . . ." Marlow started, shrugging. He looked like he was about to burst into tears. "He's *French*."

Pan shook her head, turning her attention to Herc in the seat in front of her. The rucksack sat next to him.

"What's in there?" she asked.

"A surprise," he said. "A little present for Mammon."

She didn't have the energy to pursue it. "So, what do we know?"

"What do we know?" Herc replied, leaning his elbow on the back of his seat. "Nothing. Absolutely nothing. But we can guess. One thing we always suspected was that wherever the Engines are, you can be sure to find death."

116

"Death?" said Marlow, leaning across the aisle. "How do you mean?"

"Death," said Herc, shrugging. "Like, not living. It's why you'll find the Red Doors in big cities, old cities. The Red Doors pump out bad vibes like a faulty nuclear reactor pumps out radiation. Murder rates skyrocket near every place the door opens to; assault, suicide, everything you can think of. And that's just the *door*, not the Engine."

He smoothed a hand down his stubble, contemplating something.

"You have to understand that the Fist has been hunting for the actual location of the Engine for centuries."

"Mammon's Engine?" said Marlow. Herc shook his head.

"No, our *own*. Nobody has ever known, they have just accessed it through the Red Door. The door essentially teleported them to the Engine's location."

Pan thought of the way it pulled you apart, the way it put you back together, layer by layer, cell by cell.

"Even with today's technology, *nada*. Ostheim has spent a fortune scanning beneath cities, using satellite imaging and that sort of thing. But whoever built the Engine—the Engines—wanted to keep them hidden."

"I thought they wanted people to find them, though," said Pan, holding on to her seat as Taupe steered them around another corner. "To use them."

"Find the door, yes," said Herc. "Find a way inside so they can make a deal, yes. But find the actual Engine, no. It would make it too vulnerable, too easy to locate and destroy. The Red Door was smart, you always knew that bastard thing was watching you, that it could, I don't know, *read* you somehow."

Pan's flesh crawled at the memory. The door had been an evil piece of work, no doubt about it. Clever, too.

"But the Engines, both of them, they were hidden some-where deep, somewhere almost impossible to find. They were—"

Something smashed into the window by Herc's head, spray-ing glass. He swore, turning to yell at a crowd of teenage boys in the street. They lobbed another couple of bricks but Taupe put his foot on the gas, the bus roaring out of reach.

"Damn things," Herc said, brushing the shards from his head. "Where was I?"

"Engines impossible to find," said Pan. *"We don't stand a chance.* You know, boosting our morale."

"They *were,*" he said. "But not anymore. Mammon is trying to bring the Engines together, his and ours. In order to do that, far as we can tell, they *have* to move. It's just physics, plain and simple. It's like a hunter waiting for its prey to break cover— invisible when it's still, but as soon as it moves you get your shot."

Yeah, you get a second or two, then it's gone forever.

"So, death?" Marlow said.

"Oh, yeah. Death. There's one thing, so far, that all of the Red Door locations have in common. They're in, or close to, churches."

"Ironic," said Pan.

"Yeah, sure," said Herc. "Makes sense, though. If the Red Doors corrupt then why not consecrate the ground; try to, I don't know, unsalt the earth."

"Good way of hiding them, too," said Pan. "You don't look for the devil in a church."

"True," said Herc. The bus lurched as it plowed into some-thing, Taupe not slowing down. "Not just churches, either, but graveyards, cemeteries. The Red Doors were always sur-rounded by the dead."

"Corpses?" asked Marlow.

"The more dead bodies, the better," said Herc. "The church in Prague was built over a boneyard, an ossuary. If you'd kept walking down those basement tunnels you'd have found the skeletons of a few thousand people."

"And you let me use the bathroom down there?" yelled Truck from the back.

"Paris has tunnels filled with bones?" said Marlow. Herc nodded.

"The city is built on them. There are six million dead beneath us right now."

"What?" said Marlow, shaking his head. "Nope."

"The Catacombs," said Herc. "A thousand miles of tunnels that cross the city, built from bones. The world's biggest grave-yard."

"Nope," he said again.

"And somewhere down there, as far as we can tell, are the Engines."

"Just nope," said Marlow.

"So this place is the world's biggest graveyard and you've never thought to look here?" asked Pan.

"Of course we've looked," Herc replied. "We've had teams down there for years, mapping the tunnels, cataloging the contents, and looking for clues. Ostheim has had tectonic ultra-sounds made from the basement of pretty much every building in Paris, probing. But you've got to understand, these tunnels, they're old mines, connecting to even older cave systems. They're deep."

"We've lost more than one person in there," yelled Taupe. "Just vanished into the walls, like the dead pulled them in, de-voured them. Hang on."

His cell was ringing and he pulled it from his pants pocket, the bus lurching as he let go of the wheel.

"Because the Engines, they have ways of protecting themselves," said Herc. "*Hiding* themselves."

Pan blew out a sigh. Six years she'd been running missions for Ostheim and Herc, six years she'd been a member of the Fist, and she felt like she knew less now than she ever had.

"It's our best shot," said Herc. "Right now it's our *only* shot."

"And we've just had confirmation," Taupe said. "The code readers, they've found a cluster of anomalies at the entrance to the Catacombs. Engineers."

"And they know we're coming," said Pan.

"Let's go crush some ass, then," said Truck.

The bus roared around a corner, Pan sliding across her seat and nearly falling into the aisle.

"Hang on, hang on." Herc shook his head. "No way, it's too easy. Stop the bus, Taupe."

The Frenchman did as he was told, bumping them up onto the curb. Over the idling engine Pan could hear more shouts from outside, a scream.

"What?" asked Taupe, looking back.

"We have to assume Mammon knows we're here, and that we'll be looking for anomalies. So he sends all his Engineers to the entrance to the Catacombs."

"To protect them," said Truck. "Like Marly said, he knows we're coming."

"Or to pull us off the scent," said Pan, and Herc nodded.

"We head straight to them, and even if we do get past the guards we're in the wrong place. He's lured us away from where we need to be."

"Or he's just protecting the *right* place," said Marlow. "How do we know?"

Herc popped his lips. "You heard from Ostheim?" he asked Taupe.

The other guy shook his head.

"What about any other blips, smaller ones?"

"A couple," said Taupe. "One on the Seine, another in a Metro station."

"Which Metro station?"

"Uh . . . Châtelet, Rue Saint-Denis, near—"

"I know where it is," said Herc. "Head there, that's where we need to be."

"Why?" Taupe asked. "It does not make sense, scurrying around like this. We should meet Mammon head-on."

"It's what he wants us to do," Herc said. "I know him, I've been smacking heads with that asshole longer than any of you been alive. I'm telling you, it's a trap."

"I think not," said Taupe. "We carry on."

He gunned the engine, the bus thumping down onto the street and into traffic. Pan and Herc shared a look, and Pan flexed her fingers to shake up a charge. Taupe may have been a legend. He may have been the best-looking guy she'd seen in a long while, but times changed and people changed. In this line of work, you couldn't trust anyone.

Herc must have been thinking the same thing because he'd unbuttoned the holster of his sidearm, pulling out a Desert Eagle. He aimed it at the back of Taupe's head.

"Hey, Taupe," he growled. "I need you to turn this bus around."

Taupe glanced in the mirror, then looked over his shoulder.

"Hey, Herc—chill, man. This is the right move."

Herc cocked the hammer, finger on the trigger.

"That's an order, Taupe."

"You stopped being able to give me orders a long while ago, old man."

He's working for them, Pan thought. *He's on Mammon's*

payroll and he's taking us right to him. A spark escaped her fin-ger and fizzed across the floor of the bus.

"Ostheim said whatever it took, Herc," Taupe said, the bus going even faster, glancing off the side of a parked car. "He said this was going to be brutal. Mammon is preparing for a fight because he knows we're onto him. I'm telling you, if we head to the Catacombs, to where his Engineers are waiting, then we've as good as found the Engine."

"Taupe!" Herc yelled. They swept around a corner hard enough to shunt Herc from his seat. His gun fired, a round ricocheting off the roof. Taupe was whooping now, gunning the bus up to forty, fifty, sixty miles per hour—Paris just a blur outside the window.

Then he slammed on the brakes and Pan's head snapped forward, her forehead connecting with the seat in front. The crossbow swung over her shoulder, landing in her lap. She blinked away the stars, pushing herself up and groaning. The electricity was a cold current in her arms and she clenched her fists to hold it back. She was going to fry Taupe alive, but not before she'd gouged every last truth from his evil, ridicu-lously good-looking face.

"Goddammit, Taupe," said Herc, collecting his gun from the floor and leveling it. "Please tell me you didn't sell us up the river."

"Never," he replied with that flawless grin. "Not you, Herc. I'm here to fight, I'm here to stop Mammon before he opens the gates of hell and we all get pitchforked to death."

Pan held her breath. Holding back the charge was like hold-ing a pulled bow—her whole body was shaking with the effort of it. Taupe glanced out the window. They were sitting in the shadow of a huge statue, a bronze lion, and past that there was movement.

"But if I were you, I'd be pointing that gun over there," Taupe said, grabbing the edge of the driver's seat in white-knuckled hands. "Because we've got company."

And Pan barely had time to look before something collided with the bus and her world flipped upside down.

ALWAYS OUTNUMBERED,
NEVER OUTGUNNED

It was like a train had hit them, the bus rolling onto its side. Marlow didn't even have time to scream as he slammed into the window, then onto the ceiling as the bus flipped again. The air was a tornado of glass, grinding into his skin, his lungs.

Another impact, a squeal of metal as the bus was shunted across the street. One side of the bus caved in, like they were inside a compactor. Pan was ahead, picking herself up from a puddle of blood, the crossbow strapped on her back. Her nose was streaming and she wiped it with her hand. Then she aimed her fingers at the windows and unleashed a charge of energy that blazed into the street. A boom of thunder detonated inside the bus and there was nothing in Marlow's head but static.

He stood, banging his head on one of the seats that now hung above him. It was like he'd been packed in cotton wool, everything muffled, everything fuzzy. Pan was standing in a cloud of vaporized blood and smoke, a shimmering vision who pulled back her hand then thrust it forward. This time Marlow turned away from the wave of cold fury, pressing his hands to his ears against the boom that followed.

Somebody ripped the rear doors from the bus, letting in a wave of blinding sunlight.

"I got them," said a silhouette, climbing inside.

"Move!" came a muffled cry, Herc pushing past Marlow, his Desert Eagle barking. The silhouette lurched, groaning as he fell back through the doors. Herc grabbed a handful of Marlow's T-shirt, hauling him along. "We're sitting ducks, we gotta get out of the bus!"

Marlow did as he was told, his heart trying to jackhammer its way through his ribs. Truck was moving, shotgun roaring as he stepped into the day.

"Herc!" yelled Taupe, lobbing the bazooka up the bus. Herc let go of Marlow and snatched it, then struggled to get the rucksack on. Marlow left him to it, stumbling toward the open doors of the upside-down bus.

More thunder, an assault rifle spitting rounds. Marlow almost threw himself to the floor before he realized it was Taupe, spraying hell from the front of the bus. Then he was out, blinded by sunlight as he stepped onto the street.

"Marlow!" Truck yelled, enough warning for him to twist around and see the punch coming. He dodged and the fist glanced off his chin, still hard enough to make it feel like his head had come loose. The silhouette was there—not a shadow anymore but a young guy who had to be bigger than Truck, his night camo overalls bulging with muscles. He lunged in again, a vicious uppercut that connected right where it meant to.

Marlow was airborne, feeling like he'd been launched from a catapult. He flipped twice, landing awkwardly on his shoulder. The agony was arm-in-a-blender bad but he could still move, nothing was broken. The Engine in his blood was protecting him.

He pushed himself up, the guy running at him over the

cobbled street. Behind him another searing fork of lightning burst from the bus, rippling across the street and into the side of a building. The man flinched at the sound of it, losing his footing.

Marlow ran, time slowing. He glanced right to see Truck frozen still, a plume of fire sticking out from the end of his shotgun. To the left was a rippling line of bullets, hanging in the air between the bus and the buildings and glowing like fairy lights—Taupe shooting across the street to where a girl stood, dressed in the same black-and-gray camouflage. She couldn't have been older than fourteen. Herc was halfway out of the bus, a face like grim death.

Then Marlow reached the man and time snapped back in a hurricane of noise and movement. The guy blinked in surprise as he saw Marlow materialize.

He's new, Marlow understood. *He's just been recruited.*

He let loose a punch that connected with the guy's face. He had a jaw that belonged to a cast-iron bull but it didn't save him, the impact from Marlow's fist like being hit by a wrecking ball. He flew back, skimming over the street and slamming into a green metal outbuilding by the side of the road. There were people everywhere, Marlow noticed, normals who were fleeing from the carnage.

And there, streaming from the same green building, two more teenagers in black.

"Incoming!" Marlow yelled, then something crunched into the back of his skull. He staggered forward, feeling like his eyeballs had been knocked loose. When he turned around again there was nobody there, but it didn't stop something pounding him in the head, once, twice, his vision full of white noise.

What the—

Another phantom punch connected with his kidneys and

he broke into a run to escape, time stretching out before him. He glanced back as he sprinted, seeing a shimmering blur, one that flickered and jarred like a video glitch. Somewhere in the movement he made out a girl, the same girl that had been standing on the other side of the street. She must have traded for invisibility.

Marlow skidded back into real time, breathing hard. The bus was on fire now, Taupe clambering through the shattered windshield. Pan scrambled out the back, shaking smoke from her blackened hands, her face etched with pain. She saw Marlow, jogging to his side. Truck was there, too, lumbering over, his face slick with sweat.

"Watch out," Marlow said. "There's a—"

Truck yelped, toppling like a felled oak. Blood squirted from his lip as it was hit by an invisible fist. Marlow didn't hesitate, lunging forward, feeling for the girl, connecting with a bag of cloth and flesh. She screamed and he felt a hand on his arm, teeth in his flesh. Grabbing tight, he swung himself around in a circle and lobbed the girl like he was throwing a hammer. One of the trees along the side of the road bent and swayed as she hit it, then she flickered back into view, sliding along the ground.

"Watch your four o'clock!" yelled Herc.

Marlow looked left, saw nothing.

"Four, you idiot. Look *right*!"

He did as he was told, seeing the two black-suited Engineers jogging across the road, heading right for them. Another three were pushing their way out of the half-demolished green building.

One of them with bright red hair.

"Oh God, not this bimbo again," said Pan.

The redhead pointed at them, her face alive with fury. Then

she broke into a run, pulling a copper-colored blade from her belt.

Oh no.

Pan splayed her fingers and fired out a jagged current of electricity, one that tore up the street in a tidal wave of cobbles. The girl screamed, vanishing into the blast, and for a second Marlow almost cheered. Then she was out, running right for the statue that stood in the middle of the street. She leaped up, jammed the knife into the body of the bronze lion.

The statue groaned like a living thing, the bronze bending, stretching. A face appeared in the lion's ribs, a demon pushing its way through from the other side.

"Oh boy," said Truck as Pan helped him to his feet.

"There's a monster from hell taking possession of a giant metal lion, and the best you can do is 'oh boy'?" said Pan, raising an eyebrow.

It fell just as fast and she let out a curse of her own.

Marlow followed her line of sight to see one of the other Engineers stop in the middle of the street—an older girl, maybe Pan's age. She grimaced, then her entire body burst into flames.

This is new.

The burning girl stretched out her hands and a plume of fire burned out of them, flamethrower fierce. It sluiced across the street, the force of it pushing Marlow back, scattering them. The ground was trembling as the demon-lion thing leaped from its pedestal, shaking itself like a wet dog before breaking into a lopsided run. Still more Engineers were pouring from the half-demolished shed, an army. Then Marlow lost sight of them behind another wall of flame.

It was hopeless.

"We're outnumbered," he yelled, choking on smoke, not even sure if anyone could hear him in the chaos. He thumped into something big and flailed against it, only to hear Herc's voice.

"Always outnumbered," he growled, hefting the bazooka onto his shoulder. "Never outgunned."

The old guy took a deep breath, then pulled the trigger. A pillar of exhaust flame burned from the back of the tube as something shot out of the front. The missile whistled as it cut across the street, punching a hole in the front of the green building just as another Engineer was running from the door.

The building exploded, a fist of heat and sound that knocked Marlow to his knees. The air was suddenly an orchestra of screams, and through the sun flares in his vision Marlow saw pieces of black cloth and burning flesh scattered across the street. He dropped onto all fours, retching, nothing inside him but bile.

"Pan!" he heard Truck shout. Marlow looked with watering eyes to see the demon lion running right for her. She fired off a blast of energy with one hand, trying to pull free her crossbow with the other. Then a billowing cloud of smoke rolled over them and they vanished.

Get up, he told himself, but his legs were made of ash, not enough left there to carry him. He crawled instead, silently yelling *get up get up get up* until he somehow managed it. The entire street was an inferno, trees popping in the blistering heat, electrical wires sparking. It wasn't all from the explosion, he realized. The ground near the green building was glowing like molten rock, so bright that he could barely look at it. A car parked near the curb was already sinking into it, along with the corpses of anyone who had been caught in the blast.

There was something else in the air, too. Something worse than the smoke, worse than the stench of burning flesh.

Sulfur.

The smoke on the far side of the street was suddenly split by lightning, Pan shouting something from in there. He limped toward the sound of her voice. The lion demon screamed, the noise echoed by something that pushed its way from the street—an asphalt torso, a shell of cobbles like a turtle. It shook its head until a snout had formed, teeth snapping.

Demons, coming to collect their dead.

The asphalt monster ran, snatching up burning limbs from the molten earth. Marlow could hear more shrieks, knew that they weren't coming from anything living. It was the souls of the enemy Engineers being dragged into hell.

Gunshots. Marlow followed the sound of them, heading into the choking smoke. It cleared for an instant and he saw Pan there, dodging the lion demon like a bullfighter, trying to find a clear shot. She dived beneath its foot, rolled an instant before it came crashing down. Taupe was there, too, assault rifle bucking in his grip as he fired rounds into the demon's hide. Truck burst from the smoke, looking like he was about to cough up a lung. He aimed his shotgun and fired, the rounds ricocheting off the creature's metal hide like a handful of sand.

Where the hell was Herc and his big girl?

The beast roared, its jaws snapping shut a hair's width from Pan's face. She staggered away, eyes screwed shut, a trickle of electricity dribbling from her palms. Marlow put his head down, calling her name as he charged. Even with the Engine inside him he didn't think he stood much chance against a solid metal demon beast.

But it was *Pan.*

He thumped into it like a linebacker, bouncing right off with a headful of stars. The demon swung around lazily. It had no

eyes, not really, but Marlow felt it look at him, felt it try to figure out what he was. It was like somebody had let loose a
clutch of spiders inside his soul, and despite the heat of hell
around him, his blood ran cold. The demon sniffed the air,
growled, then began to run right for him.

Oh f—

He threw himself to the side, the demon passing him like
a locomotive. He scrabbled up, waiting for the attack. But the
creature was running away, heading for the molten ground and
throwing itself into the fray. There were other demons there
now, maybe a dozen of them, more still pulling themselves out
of the stone buildings that lined the street. The bronze lion
joined them, howling like a coyote. It picked up a smaller
demon in its jaws and threw it to one side, pushing its face into
the glowing earth and digging out a body.

"Bastards," said Herc. He'd reloaded the bazooka and he
got down on one knee, firing another missile. This one struck
the back of the lion demon and the whole scene was obliter-
ated by light and heat. Herc was already running again, yelling, "Go go go!"

Marlow followed him, every step an effort. They cut left,
giving the demons a wide berth. Marlow could still hear them,
the gargled cries, the snapping of jaws, those awful, endless
screams from Mammon's dead and dying Engineers.

Another scream, this one very much alive. He glanced over,
saw a shape in the flames. It was the girl, the young one, no
longer invisible. She was curled up into a ball on the curb. She
hadn't died, and her contract hadn't expired, but in a feeding
frenzy like this there was no guarantee the demons wouldn't
tear her to pieces for the fun of it.

Marlow stopped, shook his head.

Don't do it.

The others were heading across a patch of grass behind the green building. Nobody looked back.

Keep running.

Marlow looked again, the girl cowering. Even with her powers, she didn't stand a chance.

Just a kid.

And the last time he'd tried to help someone, Night had died.

But just a kid.

Just like me.

He doubled back, forcing himself into a sprint. Time slowed reluctantly this time, he could feel the shudder and shake of it, an overwhelming groan like the universe was about to spin off its axis. In the sudden quiet the horror of the scene was almost too much, two dozen demons teeming over one another in slow motion, reducing flesh to mincemeat as they dug for souls.

He skidded down beside the girl, ignoring the ear-pulping roar of reality. He didn't stop to introduce himself, just scooped her up and doubled back. Somebody was shouting behind him and he felt another fist of heat strike him on the back—the flamethrower girl. Then he was around the corner, fumbling across the grass. The girl was struggling in his arms but he held on tight. There was no sign of the others, but before his stomach could fall all the way into his feet he heard a hiss, looked to see Herc peeking up from behind a brick wall. The old guy lifted his hands to say, *What the hell?*

"Just . . ." he said, and he couldn't find the breath for any more. He tossed the girl over the wall as gently as he could, then vaulted it himself. They were in a courtyard, a gated passage opposite. Pan, Truck, and Taupe were already there. Pan took one look at Marlow, then another at the girl, shaking her head in disgust. The girl was scrabbling back across the ground, scrunching her eyes shut like she was trying to blink her way out of the world.

"Could use you over here," yelled Truck, his hands on the bars of the gate. "My arms haven't got the horsepower they used to."

Marlow nodded, gulping down air as he crossed the courtyard. He grabbed the gate, planted his feet, and pulled. It resisted for all of three seconds before the bolts exploded from the brick walls. Marlow threw the gate away, letting Pan go first, then Taupe, then Truck.

Pan looked back long enough to yell, "You're not bringing her." Then she was gone, clattering down some steps.

Marlow glanced back. They were on the other side of the green building, he noticed. It was up in flames, and the sound of screaming demons was just as loud here as it had been on the street. The building would be rubble and ash in a minute, maybe less. The girl was backing toward it, glaring at Herc, then at Marlow. Herc shrugged at her.

"You can take your chances with us, or with them," he said, offering her a big, calloused hand.

A roar that could have come from a jumbo jet. The sound of shearing metal and crumbling brick. The girl looked back, then got to her feet, running past Herc, then past Marlow, and disappearing into the passage.

"And I thought *I* was soft," Herc grumbled as he passed them, the bazooka still mounted on his shoulder, the rucksack jiggling on his back like he was a pack mule. "Come on, Mother Teresa."

Marlow followed, hearing the roar of the building as it collapsed behind him, the screams of the demons and the shouts of whatever enemy Engineers had survived. He skipped down some stone steps into a cold, dank corridor. It took him a moment to realize that the walls were made of bones.

"Brace yourselves," yelled Herc, his voice echoing. He aimed the bazooka back up the stairs.

"Wait, Herc, no!" yelled Pan.

Too late. He fired, the sound deafening in such a small space. The exhaust jet spat back, so hot that it ignited Pan's hair. She didn't even have time to yell before the missile hit the top of the passageway, detonating. Marlow threw himself onto the ground, everything shaking, as if the whole world were collapsing around him, as if they were being buried alive. It seemed like forever before it stopped, but eventually it did, plunging them into the cold, dark silence of the world's largest graveyard.

CITY OF DEATH

There were no working lights down here, Pan realized, but seeing wasn't exactly a problem, because her hair was on fire.

Her *hair* was on fire.

Pan slapped at her head, gagging at the stench. The flames illuminated the bones that made up the walls, the grinning skulls—not that she could see much past the eye-watering pain of it. Her scalp stung like she'd been apple bobbing in a vat of acid, but after a second or two the fire fizzled out.

"Goddammit, Herc," she said to the sudden darkness. "A little warning?"

"Sorry," said the big guy. "It was a time-sensitive shot."

Pan heard rustling, then a rattle. There was a soft click and the corridor popped out of the dark again, illuminated by the huge Maglite in Herc's hand. He beamed it back and forth, blinding her. She blinked, feeling instinctively for the crossbow strapped to her back. She hadn't used it in the battle outside, even when the lion demon was trying to bite her in two. With only three bolts, she wanted to save it for when she was face-to-face with Mammon.

Only now, in the relative quiet—she could still hear muted roars from outside, the patter of dust and rubble, the deep, ragged breaths from around her—did her body seem to remember that it had been injured. The pain crept back in slowly but insistently, starting in the pounding muscles of her calves, moving up through a sprained knee, a torn muscle in her lower back, bruised ribs, and a nose that might have been broken.

It was just pain, though. As familiar as an old friend.

And welcome, too, because if you were hurting, it meant you were still alive. It was Herc who'd always said that to her after a mission.

"Man, that was bad," said Truck, pacing back and forth between the walls. He reached out and placed his hand on them, then seemed to notice the bones there, recoiling. She knew exactly what he was thinking.

This could have been us, dead and buried.

Give it time, Truck, she thought. *The day isn't over yet.*

"Nobody missing any body parts?" Herc asked.

There was a collective clapping of hands on flesh as they all patted themselves down. Pan could already feel the power of the Engine coursing through her, the contract keeping her alive, repairing wounds.

"I'm cool," said Truck. He had no contract, but he'd been in enough scrapes to know how to handle pain.

"All well and good," said Taupe.

"Nothing missing," said Marlow. "But everything hurts."

"Well, that's good," Herc replied. "If you feel pain, it means you're still alive."

Pan couldn't help but smile at the old guy's predictability.

"Where'd the girl go?" he asked.

"You brought her *in*?" said Pan. "You idiot, Marlow, didn't you learn anything from the train?"

Always trying to rescue people, how could anyone be such a selfish *jerk*? She looked behind her. In one direction the tunnel was a mound of rock, debris still falling from the collapsed ceiling. The other way stretched into darkness, no sign of anybody else. "That was real stupid, Herc. If this is the path to Mammon then she's going to be halfway to him by now. Bang goes our element of surprise."

"Pan, we just blew up half of Paris," Herc said. "God knows how many of his Engineers died out there. A giant metal lion was eating people. Our element of surprise went out the window a while back."

Pan shook her head, shooting Marlow a look she hoped he could feel. She leaned back against the uncomfortable wall so that she wouldn't crumple onto the floor, shatter like bone. The shakes were starting, the adrenaline runoff making her feel unbearably tired. They were lucky to have made it through the last few minutes. *Really* lucky. That many Engineers, that many powers, plus the redhead with her impossible dagger. Thinking about it now, she had no idea how they'd gotten as far as making it out of the bus.

And they hadn't even reached Mammon yet.

"You think this is the right place?" Truck asked.

"I do not know," Taupe replied. "If I were you, I would have picked a different route, maybe one less dangerous. It was crazy going up against all those Engineers."

Everyone turned to the Frenchman, glaring, and he broke into a smile that was brighter than the flashlight. He held up his hands.

"Joke, joke. I am sorry. Yes, I do believe we made the right decision."

Herc shrugged.

"I can't see Mammon putting that many people here if he didn't have something to hide. Chances are we're on the right track. Not like we have a choice now anyway."

Pan looked down the passageway again. There was something there, something in the way the walls seemed to shift and blur—nothing to do with the wavering flashlight. It was the same sensation she'd felt up top, a pulse of rancid, gut-churning energy that made her want to tear out her own insides, there and gone again, there and gone again, like a heartbeat.

"We're on the right track," she said.

"Yeah," said Marlow, one hand on his stomach. He looked paper-thin, like he might just fold away into nothing. He met her eye and she knew he felt it, too. The Engine was inside them both, and something was calling to them.

"What's the plan, then?" she asked. "We should call Ostheim, let him know where we are."

"He knows," said Herc, pulling a small black box from his pocket. "Transponder. Not sure if it will work beneath the ground but he'll know our entry point."

"Then we wait for him, *oui?*" said Taupe, brushing dust and ash from his jacket.

"Why?" said Truck. "Old geezer couldn't win a wrestling match against a pudding."

"Truck!" yelled Herc.

"You saw him, dude. He's about as useless to us down here as a fart in the wind."

"Truck!"

"What?" Truck said, holding up his hands. "Am I the only one thinking it?"

"Got a point," said Pan. "Looked like he wouldn't have said boo to a goose."

"Looks like he would have crapped his pants if he'd *seen* a goose," added Marlow.

"He's still the boss," said Herc, jabbing a finger at them. "But no, we're not waiting for him. Our job is to find the Engine, one of them, both of them, I don't even know. Find it and work out a way of destroying it. Time is ticking, people. Let's go."

He heaved up his backpack, fumbling with the Desert Eagle and the flashlight. "Any of you lazy bastards want to help?"

Marlow took the flashlight from him, shining it down the tunnel. There was barely a scrap of wall that wasn't bone, making Pan feel like she was descending the throat of some huge, ancient creature. Skulls stared at her with big, empty eyes. Everything shuddered again, a ripple of bad energy rolling past her. This time it had audio, whispers scuttling around the bowl of her skull like insects.

The same sensation she always had standing next to the Red Door.

"Can we go?" she snapped, scratching at her head. If she had to stay here for much longer she was going to lose her mind. She didn't wait for a reply, just started walking, her shadow leading the way. She conjured a handful of sparks that fizzed over her palm, illuminating the tunnel. Interspersed with the bones were various plaques—touristy stuff that seemed so out of place here, it was laughable.

"This is the public face of the Catacombs," Taupe said, jogging to her side. "A museum, really. But the tunnels stretch for nearly two hundred miles, maybe more. Nobody really knows."

She nodded, although she wasn't really listening. It was taking everything she had to put one foot in front of the other. The stench of smoke, of sulfur, of vaporized blood hung in her sinuses, every breath she took reminding her of death. The tunnel seemed to shrink around her, the whole weight of the world pressing down, and suddenly she couldn't breathe at all.

"Have no fear, Pan," said Taupe, and his arms were around her, reassuringly solid—a cage in an ocean full of sharks. She pushed her face into his chest and inhaled, breathing in the pleasant, unfamiliar smell of him until the panic attack passed. "We are here. We are alive. We are together."

He squeezed her, gently, then let go.

She nodded, smudging away tears that she hadn't even noticed were there. But the passageway did seem wider, the layers of rock and bone overhead a little lighter. Everybody had come to a standstill again, all eyes on her.

"Nobody said saving the world would be easy, kiddo," said Herc, his flashlight blinding her.

"Piss off," she said.

Then Marlow was there, walking to her, his arms wide like he meant to swallow her up. She turned away. "And that goes for you, too, Marlow."

When you're going through hell, just keep walking.

She did, the tunnel splitting in two. She didn't even hesitate, her blood swelling like an ocean in high tide, pulling her to the left. A red rope stretched from wall to wall, a sign hanging from it saying NO ENTRY in half a dozen languages. She stepped over it, the sparks dripping from her fingers and hissing out on the wet floor.

"Sure this is right?" said Herc as they reached another fork and Pan led them left.

"This is right," she said. She'd never felt the pull of the Engine like this, not even in the moments before a contract, standing next to the black pool. It was like it had a hand in her soul, physically dragging her along. Her guts were churning but it wasn't necessarily a bad thing. It was the same sensation she always had before seeing the Engine—dread, yes, and terror, and panic, and confusion.

But excitement, too. Always excitement.

There was a spiral staircase ahead and she ran down it, careful not to slip on the stone. Her fistful of lightning brought the bones to life, making the skulls seem to chatter. There were more whispers now. So many of them, as if the dead were talking to her. Other noises, too. Phantom groans, the click of insect tongues, the wet thumps and slices of a butcher's shop. Not sounds, nothing she could pick up with her ears. But she didn't need ears—these were inside her soul.

"Jesus, it's cold down here," said Marlow, shivering in his T-shirt. "How deep do they go?"

"Nobody really knows," said Taupe. "Nobody has explored the whole thing."

"Great," Marlow muttered. "Thought you were an expert."

"I have spent more time underground than anyone else I know," Taupe spat back. "You will not find a better guide to the city of the dead."

"It's why his name is Taupe," said Herc. "French for Mole."

"Mole?" Marlow said, improvising. "I thought that was because of his big nose and squinty eyes."

Taupe spun around, jabbing a finger back up the stairs.

"You should watch your mouth, *petit garçon*," he said.

"Or what?" Marlow dropped down another couple of steps so they were face-to-face. "You gonna dig a tunnel underneath me?"

"*Tu chien insolent—*"

Something clattered down the steps above them, a pebble. It skipped past Pan's feet and disappeared around the corner.

"Shut up," she said to the bickering boys. Then, when Taupe kept speaking, she reached up and grabbed his arm, hard. He turned to her. "That girl," she asked Marlow. "Was she the invisible one?"

A scuffing sound from the way they'd come. Pan broke into a run, pushing past Marlow so hard he toppled onto his ass. She swiped her arms in the air before her, searching. Then she flicked out a bolt of lightning that burned into the stone. Another, and another—this one making contact with something that wasn't there.

A soft scream inside the rolling waves of thunder, the girl materializing in the dark. She collapsed, her body spasming like she'd been Tasered. Pan stumbled up the steps and grabbed her before she could vanish again. Christ, she was young, thirteen maybe, twelve even. Her eyes had rolled up in their sockets, her hands groping the air. Then she was back, her face a mask of terror as she realized she'd been caught.

"*Non,*" she said, then she was gone—just stone and darkness where she had been lying. Pan still had her, though, her fingers wrapped around two stick-thin arms. She loosed another jolt of energy and the girl screamed, reappearing.

"Don't," said Pan. "The more you struggle, the worse this gets."

She shocked her again, just enough to make her pay attention. The girl stopped squirming, then burst into tears—great, heaving sobs.

"*Maman,*" she said. "*Maman maman maman.*"

"Shut up," Pan said, another shock. The girl started fitting, bucking hard on the steps, foaming at the mouth.

"Pan!" It was Marlow, by her side. "She's just a kid."

"She's one of *his,*" she spat. "If she's old enough to make a contract then she's old enough to know what she's doing. Where is he?"

Another jolt, and this time Marlow grabbed her, pulling her away. She lost her balance on the narrow stairs and fell into the wall. Marlow wrapped his hands around the girl and the look in his eye was crystal clear.

Don't try it.

"You gonna let your pathetic emotions decide what happens

to the world?" Pan said, pushing herself up. "You gonna let one girl's life get in the way of millions? *Billions?*"

"And what if I do?" he shouted back. "If you think a single life is worth sacrificing then how are you any different from Mammon? How are you any different from *him*?"

She opened her mouth to fire something back, realized she didn't have any ammunition.

"Screw you, Marlow," she said.

"*Maman,*" the girl whimpered.

"Yeah, where is he?" Pan said. "Tell us where he's hiding."

"She's not saying Mammon," said Taupe. "She's saying *maman*. It means mother—*mom*. She is scared senseless."

"It's okay," said Marlow, still holding her. "We won't hurt you. But look, we need to know where he is. We need to find the Engine. I don't know what Mammon told you, but you can't want this, can you? You can't seriously want him to win this war?"

The girl shook her head, her sobs softening. She stared at them all, her eyes so full of tears they could have been made of glass—a doll's eyes.

"He promise me," she said in broken English. "He promise us all, we would not hurt. I did not . . . did not think . . . *Il est un démon, il est le diable, non?*"

"He's a demon," Taupe translated. "The devil."

"You've seen him? Mammon?" Herc asked.

The girl nodded, pointing at the floor.

"*Ici.* Here. *Très profond.*"

"Deep," said Taupe. "You know the way?"

"He will kill me," she said. "Those things, *les monstres*. I did not think it was real. I did not think it was real."

"It's real," said Pan. "About as real as it gets. You need to take us to him."

She started to cry again.

"*Non,*" she said. "He told us what you would do. He told us what would happen if you took the Engines for yourselves."

"And you prefer his way?" said Pan. "You think that's better?"

"His way keep me off the street," she said. "His way keep me alive."

Pan spat out a laugh, sending another bolt of blinding light thudding into the ceiling.

"You wanna bet on that?" she said, sparks raining down. "Listen to me. You've got one chance. You either take us to him, or I kill you right here, and right now. You ever seen a watermelon that's had a thousand volts pumped into it? It's messy."

"*Non,*" she said. "*S'il vous plaît, s'il vous plaît.*"

"One," said Pan, rippling curves of light dancing on her palm. Her whole arm ached with the pressure of it, her skin tingling with the electric charge. The girl had obviously been brainwashed by Mammon the same way all of his Engineers had been, but she must have known. You don't make a deal with the devil and not suspect something. "Two," she said. "Last chance."

"It does not matter," she said. "It does not matter anymore."

"It matters to us," Marlow said. "It matters to the world."

The girl looked up at him, frowning.

"It does not matter because you are too late," she said.

"That's a lie," said Pan.

"It is the truth," the girl said. And this time she met Pan's eye and didn't blink. "You are too late. Mammon has already joined the Engines. They are one, and all of this, this stupid war, this stupid fight, it is over." She closed her eyes, squeezing out tears that shimmered in the lightning storm. "It is done."

IT'S OVER

"You're a lying bi—"

"No!" yelled Marlow. Pan was storming toward the girl, her hand crackling, and he threw himself between them. The power leaking from her was enough to make his hair stand on end. The spark she'd thrown at the ceiling had gouged out a star-shaped crater in the rock, and he didn't want to think about what it would do to the contents of his skull.

"She wants it to be over, then it can be over for her, no sweat," Pan said, her face twisted into something that didn't look human, that looked almost demonic. Marlow had never seen her like this, never seen her so full of fury. Even after everything he had been through, every horror he had witnessed, it made him feel jellyfish scared, like every bone in his body had turned to seawater. He didn't move, though. He knew that if he did then Pan would blast the kid to atoms, that they'd all be brushing her ash from their clothes and coughing it from their lungs. "We need her," he said. "She can still take us there."

"Marlow's right," said Herc, clapping a hand on Pan's shoulder and making her flinch.

"You honestly think she will? You think she's going to just lead us right to the Engines? She'll take us the other way, or right into a trap. She's one of his, Herc, she's so full of crap. How can you not see that?"

"Why do you say it's over?" Marlow said to the girl. "How do you even know that?"

"Because he told us," she replied. "He said that we had only one more battle to fight. One last defense, and his war would be done. He just needed us to keep you away—just for a while, just so they could finish. And they have. The Engines are united."

No demons pushing themselves through the walls, no ocean of blood and fire churning down the street. If Mammon had succeeded in uniting the Engines then why hadn't he opened the gates?

"Nothing's different," Marlow said. His fingers were cramping where he was holding the girl and he relaxed them. He still felt her shrug.

"It takes time," she said. "It does not happen instantly."

"Screw her," said Pan, turning and stomping down the steps. "We don't need her to find the Engine. It will pull us right to it." She disappeared around the corner of the spiral staircase, her shadow following her. "You want her, she's your problem."

Taupe followed her, then Truck, muttering something about how much he hated stairs.

"Bring her," said Herc. "Better we keep an eye on her. You pull that vanishing act again, kid, and you're toast. Got it?"

The girl nodded, the fight beaten right out of her. She sniffed, knuckling her eyes. She was looking younger by the second. Herc turned and followed the others and Marlow stood, holding out his hand to the girl. She took it, letting him pull her to her feet. She dusted herself down, hauling in a long, broken breath.

"I'm Marlow," he said.

She studied him for a moment with dark eyes.

"Claire," she said.

"Well, Claire," said Marlow as he started to walk, keeping hold of a fistful of her jacket. "I have to say, you're not the kind of soldier I was expecting to fight for Mammon."

"You are not who I expected either," she said.

They made their way down the stairs, just enough light ahead to see by and a wave of impenetrable darkness on their heels. Marlow kept glancing back into it, expecting to see a razor-toothed jaw open up there, or Mammon's face pushing through, eyes blazing. He shuddered, upped his pace, almost slipping on the wet stone.

"So, what made you fight for him?" he asked, just to stave off the suffocating silence. "Mammon isn't exactly nice. And what are you? Fourteen?"

"Nearly," she said. "In like a year and a half."

"You're *twelve*?" he said.

"Oh, and you are much older, yes?"

"Fifteen," he muttered. "Loads older."

Claire said something in French but he didn't exactly need a translation to know she was making fun of him. She sniffed again, shivering. The stairs kept going, spiraling endlessly. Marlow's internal organs were fighting a no-holds-barred cage match, his whole body ringing with the force of the Engine. *Engines.*

"How did you even end up here?" he asked, doing his best to ignore the sensation.

"I was, um, how do you say, without a home. I live on street. Me and friends, the ones . . ." She swallowed hard. "I do not think they survived."

"Sorry," said Marlow.

"I do not know them long. I ran away, bad father. Somebody came to see us, just the day before today. A girl."

"Red hair? Face like a smacked ass?"

"A smacked what?" she said, frowning at him. He waved it away and she nodded. "Red hair, yes. She told us that if we helped her for one day then she would get us off the street, that she would make us rich. She did not say what it was she needed us for. She did not say there would be . . ."

She choked on her words, brushing away tears.

"But you saw the Engine, right?" Marlow went on, almost slipping again. How deep did these stairs go? He glanced up, seeing a weird star-shaped mark on the ceiling. Why did it look familiar?

"*Oui*," Claire said, nodding. "It is horrible. It is the work of the devil, *non*? Mammon threw us into the black water, we could not refuse him. And there was something in there, something impossible."

Marlow knew, he'd seen it, too. An entity of darkness, as big as a mountain, watching him with insect eyes.

This is what you desire? it had asked. The memory made his head ache and he felt something creep its way down from his nose—blood. He smudged it away, focusing on the stairs, on their endless downward passage, on another black mark on the ceiling. He frowned, looking back, nothing but darkness. Reaching out, he pulled one of the skulls from the wall. It came loose with a pop, two of its teeth scattering. He laid it on the step beside him and carried on, ignoring Claire's questioning look.

"Then what?" Marlow asked her.

"He said we could have anything we wished for, but that we needed to wish for something that would make us strong, make us powerful. Something we could fight with. I did not believe him, but when I was there I panicked. I just wanted to escape. So I wished to be not seen, to be, uh, what is your word?"

"Invisible," he said.

"That is the same as we say. To be *invisible*. I thought that if this was true, and not some nightmare, then I could sneak away. But he could still see me. He sees everything. He took us up to the surface and told us that we needed to fight. If we survive, he said, then we will have anything we wanted."

"How many of you?" Marlow asked.

"I do not know," she said. "There were seven of my friends, but there were others there, too, many others."

Too many for Mammon to ever be able to cancel their contracts, Marlow thought. There just wouldn't be time. He'd set them up to die—worse than that, he'd set them up so their contracts would expire, so that they would be dragged into hell.

But what else had he expected from Mammon?

"Listen, I need to know if you saw my friend. The guys down there, was one of them called Charlie?"

"Charlie?" she said, pronouncing it *Sharrrlie*. "I do not think so."

"My age," he said, pressing. "Dark hair, brown eyes. Short. American."

Claire stopped walking. Her eyes had grown twice as big, so huge they looked like they might just roll out. The horror on her face was contagious, filling Marlow's heart.

"What?" he asked.

"The boy you describe, he was there."

Thank God, Marlow thought, saying, "Alive?"

"I do not know," she said, shaking her head. "He was . . ."

"Was what?" Marlow said. She pushed past him.

"I cannot talk about it," she said. "I cannot."

"Hey," he called after her. "Claire, he's my friend, I need to know."

"Watch your feet," said Herc beneath them, and Marlow

turned the corner and almost stepped on a skull that lay there. He put a hand to the wall, to the space he'd ripped it from. Then he looked up, knowing what he'd see there.

A burn mark, star shaped, where Pan had fired a bolt of lightning into the ceiling.

"Hey, guys," he yelled. "Hold up, something's wrong."

He heard grumbling beneath them, then Herc's face appeared, the beam of the flashlight like an explosion in Marlow's retinas—so bright he could see the veins there.

"What?" he said.

"We're going around in circles," he said.

"Duh," came Pan's voice from below. "It's a spiral staircase."

"No, I mean we've been walking on the same bit of stair for a while now"—he struggled to find the words—"like, something weird is going on."

Pan appeared next to Herc. She shrugged impatiently and Marlow pointed to the skull.

"I just pulled that out of the wall, and that mark, you made that, Pan."

Pan shook her head, turning and walking off. Marlow heard her footsteps thud downward, fade, then start again from overhead. And suddenly Pan was there, above him.

"Oh," she said.

"Temporal loop," said Herc, putting a hand to the bone-covered wall. "Try going up again."

Pan spun around and jogged up the stairs, into the darkness. She reappeared a few seconds later behind Herc. Marlow felt the terror shift inside him like a tectonic plate, unfathomably huge. He turned, tripping on a step as he struggled up. It was hard to feel anything past the constant churning horror of being this close to the Engine, but there was a buzz in his ears, a rash of gooseflesh on his arms, and then he stumbled into the back of Truck. The big guy said something but Marlow pushed past him, past all of them, twisting around the staircase, ever upward.

And there was Truck again, his bulk just about blocking the path.

Marlow swore, pulling another bone from the wall, and another. There was nothing beneath them but solid stone.

"Hey, calm down," said Herc. "Just let me think."

"What the hell is going on?" Marlow said, ripping a skull away. It hit the ground and chattered down the steps, gaining momentum, appearing above them as it bounced to a halt.

"It's part of the Engine's defenses," Herc said. "This must be the outer boundary, the thing that keeps the Engine hidden. Hey, kid, you know anything about this?"

Claire shook her head. She had shrunk back against the wall, draped in shadow. Even though she wasn't invisible she was pretty hard to see.

"We came this way," she said. "But this . . . this thing was not here."

Marlow had cleared a patch of wall now and he pushed at the stone beneath. It felt solid, and cold. How deep were they? Maybe a hundred meters by now. The earth was a solid mass on every side, above and below. He could almost hear the vast weight of it groaning, pushing down on them. He snatched in a breath, no air down here, and the panic was an acetylene torch held against his eyes.

"How do we get out?" he said, turning to Claire.

"I do not know," she said, shrinking away from whatever was in his expression. "I do not know."

He reached for the girl but she backed away, sprawling on the step.

"How do we get out?" he roared, and this time he lashed

out, his fist striking the wall, splinters of bone detonating. He punched it again, the stone cracking. Dust rained down from the ceiling like a handful of soil on a coffin. He punched again and this time the stones moved, crumbling outward. The fourth attack left a hole in the wall, darkness pouring through from the other side. The entire stairwell trembled, the pressure changing so fast that Marlow's ears ached.

Time, snapping back.

"Marlow one, wall zero," said Truck, stepping up beside him and planting a calming hand on his shoulder. "Feeling better?"

The dark wasn't the only thing entering the stairwell. There was a breeze, too, cold and stale but still beautiful. Marlow inhaled until he thought his lungs would burst, the monster inside him shrinking away. Herc stepped up and stuck his head through the hole Marlow had made.

"Can't see a damn thing," he muttered. He opened his backpack and rummaged around inside, pulling out a flare. Striking it on the wall, he lobbed it out. "Ground, not too far below. Can't make out much else. You know what's down there, kid?"

Claire didn't need to answer. It was pretty clear what was down there. Marlow's flesh crawled with it, like a churning foam of spiders had ridden in on that wave of darkness, crawling on his skin, chittering their way into his nose, his ears, his eyes. He scratched, groaning, his head suddenly full of whispers and screams. He dug a finger into his ear to find an impossible itch, would have happily stuck a knitting needle in there and pushed it into the flesh of his brain.

No, she didn't need to answer, but she did anyway.

"Hell," she said, her voice almost drowned out by the madness that roiled inside Marlow's skull. "Hell is down there."

THE LIMINAL

Pan clung to the edge of the hole, the world around her burning brimstone bright from the flare. She knew she had to drop, but her fingers weren't going to obey her. They knew the truth.

If she let go now, then she was going to fall right into hell.

"Hey, Pan," yelled Truck from fifteen feet or so below her. "Stop hanging around, we've got to go."

He laughed at his own joke.

"Hold on," punned Marlow. "Give her a chance."

"You guys insane? Kidding around in this place?" growled Herc. "Besides, you all know she doesn't like heights. It's one of her *hang-ups*." He snorted, trying to cover it with a cough.

She had no idea why they were making jokes. They had breached the outer wall of the Engine. They were about to throw themselves into a battle against one of the most powerful entities on the planet. What was funny about that?

And yet the sound of their muffled giggles was contagious. The Engine wasn't the only thing with defenses, she understood. People had them, too. Laughter was powerful. It was pretty much the most human thing you could do. Even now, with chips of broken bone and stone digging into her palms, her stomach threatening to cramp, and that godawful endless idiot chatter of the Engine in her head, she couldn't help but smile.

It gave her strength and she let go, her stomach lurching into her throat. She managed a scream, the drop higher than she'd expected, so high she thought she might have fallen right through the floor, falling right into—

She landed lightly, a pair of strong arms grabbing her from behind and reducing the shock. She leaned into them, happy to be held and not wanting to be let go. When she turned to thank Taupe, though, she saw Marlow instead. She scowled at him, pulling loose.

"Sorry," he said, backing away like a beaten dog.

They were standing in a cavern. She had no idea how big it was because it was drenched in darkness—darkness so heavy, so deep, that it felt like a physical thing. It seemed to press down on her, to put a cold hand over her mouth. To one side was the wall they had just passed through. Every inch of it was covered in bones, the floor, too. Herc's flare sputtered, spitting out an infernal red light.

"Now—"

She stopped, feeling something wriggling inside her throat. She hawked it up, spat, seeing the glistening body of a fat, squirming maggot slip between the bones on the floor. Her stomach tightened, her body trying to turn itself inside out.

"Now what?" she managed, smearing her hand over her trembling lips.

"We did not see this place," said the girl. Her voice, with its annoying accent, seemed like it came from a million miles away, as if they had dropped to the bottom of the ocean. "We passed through a . . . a church, then a tunnel, then entered the stairs. This is new."

"The Liminal," said Herc. "The space between. The Engine is surrounded by it, it's what keeps it out of reality, keeps it hidden."

"The space you pass through when you go through the Red Door?" Marlow asked, his voice as muted as everyone else's. "No wonder I feel like my guts have been trampled by an elephant."

He wasn't wrong. Pan flexed her jaw, something buzzing inside the skin of her cheek, and she imagined a clutch of flies had just hatched there. It was unbearable, and the only thing that stopped her firing a crossbow bolt into her own head was the fear that she might be stuck down here, trapped in the Liminal for an eternity.

The thought of that was somehow even worse than the thought of being taken by the demons.

Herc's flashlight wobbled and he gave it a slap, shining the beam into the heart of the darkness. It reached maybe fifteen feet then stopped dead, too afraid to reveal what lay there.

"How far away is it?" Truck asked.

"The Engine?" Herc shrugged. "No idea. Time and space, they're different here. One way to find out, though."

He set off, bones crunching beneath his boots. Pan adjusted her crossbow and set off after him. She was exhausted, everything drained. She wasn't sure she could even conjure up enough for a burst of charge. Something popped beneath her and she looked down to see a skull. *That used to be somebody's face*, she thought as she pulled her foot free, shaking the dust away. A sudden, alien scream loosed itself inside her head, like somebody had split it open and was crying into it. She gouged her nails through her hair, breathing fast, the darkness a spinning vortex around her.

In front, Marlow doubled over, groaning. She grabbed his arm, as much to keep herself standing as him. They stumbled on together, Herc's flashlight a boat of light in the river of darkness. Behind them, the flare sputtered out. There was no way back.

Not that there ever had been. You didn't start a mission like this expecting to retreat.

"What is that?" said Taupe up ahead. Pan could hear the fear in his voice. When she reached him she saw that he was looking down at the ground and something was moving there.

One of the bones.

It was vibrating, softly. Barely noticeable, other than the buzzing noise it was making. It stopped, then started again, reminding Pan of a bluebottle trying to fly with torn wings.

"I really don't like this," said Truck.

"Come on," said Herc, hoisting up the duffel bag. "We got to keep moving."

They had only made it another few feet, though, before something else clattered over the ground. It was another bone, a small one that might once have been somebody's finger. It was jittering like there was an earthquake, bouncing a couple of inches then lying still.

"I really, *really* don't like this," said Truck. He stamped down on it, grinding it to powder.

A voice, up ahead. Somewhere distant. It sounded like a man crying out in pain. Pan's skin crawled so badly she thought it was trying to slither right off her.

"Someone's there," she said, pulling the crossbow from her back. It was loaded with a bolt, one that had been carved from the fabric of the Engine itself. The metal was old, etched with runes. And it was powerful, especially against the undead. Fire one of these into a demon and it would be like it had swallowed a grenade.

Then why did she feel so exposed, and so helpless?

Another faint cry, more bones scuffing across the ground as though they had minds of their own. Pan squinted into the darkness, no sign of anything.

"Stay sharp," said Herc. "Anything is possible in here."

They huddled together, insect-small in the vast space. The shout up ahead was being answered by another that could have been a crow's caw. More rose up in the dark, a swelling tide of noise. These weren't the call of the Engine, Pan understood.

They were real.

Something snatched at her foot, a cluster of long bones. It punched a grunt of horror from her throat and she shook free, kicking the hand onto its back where it trembled like a dying insect. This one was decorated with smudges of rust-colored blood that looked centuries old.

Truck swore. He was skirting around a skull that was moving inside its nest of bone, its lower jaw twitching wildly like it was telling a joke. A scraggy cap of blond hair hung over its side. The big guy was smearing his palms down his T-shirt, again and again.

"Ignore it," Herc said.

"*Ignore the moving bones,*" Truck said, and Pan could hear the hysteria in his voice. "Yeah, su—" His foot suddenly plunged into them, ankle deep, and his scream soared into the cavern like it was a trapped bird, fading fast. "Goddammit." He pulled his leg free and aimed the shotgun at the skull, firing off a blast that made Pan's ears ring.

And in the flash of the muzzle she saw something to her side—there and gone in an instant.

"Herc, your three," she said, and Herc swung the flashlight.

It looked like a huge moonlit ocean over there, bone white and restless. There was still no sign of the end of the cavern, or the roof, but she could hear the endless, crashing crescendo of churning water.

Water?

"Oh, Jesus," said Marlow. "That can't be . . ."

Pan stumbled on, unable to believe what she was seeing. The ground before her seemed more agitated with every step, bones writhing against each other, scratching at the air, at their legs as they passed. Some of the skeletons had scraps of flesh and muscle, like leftover meat on a barbecued rib. One of the skulls had an upper lip, as fat and wet as a slug. It moved up and down in silent speech.

Then she saw a face. A *real* face.

It sat in the ground like it had been buried up to its neck, an old woman with patches of silver hair. The skin was withered and torn, one eye fused shut. But the other was a weak, watery gray thing that fixed on Pan and blinked furiously. The woman's mouth opened, and through it Pan could see the floor. Her scream was just a gust of dry air, but it felt deafening.

Pan's terror was too big to fit up her throat and she beat it back, forcing herself to stay numb. She felt a tickle of insanity in the corner of her mind, wondered how close she was to the abyss, to falling into that madness and drowning there.

The closer she got to the ocean, the more she saw that there was no water there. It was a sea of flesh and bone, of things that could not possibly be alive and yet were. Arms dug at the dirt, shedding fingernails in their desperation. Feet kicked at the ground, at the air, like the final, awful movements of somebody trapped in a landslide. Limbless torsos twitched and trembled.

And the faces. So many of them. They stared with red, bulging eyes, fat tongues sticking from their mouths as if they'd been hanged. They were obviously aware that they had company. Some of them cried, some of them called out in a language Pan did not recognize. Most of them screamed, a rising wave of sound that rippled outward, surely loud enough to bring down the walls of the cavern, to bury them all forever.

They screamed and they screamed, and Pan put her hands to her ears and screamed, too.

Herc kept moving, shaking off the hands that grabbed at him as he waded deeper into the ocean. Pan's foot slipped on something wet and she looked to see a man's face there, gulping at air that he couldn't need because he had no body. His eyes scrolled blindly back and forth.

Sorry sorry sorry, she thought, but could not find the strength to say.

"There," yelled Taupe, his shout reduced to a whisper by the roar of the dead. He was pointing ahead, and when Herc shone the flashlight Pan could just about see a column of rock stretching up.

Pan set off for it, moving too fast. Something grabbed her leg and she was falling, landing in the grasping ocean of wet flesh. Her fist plunged into a decaying torso—one that squirmed beneath her, which pulled at her. She was face-to-face with a man who had only half a head, the bowl of his skull gleaming. His one eye rolled her way and a toothless mouth moved against the air, like he was trying to kiss her.

She tried to get up but something was holding her tight— fingers sprouting from the earth and groping for her, a leg winding around her waist like a wrestler's, another fistful of fingers probing into her mouth, tasting of spoiled food and old blood, another yet in her hair, filthy nails scraping her scalp. And the man, his lips searching for her, breathing on her with the stench of old meat, that one eye rolling madly in its puckered socket.

The fire burned up inside her, too much of it for her to control. She closed her eyes and let loose a pulse of electrostatic energy, one that blazed out of her in every direction. The man's face erupted into ash, the ocean of limbs crumbling, freeing her. She pushed up, shaking the sparks from her smarting fingers. Her mouth tasted of copper, tingling like she'd bit down on a live wire.

"Easy, Pan!" said Herc from somewhere behind her, his voice jittery. She ignored him, moving as fast as her legs would let her, not caring that her boots were crunching through faces, not caring about the crack of breaking bones and the slap of wet meat beneath her. She just ran through the living corpses, through their endless screams, heading for that wall of rock.

It rose from the living ocean, catching the swinging beam of Herc's light. She couldn't see to the top—or anywhere near it—but she could *feel* how tall it was. The height was vertiginous, like she was standing in the shadow of the Empire State Building. There were openings in it, a collection of mouthlike caves running along the bottom. They looked like they might hold spiders, but they couldn't be worse than this.

Nothing in all of hell could be worse than this—the countless, shrieking dead.

The caves along the wall grew vast as she approached them, each the size of an apartment block. She stumble-ran into the nearest, the Engine still pulling at her, still guiding her. Herc and the others were shouting but she didn't care. She just wanted to be out of this nightmare. She felt that she would throw herself into the black pool, would gladly give her soul to whatever lay there, just to be free of this place.

No light here, just more groping fingers and howling mouths. She pushed on, the ground sloping beneath her, gently at first and then hard. She lost her footing, sprawling. But the drop was too steep, the dead didn't have the strength to hold her. She rolled, bouncing between the moving corpses. She fired as she went, sparks of electricity exploding like a camera flash—glimpses of bared teeth, of rabid eyes.

Then she was falling into something rabbit-hole deep and lined with fury—a pit of snatching limbs and jaws. She reached for them, trying to halt herself, but she was going too fast. The hole was narrowing, too, arms and legs slapping against her from all sides. The sound of their panic was like a choir of the damned, enough to reduce her brain to a pulp.

She would be buried here. Buried alive, because she would not die, not in the Liminal. She would lie here for the rest of—

Light, somewhere beneath her. Just a faint glow. The forest of teeth and hands was silhouetted against it, everything still trying to grab her. It was working now, too, trapping her fall like a spiderweb traps a fly. She felt one of them bite into her arm, shouting at her through a mouthful of her blood.

She had stopped. They had her.

She pushed downward, clawing her way past the corpses like she was trying to pull herself from a tar pit. Another set of teeth grated the side of her head and she growled, almost losing herself inside an ecstasy of terror. They were tearing chunks from her, they were trying to devour her. But the light was growing, it was just there, *just there.*

Gravity took hold of her, and she was out of the hole, falling again. She hit the ground, squirming onto her back, her heartbeat thrashing itself into a frenzy. Above her was a sloping ceiling of red rock, a fissure splitting it in two. Gray, bloodless hands explored the edges, and past them was the flash of teeth and bone and wide, frightened eyes. Groans and howls slipped after her, like they meant to pick her up and pull her in. She scuttled back as far as she could, until her hands gave way beneath her.

Only then did she force herself to calm down, both hands on her chest as if she could massage her pulse back to normal.

Her eyesight was boiling at the edges but with each breath the panic subsided.

"Get off me!" came a muffled voice, then Truck tumbled from the fissure in the ceiling, landing with a splat. Marlow and the young girl dropped out next, arms wrapped around each other, the big guy cushioning their fall. Marlow scrambled up and out of the way, spitting, and Truck was halfway to his feet when Taupe slid free, falling on him.

"Dammit," Truck yelled. "Let me get—"

Herc was last, screaming as he crunched down onto Taupe and Truck. He rolled onto his feet, his breaths half pant, half scream. His eyes were drenched in fear, the eyes of a madman, and when he met Pan's gaze she barely recognized him. Then the old guy blinked, twice, three times, and each time he slipped further back inside himself until it was just good old Herc standing there. He sniffed, adjusting the straps of the bag on his back.

"Everyone okay?" he asked.

"No," said Truck.

"*Non,*" said Taupe and Claire together.

"Not even close," said Marlow, brushing the grime from his clothes. "What was that?"

The French girl had been right.

That had been a little slice of hell.

"The Engine needs death," said Herc, his voice still shaking. "It needs suffering. We all knew it, we all knew it would be bad. Now, where are—"

He stopped, and actually smiled. Pan followed his line of sight.

They might have been inside a cathedral, but one made from rock and flesh. The space they were in was the size of a football field, another vast underground cave. This one, though, was lit by torches. Thousands of them, mounted on the forest of pillars that filled the cavern. Each torch was set inside the mouth of a body mounted on the stone, their limbs seemingly fused there. The sight of it reminded Pan of Patrick Rebarre, of what had happened to him back in New York—teleporting inside the ground, and becoming part of it. It made her shudder.

Not as much, though, as when she realized that each of those poor souls had his eyes open. They stared down at her, their dirty faces marked by rivulets of tears, their mouths infernos that spat and crackled. The constant susurration of their blinking eyes was like a flock of distant birds taking off.

The columns stretched up to a vaulted ceiling decorated with sculptures that might have been people. The walls, too, could have been red stone, or could have been skinless bodies. Thankfully none of them were moving. There was only one more thing in the giant space, embedded in the far wall—something that filled her with fear, but which also flooded her mind with relief, because in the unimaginable horror of what they had just waded through, even something as rotten and wrong as this was still beautifully familiar.

"Well, what do you know," said Herc, walking to her side. "We only went and did it."

"Look at it," said Truck, appearing on her other side. "Just sitting there all evil and stuff."

"Wants us to open it," said Marlow. "I can feel it."

He was right. She could feel it, too, a nagging itch right in the center of her brain, and a graveyard voice that whispered, *What is it you desire?*

"So let's give that bastard what it wants," she said.

And as one, they made their way across the cathedral, to the Red Door.

HOME SWEET HOME

"Dibs on not being the one," said Truck, holding up his hands.

"Same here," said Pan and Herc together.

"What?" said Marlow. "Wait, that's not fair."

They stood in front of the Red Door. It must have been happy to see them, because it was blasting out images that belonged in the sickest of horror movies—images and sounds and thoughts that turned Marlow's stomach. It seemed impossible that this was the same door they had used back in Prague and Budapest, but there was no denying it. The same slab of patterned wood, the same glossy, lacquered paint the color of blood, the same antique brass handle.

The same gut-wrenching evil.

"What about Mole, he didn't call it?"

"We do not have this dibs custom," said Taupe.

"Yeah, the Frenchies are exempt," said Herc. "Just do it, Marlow."

Marlow reached out, then pulled back, like the door might be electrified.

"I thought there was no way of opening it from the outside," he said.

"From anywhere else, no," said Herc, adjusting his bag again. "But this is the real door, and the real Engine."

Marlow reached out again, his hand hovering there.

"What if it—"

"For God's sake," said Pan, barging past him and grabbing the handle. She twisted it, shunting it with her shoulder. It opened like Pandora's Box, spilling a freak show of noise and terror into Marlow's head. He balled his fists, let it ride over him.

They were just images, after all. It was like a Disney show compared to what he had just crawled through on his hands and knees.

The door opened silently, smoothly, like its hinges had been greased. Whatever Marlow had been expecting on the other side, this wasn't it. No Engineers, no Mammon, just that familiar gray corridor stretching toward the elevator shaft.

"Home sweet home," said Truck.

The cacophony inside Marlow's head had muted, but there was something else there, a noise that he couldn't quite put his finger on. It was something industrial, something far away, something *loud*. He wasn't sure if he could even hear it, or if he could just feel it, a thunderous tremor that ran up his bones and reverberated around his skull. It came again and dust drifted down from the ceiling inside. He glanced at Pan and knew she heard it, too, knew what she was thinking.

This is something new.

It came again, like artillery fire. It was definitely an explosion of some kind, and Marlow couldn't help but think of somebody trying to blow open a vault door.

Or trying to blow open the gates of hell.

Pan walked through, one hand on the wall to brace herself. Marlow followed, feeling nothing as he crossed the threshold. Why would he have, though? There was no need for the Red Door to teleport him this time. He'd just crossed the Liminal on foot.

But something weird was happening inside the Pigeon's Nest. Nothing seemed particularly solid. The walls were shifting, the movement too subtle to really see, just a flickering in the corner of his vision. The floor, too, didn't feel solid. The concrete passageway was pumping out a hum that made his teeth ache.

"Just don't let your guard down," said Herc as he joined them. "This doesn't feel right."

"It feels like a trap," said Taupe. "Too easy."

It *was* too easy. Marlow passed one of the swastikas painted on the wall, left over from when the Nazis had occupied the bunker during the war. Even as he looked at it, it vanished—just for a second, then it was back, like a video game glitch. He leaned in, putting his hand to it. The pattern of the concrete wall was shifting, scratches and scuffs appearing then disappearing. He could make no sense of it. Was this the same thing that had happened back on the train? Mammon making a building grow from the locomotive? He didn't think so, but how could he be sure of what was real and what wasn't?

She's real, he thought, looking at Pan. *If in doubt, just look at her.*

And he did, watching the way she leaned against the wall, the way she balled her fists to stop her hands from shaking. He saw the exhaustion there, in every line etched in her face. She rubbed the scar on her chest, then spotted him looking and scowled.

Yeah, she's real, all right.

"Keep your eyes open," Herc said as he walked past them, stooped beneath the weight of the duffel bag. He had his Desert Eagle clenched in one sweaty fist.

"Where are the Engineers?" Marlow asked. "I don't get it."

It didn't make sense for Mammon to throw all his Engineers up onto the street. This corridor was the perfect place to defend—narrow, just one way in. Mammon could have rigged the whole thing with explosives and killed them all the moment they stepped inside.

It's because we're too late, he thought. *He doesn't need to fight us anymore, because the Engines have been united.*

A peal of distant thunder again, from deep beneath them— one that made the corridor flutter out of reality for a moment, everything blurring. Marlow's stomach did a loop like he was riding a roller coaster.

Something was happening to the Engine.

They reached the elevator and Herc pulled open the gate, craning inside.

"Think it's safe?" Pan asked, cradling her crossbow to her chest.

"Bloody thing has never been safe," he said. "But I can't see any sign it's been tampered with. I don't think Mammon would want to risk being trapped down there."

"Why is it up?" Marlow asked. Herc frowned at him. "I mean, those Engineers needed to get to the surface, right?"

"Sure," said Claire. "We came this way."

"But why leave it here, why not pull the elevator back down, make it harder for us?"

Nobody had an answer.

The world rumbled again, a buzz that seemed to rattle Marlow's skull.

"There is no way in hell I am going in there," said Truck.

Herc daintily placed a foot inside the elevator, tapping his toes against the floor.

"Up to you," Herc said. "Take the stairs if you'd rather."

Truck glanced at the access door to the stairwell, frowned, then shook his head.

"The elevator looks safe enough," he muttered.

Herc went first, the cab rocking as he entered. Pan followed, the fear flowing from her in great big waves. Marlow pictured the elevator coming loose, suddenly plunging into darkness. And it was because he didn't want to lose her that he stepped inside. There were grumbles as the others joined them, all except for Claire. She stood in the corridor, chewing her nails like she hadn't eaten in a month.

"Come on," said Marlow.

"I cannot."

"Better in here with us than out there alone, right?"

"But you do not know what he is like," she said. "You have not seen him."

Marlow thought back to the fight outside his school. Mammon had been an impossible shape of darkness pushing up the street—an icebreaker shattering its way through reality. And again on the train, he had torn the world apart, a glimpse of what was to come if the gates opened, if hell broke free.

"He is not human," she said. "He cannot be beaten."

"He might not be human anymore," said Pan. "But he *can* be beaten."

"We can crush his ass," said Truck.

"It is not just him," she said. "His soldiers."

"We'll crush their asses, too," Truck said.

"Come on," said Herc, his hand on the gate. "Last chance."

She backed away even more, hitting the wall.

"I am sorry."

Herc sighed as he pulled the gate shut and slammed the button. Marlow put his hands on the grille, looking at the young girl outside.

"We'll be back," he said. "Just wait here."

"You asked about your friend," she said.

"Charlie? Yeah, he's down there, right?"

The gates locked, the elevator starting its slow journey down.

"He is there," she said. "But be careful, Marlow."

She walked to the gates, looking down at them.

"He is not like you," she said. "He is like *him*."

"What?" Marlow yelled. He pushed the button, trying to make them stop, but the elevator kept moving. "What do you mean?"

"I mean Mammon is not the one who is uniting the Engines," she shouted over the whine of the gears. "Charlie is. He is the one who is bringing them together."

Then she was gone.

Marlow spun to the others, their faces like Halloween masks in the half-light.

"What does she mean?" he asked.

He was answered by another booming pulse of not-sound, one that pounded his internal organs.

"What does she mean?" he said again when the sensation had passed.

"You tell us," Pan replied. "You tell us who he really is."

Charlie, just Charlie, *always* Charlie.

And there was no time to answer anyway because the elevator began to slow, rattling to a halt on the next level down. Slowly the bullpen rose into view, the huge space buried in shadow. All but a handful of the lights on the ceiling had blown but Marlow could still see the stains on the concrete floor—dried copper-colored puddles that must have once been the Engineers, been the Lawyers, been Betty, been Seth.

He swallowed a throatful of bile but his rage pushed it back up again, choking him.

How could Charlie have done this?

They crunched to a halt and Herc grabbed the gates.

"You shoot first, ask questions never," he said, his fingers flexing on the pistol. "Marlow?"

Marlow remembered the gun, pulled it out. His palms were so sweaty he almost dropped it. Herc reached over, flicked something on the weapon.

"Safety's off," the old guy said. "Just point and shoot."

"Point and shoot," Marlow repeated.

Herc grabbed the gates and wrenched them open. Down here the thrum of the Engine was worse than ever, each pulse like something had been detonated inside Marlow's soul. He waited for Herc and Pan to move then he stepped out into the bullpen. There was no sign of life but most of the basketball-court-sized room was cloaked in darkness, and anything could have been hiding there, watching them.

"Oh, crud," said Pan. Marlow followed her gaze to the side. The bank of supercomputers that sat there had been smashed to pieces, glass and metal and plastic strewn everywhere. It took a second for it to sink in, and when it did he thought he felt his heart actually crumble to dust inside his chest.

The computers were what the Engineers needed to crack the contracts.

Without them, they didn't stand a chance.

"Doesn't make sense," said Truck. "Why haven't they busted Marlow's contract?"

Herc had pushed himself out into the dark like a boat leaving harbor. Even with the muscles, even with the gun, he looked too vulnerable out there.

"Maybe they were worried we'd come," he said. "Maybe they thought we'd take it back."

"Hardly."

The voice came from the other side of the room, a girl's voice, and the shock of it made Marlow jump. He dropped the gun and it clattered onto the floor. By the time he'd scooped it up again some more of the bulbs overhead had blinked on, pockets of light appearing in the night. Each one contained a handful of Engineers, all dressed in black. By the time the final light had sputtered to life there must have been twenty of them, more maybe.

Marlow held up the gun, and the sound of it rattling in his hands was the loudest thing in the room.

"I wouldn't," said the same voice. The redhead stepped into a spotlight, brushing her hair from her eyes. She was bleeding from the battle on the street, and she looked as pissed off as ever. She still held one of her impossible blades. "Drop the guns. Then put your hands behind your back. Try anything else and it will be the last thing you do before the demons come collect you."

The Engine pulsed beneath them, a vibration that made the whole room shiver, which made the light fittings swing. It was like they were in an air raid shelter, bombs raining down. Herc stood there with his gun, Pan with her crossbow. Everybody armed, nobody moving.

"Last chance," the redhead said.

"We drop our guns, you kill us anyway," Pan spat back. "Might as well go out fighting."

"If we'd wanted to kill you, we would have killed you," she shouted back. All around her the other Engineers shifted uneasily. The tension in the air was electric, making Marlow's hair stand on end. Just how much power was in this room? And what *kind* of power? If every one of those Engineers had traded for something then they would be unstoppable. "On the train, in the street. We *could* have killed you."

"We kicked your scrawny ass on the train," said Truck.

"Yeah?" said another voice, a guy stepping out of the crowd. It was *him*, the Magpie who had pulled Night to her death. He must have teleported out of the other girl's body before they hit the ground. "Tell that to your little friend."

Truck moved, fast, his fists clenched. Herc shot out an arm and grounded him, growling out an order.

"You're too late, anyway," the girl said, placing a calming arm of her own on the other guy. "The Engines are united."

As if on cue the room shook with another bone-shattering pulse of sound—an almost subsonic howl, like the entire planet was screaming.

"I don't believe you," said Herc. "World's still here."

The girl shook her head.

"You really are that stupid," she said. "All this time and you still don't know. Mammon said that's what it was, but I didn't think there was any way anyone could be so deluded."

"Look, this is nice and all," said Herc. "But you either tell us where Mammon is and get the hell out of the way, or you kill us. I'm old, and tired, and you are really starting to piss me off."

"Mammon is here," said the girl. "He is down in the Engine. He would like to speak with you."

What? Marlow shot a glance at Pan and she met it, her thoughts carved into every line of her face.

This has to be a trap.

"Charlie is there, too," said the redhead, looking at Marlow. "He needs to show you something."

"Yeah?" said Marlow, the tremor in his voice echoing around the room. "Show me what?"

"The truth," said the girl. "The stupid, awful truth."

"That you're about to open the gates of hell," said Herc. "That you're about to drown the world in demons and fire."

She shook her head.

"No, Herc, the truth that we're trying to *save* the world," she said. "We're trying to save it from *you*."

THE TRUTH

"Bullshit!"

Pan's fury ignited inside her, bursting from her mouth as a scream and from her fingers as a blast of white lightning. It snapped across the room, whipcrack fast, punching into the redhead and sending her tumbling backward into the dark. She aimed her other hand and blasted out a second strike, this one aimed upward.

The lights exploded, a fireworks show of sparks ripping across the ceiling. Then darkness, punctuated by the blinding bark of Herc's Desert Eagle and the flash of Truck's shotgun.

Somebody yelled in pain, in panic, the enemy Engineers scattering. A pulse of burning plasma appeared from the shadows, crackling as it tore across the floor—somebody fighting back. Pan fired again, blindly, then felt a hand on her shoulder.

"Get down to the Engine," growled Herc. "Take Marlow. You two are the only ones with powers, the only ones who can beat him."

Something swooped through the air above them, a dark shape that cried out with a human voice. Pan could hear Taupe shrieking something in French, the sound of his assault rifle deafening.

"We'll hold 'em off best we can," Herc said, firing another couple of shots across the room.

Pan nodded, retreating. She backed into Marlow and he grabbed her arm, both of them running into the open elevator.

"Pan," Herc yelled, his face a blur against the dark, his eyes two shards of steel. "Whatever happens down there, whatever he says, just remember who you are." He ducked as another wave of plasma seared its way across the room, igniting somebody. Friendly fire. The enemy Engineers were attacking one another in their confusion. Marlow grabbed the gates and hauled them closed, pushing the button for the bottom floor. "And, Pan," Herc called after them. "You never forget what you've done, yeah? You never forget that the world wouldn't be here without you."

Then he was gone, his voice fading behind the grinding roar of the elevator. Pan reached for the button, wanted to drag it back up and join in the fight. She couldn't leave him, not Herc, not when he needed her.

But her battle was with something else.

Something infinitely worse.

She shook her tingling fingers, breathing hard. Marlow was pacing from side to side like a caged tiger.

"We can't beat him," he said. "We can't."

She stood in his way and grabbed the scruff of his T-shirt, waiting until his big, frightened eyes met hers. The elevator rumbled downward, ever downward, carrying them right to hell's front door. The Engine was summoning her, each pulse of sound a clarion call she felt in the flesh of her brain. Her fear was so pure, so bright inside her that it didn't feel real.

It would, though, she knew, when she came face-to-face with Mammon.

"We can't," said Marlow, trying to tug loose. "You've seen him, he's too powerful."

"Marlow," she said, holding him tight. "You need to focus."

"On what?" he shot back. "On the fact that we're about to get killed? That we're going to get *taken*?"

The sounds of battle overhead had almost faded, plunging them into the closest thing to silence she had heard for a long time.

The calm before the storm, she thought, inhaling it, hoping that the sudden quiet would help calm her churning terror.

"We have to go back," said Marlow, hammering at the button. "We have to go, get to the surface. Someone else will do this, someone else will—"

She leaned in without thinking, and kissed him, pushing her lips against his until his lips stopped moving. She didn't think it was possible for his eyes to grow any wider but they did, his words drying up in his throat. He tasted of copper and mint, his breath heavy and hot against her tongue. He opened his mouth and she made to pull back, but didn't. It just felt so good to be close to somebody, even if it was him. She rested her arms lightly on his waist, feeling him tremble, feeling how fragile he was, as if she pressed too hard he would shatter like glass. He put his arms around her, too, his fingers tickling the small of her back. They stood there, connected, for a small eternity.

Then his tongue brushed against her lips and she reared back, wiping a sleeve over her mouth. The elevator was slowing, pulling her back into a world she had almost managed to forget about.

Marlow put his fingers to his lips as if there might still be a piece of her there. He was gulping air.

"You were losing it, I needed to shut you up," she explained, turning away so that he wouldn't see her cheeks blaze. "It worked."

They shuddered to a stop and she grabbed the grate, pausing for a moment. Beyond was the vault room, the last barrier between the world and the Engine. The door was several feet thick, designed to withstand an atomic blast. It could keep out even the strongest of Engineers.

And it was open.

"Maybe he really does just want to talk," she said, tugging at the stubborn gates. Marlow gave her a hand, wrenching them open. He put a hand on her arm and she shot him a look that made him let go immediately.

"You started it," he said. But the fear had gone from him, that blind panic. He even managed a smile. "One more, you know, before we die a horrible death and get dragged to hell?"

"We make it out of this," she said, "then you've got yourself a deal."

It was a safe bet to make. She was pretty sure they weren't getting out of this one.

She took a step forward, then felt his hand on her arm again. When she turned, though, the smile had gone and he was frowning.

"Look, Pan, I should have mentioned this before." He cast a look at the vault door, chewing something over. "Charlie, I spoke to him, back when he was in the infirmary. He said something."

"What?" she said when he didn't continue.

"He said that I needed to be careful, because they were lying to me."

"*What?*" she said. Mammon had told her the exact same thing on the train. "Who's lying?"

"He didn't say. That's all he had the strength for."

"It doesn't matter," said Pan. "Mammon is the liar. Ostheim always called him the father of all lies. You shouldn't believe a word that comes out of his mouth, and if he got to your friend then you shouldn't trust a word that comes out of his, either. Come on."

But the doubt followed her into the room, nagging at her. *They're lying to you.* And why had Mammon not just killed her there and then, on the train, rather than trying to talk. It just didn't make sense. She checked her crossbow, the first bolt loaded and ready to fire. If she had a lucky shot, if she buried it right in his rancid heart, then there would be no more lies.

No more lies, no more fear, just relief.

The thought of it was overpowering, propelling her across the room. She splayed the fingers of her free hand, the current dancing between them, waiting for its orders. The Engine spoke to her in the language of hell, those same images flashing across her vision, burrowing into the meat of her brain—death, torture, screams, flames, all so familiar now that she dismissed them with a grunt, forcing herself through the door.

And there it was, the Engine.

She had never seen it like this, every one of its countless clockwork parts in motion. It looked vast, stretching from ho-rizon to horizon and lit by the thousand lights embedded in the distant ceiling of the cavern. And it looked *alive*, like it might just pull itself up, collect its scattered pieces, and haul its bulk out into the world.

Something exploded deep inside the Engine, a pillar of thick, red flame curling up and pooling in the hollows of the ceiling. There was a pulse of sound, of *feeling*, and the Engine roared, the collective cry of billions and billions of cogs and gears and needles and springs. It roared loud enough to end her, to end the entire world. It roared so loud that she almost didn't see the figure standing by the black pool.

Mammon.

He stood with his back to her, staring into the dark water. He could have been mistaken for a normal human being except for the way his body seemed to shimmer, glitching from side to side like she was watching a video in fast-forward. She knew it was him, though, he was kicking out an evil stink that made her soul hurt.

She didn't hesitate, not for a second, knowing that if she did she would never be able to move again. She started down the stairs, taking them two at a time, the crunch of her footsteps lost behind the world-ending groan of the Engine.

"Find Charlie," she yelled back, feeling Marlow on her heels. "I got *him.*"

No time to wait for a reply. She was already close to the bottom, the Engine sprawling out to her side, its deafening orchestra of clicks like an army of insects about to swarm onto the rock and devour her.

She ignored it, ignored everything except for him.

Skidding onto one knee, she placed the crossbow to her shoulder.

One chance. One chance. Don't mess it up.

Mammon was starting to turn, slowly. The shape of him wobbled and blurred, like he wasn't really there. But he *was* there. She knew it. She could feel it in the way she wanted to open her head with a hammer and claw out her brains. She could feel it in every screaming cell of her body as he turned to face her.

Mammon. The man she'd been trained to fear, trained to hunt, trained to kill.

She fired, the bolt humming as it shot from the crossbow,

arcing through the air, a flash of iron as it burned toward Mammon's heart.

He snatched out a hand and caught it.

Pan, he said, his voice a skewer in her ears, puncturing her.

She swore, thrusting out a hand and loosing a raging torrent of electricity. She didn't wait to see if it hit him, just strafed right, trying to fumble another bolt into the bow with her smoking fingers.

Pan, listen to me.

No.

It slipped from her grip, rolling away, and she left it, pulling the last bolt loose. Mammon was still standing there, sparks rippling over his body like they were trying to find a way in, trying to find a way to hurt him. He lifted a hand and she felt something cold and dark in the air around her, felt herself rise from the ground. The raw sewage stench of him was unbearable.

She twisted against his invisible grip, tilted the crossbow toward him.

Pan, stop, listen to me.

She pulled the trigger. This time Mammon wasn't quick enough, the bolt slicing past his face. She felt his hold on her loosen and she crashed earthward, pain flaring in her knee as she landed. The crossbow skidded away and she scrabbled for it.

Something wrapped itself around her foot, yanking her back. Her face slammed against the floor, a tooth spinning away. For a moment there was nothing, her vision a series of dark, churning cogs like she'd been thrown into the heart of the Engine. She blinked hard and the world snapped back on. She was still being dragged over the rough stone, something locked python-tight around her ankle.

Grunting with the effort, she managed to flip herself onto

her back. Mammon was ten yards away and reeling her in like a fish. His body danced in and out of reality, his face shifting like a collection of photographs being shown at lightning speed.

You do not have to fight me, he said. *We are on—*

She punched another bolt of energy at him, this one weaker but still enough to make him lift his arm in self-defense. It crackled into him, pushing him back, and she fired another, and another. The grip on her leg vanished and she forced herself onto her feet, loosing another attack. This one hit Mammon in the chest and he staggered away, his cry like a shrapnel grenade had exploded inside her head.

Where the hell was the bolt she'd dropped?

She fired another charge, pathetically small. Her body was running on fumes but it didn't matter. She didn't have to fight for much longer. If she could just find it . . .

There, near the stairs.

She ran for it, Mammon roaring behind her. She could feel the force of his voice like the shock wave of an explosion and she almost fell again, her arms wheeling to keep herself upright. Another pulse howled its way from somewhere inside the Engine, an enormous pillar of fire curling lazily toward the ceiling. There was no sign of Marlow.

More invisible hands trying to grab her. She dived, rolling out of their reach and snatching the bolt from the stone.

No time to get the crossbow.

She gripped the bolt and ran, willing the last few charges from her fingers. The air crackled with thunder. Mammon weaved out of their way, his face—*faces*—a mask of fury. Then he was moving, too, running right for her, shattering his way through reality. His mouth stretched, *too* wide, so wide that he might be about to swallow her up. And he roared, a noise that could have broken every bone in her body.

But still she ran, no charge left. She ran and ran, unleashing a scream of her own that had been building inside her for years—since her mom had turned her back on her, since Christoph had tried to take her, since the cops had arrested her and Herc had saved her, since she'd first heard Mammon's name, since her first mission, since she'd stood by and watched all those people die, all of her friends. She screamed until there was nothing left inside her, and she ran until there was nothing left between them.

He lunged for her but she put her head down and tackled him. There was no air left in her lungs to be knocked away but she still felt it in every tendon, like she'd tried to bring down a bear. They locked in a demented dance. She held the bolt like a knife, jabbing it into his flank. But his arms were around her, crushing. She had no space to move. His touch was cold, turning her blood to ice. His graveyard stench enveloped her, choking her. He squeezed harder and she felt the vertebrae in her back creak, ready to pop.

Just stop! Mammon yelled at her. *Just stop!*

No.

She dug deep, deeper than she'd ever gone, and found something there. She grabbed hold of a handful of cloth and pulsed the last of her electrostatic energy into his ribs. A direct hit.

Room to breathe, to move. She swung her hand around again and this time the bolt found its target, sticking in the flesh of Mammon's side. It was like dropping a flare into a canister of gas, the force of the explosion spinning her away on a cushion of heat and noise. She landed on her back, skidding into the rim of the black pool.

Darkness, the overwhelming force of it trying to pull her in, trying to smother her.

Get up, she told herself.

She clawed her way out of it, her eyes bulging, her mouth hanging open. Mammon was right in front of her—no longer a shifting mirage of faces but a man. No, a *boy*. He looked younger than her, younger than Marlow, curls of blond hair falling over his eyes, his mouth twisted into a grimace of pain. The bolt stuck out of his side and his clothes were smoldering there, tongues of flame licking up.

"Just die!" Pan said. She'd meant it as a scream but it came out as less than a whisper, just a breath. She tried to stand, found that she couldn't and pushed herself onto the lip of the pool instead. Behind her the black water sat ink-thick and agitated, nothing reflected in its depths.

"Pan," said Mammon, and the sound of his voice almost sent her toppling back into the waters. It was a young boy's voice, high and trembling.

Just a trick. Just another lie.

She needed to push the bolt in deeper, right into the bastard's heart. It was the only way to finish it. She tried to move again, everything inside her drenched in pain.

"Pan, no more," said Mammon. He collapsed onto his knees, his coat billowing out around him. Gripping the bolt with one hand, he pulled. "You have to listen to me. You don't know what you're doing."

She took as deep a breath as her busted lungs would allow.

"I'm killing you," she managed. "That's what I'm doing. I'm ending this."

"You're ending *everything*," he said. "You're ending the world. Please." He stopped, panting with the effort of trying to pull the bolt loose. "Please just listen. I have tried to tell you this for so long, but he would not let me. He would never let me. He has poisoned your mind, Pan. He has poisoned everything you believe in, and everything you think is true."

"Who?" she said, finally managing to stagger to her feet. Out in the Engine another column of flame rose, illuminating the platform and Mammon's face. The kid looked up at her with big blue eyes. Was he *crying*?

"Ostheim," he groaned, spit hanging from his lips. "Ostheim. He has turned you against everything that is right. He has been lying to you. He has been *using* you. All this time you thought you fought for good, for what was right. But how did you know? How *could* you know? You took his word for it."

Despite the fire, everything inside her ran cold.

"No," she said. "Ostheim is good. He's trying to stop you from bringing the Engines together, from opening the gates."

Mammon shook his head, great fat tears rolling down his cheeks.

"No, Pan," he said. "I never wanted to open the gates. I wanted to bring the Engines together because it is the only way of *destroying* them."

"*What?*" she said. "No, that's not true. You're a liar. You're nothing but a liar and a killer and . . ."

The words abandoned her. There was no way he could be right, could he? There was *no damn way*.

Mammon cried out and the bolt came loose in a gout of blood. Pan steeled herself, trying to shake some charge into the ends of her fingers. But he just held the bolt up in one hand and threw it to her. It clattered across the stone, skidding into the raised edge of the pool.

"I am telling you the truth," he said as he clambered unsteadily to his feet. "I've *always* tried to tell you the truth. Ostheim is the enemy. He has been trying to unite the Engines so that he can bring down the wall between the worlds, so that he can open the gates of hell. He is evil, Pan."

He shuddered, patting at the flames on his jacket. His face

was starting to buzz again, separating into pieces, but he made no move toward her. He just stood there, shoulders sagging, breathing hard.

"He is evil. He has always been trying to end this world. And for years now, you have been helping him do it."

No.

No.

No.

She turned away from him, hands to her ears.

No.

It couldn't be true. It couldn't be.

Ostheim, he'd always been straight with her, always sent her on missions that would help save the world.

But were they?

All those deaths, all those assassinations. What if Mammon was right, what if she'd been killing off the good guys, the ones who wanted to save the world?

Please God, no.

She searched her head but not one single thing, not one single memory, contradicted his words.

No.

And she was crying now, her hands to her mouth. Mammon was wrong, he had to be wrong.

Because if he was right, then she was a monster.

"I'm sorry, Pan," he said behind her. "I truly am."

Only one way to know for sure.

Only one way to know the truth.

Pan climbed onto the lip of the black pool, took a breath, and threw herself in.

REUNITED

Marlow had absolutely no idea what he was doing.

Pan was running across the platform, crossbow in her hands, her whole body glowing with the force of the energy inside her.

She could take care of herself. He cut to the side, the Engine a maelstrom of movement ahead of him, a mechanical hurricane. The last time he'd been here it had been nothing like this, just an insect whisper from somewhere out there. But the last time he'd been here it had simply been forging his contract.

Now it was preparing to open a door between worlds.

He reached the edge of the platform and skidded to a halt. Beneath him the Engine whirred in a frenzy, needles and pins and cogs and springs churning. It was like standing on a cliff in a storm and he had to close his eyes against a rush of vertigo. How the hell was he supposed to find Charlie?

He opened his eyes, scanned the ocean-big mass of moving parts. The last explosion was still rising like a comet tail, something burning out there.

He jumped, landing hard at the foot of the Engine. From down here it was more like a forest, the parts so much bigger than they looked from above. The speed they moved at was terrifying, like he was standing in front of a combine harvester—blades of dark metal about to slice him apart. The noise was like nothing he had ever experienced, so loud that he could feel it in every cell.

It was almost as if it was calling to him, and when he took a step forward the section right in front of him stopped dead, a path opening up in the madness.

It *wanted* him to enter.

He hesitated, then put a hand to his lips, feeling the heat of Pan's kiss there. He wasn't sure what she'd done to him, but some of his terror had evaporated. He was still afraid, but she had given him strength. She had promised him, too. She had made a contract of her own. Get through this, and there will be another kiss.

And that had to be worth risking death for, right?

He stepped between two vast black trunks, each twice as tall as him and forged from a dull, black metal. They bristled with spikes that looked like drill bits, and were ringed by vast iron cogs. Branches split out from them, each of which had to contain thousands of moving parts—each smaller than the one it was connected to until they were so minuscule he couldn't even see them. They looked sharp enough to cut through flesh and bone. And they had to be, he guessed, because each of those pieces had the ability to open a hole in reality and change whatever lay beneath.

But they stayed still as he passed, the machine grinding to a halt, showing him which way to go. He plunged into the darkness, into the noise. Every time he passed a section of the Engine it began to move again behind him, the air thrumming with the force of it.

Not far ahead there was another explosion, one that filled the Engine with fire and made it groan like a living thing, like some huge leviathan. What the hell was happening up there?

Was that the sound of somebody breaking the seals of the universe? Opening the gate?

A section of the Engine spun to a halt and he pushed through it. On the other side was something resembling a forest that had been cleared and burned, an area the size of an airplane hangar where there were no cogs, no gears—just pieces of broken metal embedded in the ground, everything drenched in fire. The scorched earth ahead was glowing red hot, puddles of molten iron turning the air into a shimmering haze. There was so much smoke that even though his contract was still in place, his asthma cured, he was struggling to breathe. So much smoke that he could barely see twenty feet in front of him.

But twenty feet was enough. There was a shape there, a figure standing in the horror and the heat.

Not so much standing in it, as made *from* it.

"Charlie?" Marlow called out, choking on the word. He took a step into the ruin but had to stop because the heat was just too much. The shimmering silhouette ahead was walking away, disappearing into the haze. He opened his mouth and called his name again, louder.

This time the figure stopped, and turned. He stood in the inferno like he was sculpted from flame, his body a core of darkness wearing a corona of blazing yellow. He took another step, the bones of the Engine crunching beneath his feet. Closer now, and Marlow could see that where his eyes should have been there were just portals of light; it was like staring into the depths of hell itself. He felt that if he looked at them for too long he would simply end, that the sheer power there would scrub him from existence.

It's not Charlie, he realized. *It's a demon. Or worse.*

The figure kept coming, faster now. It lifted a burning hand and pointed it at Marlow, the air actually crackling and spitting with the heat of his touch.

Oh no.

Marlow turned to run, but the wall of parts behind him was spinning again, a gyroscope of blades that caged him in.

Death in a furnace or death in a blender. What the hell kind of choice was that?

He whirled back, fists clenched. Even with the power of the Engine inside him he didn't stand a chance against whatever this was. It would turn him into ash with just a thought. It took another couple of steps toward him, the roar of it even louder than the sound of the Engine, the heat of it making the hair on his head curl and shrivel even though it was fifteen feet away.

No chance, but what else could he do?

He ran, but the heat was too much. It was like moving into a burning building, his skin blistering. He slowed, squinting through his fingers, knowing that any second now he was going to erupt.

Then the demon blinked, and the flames sputtered out like he'd been doused with water. It took a moment for the splotches of light to leave Marlow's vision, but when he could see again he wasn't sure whether to start laughing or crying.

In the end, he did both.

Charlie stood there, his best friend, his *only* friend. He looked just the way he had the last time Marlow had seen him, the same messy brown hair, the same wide eyes.

Only this time he was stark naked.

His skin rippled with delicate petals of flame, his bare feet standing in a puddle of molten rock. The air around him still danced, making him look more like an illusion than ever. He studied Marlow like he couldn't believe what he was seeing, then his mouth lifted into a smile.

"Charlie!" Marlow yelled again, and he almost started running again, ready to wrap his arms around him, until he remembered where they were. "What the hell, dude?" he yelled over the sound of the Engine. "What's going on? What happened to you?"

"Same thing that happened to you," said Charlie, his voice the same as Marlow remembered, the same voice he'd listened to and shared stories with and laughed alongside for years. "The Engine."

"I don't get it, man," said Marlow, coughing smoke from his lungs. "I don't get why you'd side with Mammon. What did he offer you? Money? Whatever it was, Charlie, it wasn't worth it. It isn't worth *this*."

"Marlow, you got it all wrong," said Charlie.

"It's because I left you, right?" Marlow shouted. "Back on Staten Island. I'm sorry, man, I never should have done that. I just . . . I just didn't want to see you get hurt. I'm sorry."

Charlie shook his head.

"If you hadn't left me there then Mammon never would have found me. I never would have discovered the truth."

"You can't trust a thing he tells you," Marlow said. A section of the Engine behind Charlie gave way, metal screeching as it crashed into the glowing rock. Marlow flinched. "He's a liar, he just wants to open the gates. You've seen what happens, you've—"

"Says who, Marlow?" Charlie asked, taking a step forward. "Says Ostheim?"

"Yeah," said Marlow. "He's been trying to stop Mammon for

years, for like decades. It can't happen, Charlie. Our families, all those people, they'll die."

Charlie actually laughed.

"Mammon was right," he said, taking another step toward Marlow. "He was totally right. You have no idea."

"What are you talking about?" Marlow said. "No idea about what?"

"That you're fighting on the wrong side," he said. "You're fighting with the bad guys."

"That's a lie," Marlow said. The sweat was stinging his eyes and he wiped it away. The heat was unbearable, the inside of his mouth made of kindling. He felt that with one stray spark he'd erupt into flames. "Pan, Herc, they're good people, they're trying to do the right thing."

"Maybe," Charlie shouted back. "But they're good people following the orders of a bad man. Ostheim, he's trying to bring the Engines together. He's been trying for years. He's the one who wants to end the world."

"No," said Marlow. "No, that's not right. You expect me to believe that when you're right here, opening the gates yourself?"

"Take a look, dude," Charlie said, lifting his arms. "Just take a look. This seem to you like I'm opening anything?"

Marlow looked past him, seeing the wasteland there.

"You're not opening the gates to hell?"

"Marlow," said Charlie, one eyebrow raised. "I know I ain't exactly a saint, but you ever heard me say, *Boy, you know what I feel like doing today? Setting free a bunch of demons and maybe the devil and watch them rip the world apart?*"

"Then what the hell are you doing?" Marlow asked.

"*Destroying* it," he yelled back, and the Engine seemed to

roar in outrage. Charlie put his hands to his ears, practically screaming the words. "This was the only way. You have to bring the Engines together in order to use them, but you have to bring them together in order to take them apart, too."

Another section gave up the ghost, crumbling in the heat. Charlie took a few more steps forward until he was almost close enough to touch. Heat was still radiating from him, like Marlow was standing next to an oven with the door open.

"Mammon found me, right after you'd left," Charlie said. "Took me in, waited for me to sober up. I thought I was dead, man, I thought you'd poisoned me or something, that I was hallucinating him. Thought he was a monster."

"I've seen him, Charlie. He *is* a monster."

"No, he's not. I mean, he's messed up, all those years using the Engine, he's a ruin. I don't even think he's human anymore. Gives you the creeps, no doubt. Truth is, though, he's just a kid. Least he was, back when all this began. He told me what was happening. Told me about Ostheim, about what he wanted to do with the Engines. Told me Ostheim is a lying bastard, that he's brainwashed you and that girl and the old guy and everyone else who works for him. Made you think you were fighting for the right side."

Charlie paused, running a hand through his hair. Marlow chewed his knuckles so hard that it hurt. It didn't make any sense. He'd met Ostheim just that morning. He was harmless.

"Hate to say it, Marlow," said Charlie, like he was reading his mind. "But he's about as evil as it gets. He's old. Older than he looks. He's been doing this for years. Centuries. So has Mammon. They've been at each other like stray dogs for half of time."

"You've got it wrong, Charlie," said Marlow, but the words sounded hollow.

"Not this time, man. Mammon told me, he *showed* me. All

the stuff Ostheim has done, all the people he has killed. He told me he needed my help. He told me *you* needed my help. If I didn't say yes then Ostheim would use you the way he uses everyone, would use you to open the gates."

The world was reeling and Marlow had to screw his eyes shut for a moment. When he opened them again Charlie was even closer. He looked at his friend, saw the scar on his stomach.

"He tried to kill you," said Marlow. "Got that girl to shoot you, got Patrick to throw you off a mountain. How is that being on the right side?"

"It was part of the plan," Charlie said. "Wasn't exactly supposed to go that way, though. Patrick was broken. He was crazy after what happened to his sister. You were supposed to get me back, smuggle me in."

"So you could open the Red Door from inside," Marlow said. Charlie nodded.

"Mammon told me that as soon as I got to the Nest I had to try to get inside the Engine, it was the only way. Get inside the Engine and make a deal."

"To be the human torch?" Marlow asked.

"To have the power to destroy the Engine," he said.

"No way. There's no way the Engine would let you trade for that."

"It's just a machine," Charlie said. "The Engine does what it's told. Just a machine. I got my powers, and I opened the Red Door."

Marlow jabbed a finger at him, a fire of his own burning up from inside.

"Yeah, and you killed them," he said. "You killed all of them, Bully and Hope and Seth. Christ, Charlie, he was just an old man."

"I didn't do it," Charlie said, holding up his hands.

"Mammon did. He couldn't take any chances. He'd been waiting decades, *longer*, for a way inside the Engine. He couldn't afford to mess up. You don't get it, do you? You don't get what's at stake here. It's everything, Marlow. The whole world. What's a handful of lives compared to a million? A billion?"

It's what Pan had always said, and he thought of her now, fighting Mammon. Was he telling her the same thing? Would she listen?

It was Pan, of course she wouldn't.

Something was niggling at the back of his mind, something bad, but everything was moving too fast for him to grasp it.

"But if you're destroying the Engine . . . I mean, why now? Why didn't you just destroy your own Engine, make it impossible for them to be joined."

"Doesn't work like that," said Charlie. "The Engines can't be destroyed unless they're joined. Look, it's complicated, and this really isn't the time. I have to do this, Marlow. I have to do this now, while both Engines are here."

The palms of his hands suddenly erupted, twin blowtorches that burned phosphorus bright.

"Wait!" Marlow yelled, staggering away from the heat, from the light, from the awful, unexpected truth. "Just wait, please, Charlie. I don't get it. I don't get any of it. Where's the other Engine?"

"There is only one," Charlie said. "There has only ever been one. But it is split into two, each one frozen into its own pocket of time."

"*What?*"

"It's the perfect defense, linked but separate, the same but different. Try to destroy one version and it repairs itself from the other, it self-replicates its broken pieces."

"*What?*"

"And now they've been joined. You must have seen it, the way nothing seems right, nothing seems solid. It's because both Engines, both those bubbles of time, are here, right now, in the present. Destroy the Engine now and it has no means of repairing itself."

It roared again, all around them, the sound of the world splitting in two. Charlie looked at it, his face warped with contempt.

"Destroy the bastard now and it can never heal."

"But if you destroy it . . ." Marlow said. Charlie threw him a sad smile.

"Then there's no way of ending my contract," he said. "There's no way back. For you, or for me."

Great.

"But hey, what's one life?" Charlie said with a shrug. "And everyone else is saved. Got to be worth it, yeah?"

There it was again, that thought nestling at the back of Marlow's skull. Something important. Something *wrong.* He closed his eyes, peering into the storm.

"Mammon, he planned all this, right?" he said, looking at Charlie again. The flames were creeping over his body again. His eyes were actually glowing, and when he nodded he left sparkler trails in Marlow's vision.

"He'd been planning it for years," he said. "To get somebody inside."

"But it doesn't make sense. Ostheim had the Engine locked up tight. He'd never risk letting in anyone who could open the doors."

"Must have thought he could trust me," said Charlie. "'Cause I was with you."

"He never even knew me. I'd already put the Engine at risk once running off, why would he trust you any more than me?"

Something exploded, a deep, bone-rattling roar that almost knocked Marlow off his feet. It hadn't come from the Engine, he was pretty sure about that. It had come from somewhere overhead. Dust and debris rained down and he spat out the taste of it. That niggling thought was closer now, fluttering just out of sight like a moth against the night.

"No way," he said, as much to himself as to Charlie. "No way he'd just let you in like that. Not unless . . ."

And there it was, suddenly right at the front of his head.

"Oh Jesus, Charlie. He knew."

"What? Who?"

"Ostheim, he knew who you were, he knew which side you were on. He knew what you were going to do."

"That doesn't make any sense," said Charlie, the light in his eyes guttering out again. He blinked, frowning. "Why would he let me in?"

"Because it was the only way," said Marlow. "He's been trying to find Mammon's Engine for decades, right? To unite them. But all he needed to do was give up his own Engine, to hand it right over. He knew that when they were together they'd kick out a signal, make it easier to find them."

"No," said Charlie, shaking his head.

"We did it for him," said Marlow. "We brought them together, we brought them here. We left the door right open for him. We have to—"

Another sound from above, like the skies were falling. This time a stalactite detached from the ceiling, one that had to be bigger than a house. It fell lazily, the ground shaking as it landed somewhere out there. The Engine was moving faster now, every piece a blur, like it knew something was about to happen.

And it was right.

Marlow turned the way he'd come, everything lost behind a wall of mechanical chaos. But he didn't need to see to know that something bad was coming. He could feel it inside every cell.

"Ostheim," said Charlie behind him, and despite the power that flowed through him his voice trembled. "He's here."

WAR

The black pool engulfed her, gulped her down. She tumbled into it, no chance to prepare for the panic, for the horror. Phantom hands groped for her, hauling her deeper, deeper. The darkness was absolute, and when she could hold her breath no more and she finally opened her mouth it flooded inside like cold poison.

But she'd been here before, so many times.

She pushed the panic away, studying that darkness until it began to part. Clouds, then sweeping, awful figures half-drowned in the shadows—and there, a mountain of flesh and bone that sat a million miles away, and yet somehow right next to her, which studied her with the festering rot holes in its face.

What is it you desire? it asked, not a sound but a feeling that pulsed through the dark water. She shivered with the force of it—not disgust, not fear.

Excitement.

This place, right here in the heart of the Engine, is where she belonged.

I want the truth. She fired the words upward, toward the thing that sat there. *I want to know who is trying to bring the Engines together, and who is trying to destroy them.*

The easiest request in the world, why had she never asked it before?

I want the truth, she said again. And again, and again, a mantra hurled out into the Engine.

That is all? it asked. And suddenly Night was standing right beside her, utterly real. She reached out to Pan, her face wet with tears.

"Please," she said. "Just bring me back. It's so hot down here. It's so lonely. Please, Pan, you can bring me back."

No, Pan said. It wasn't her, it wasn't Night. *I'm sorry, I'm so sorry. I want the truth, that's all. The truth.*

It is done, said the creature inside the Engine, with another pulse of sound that could only be laughter. *And the price is your soul.* Then she was rising, out of that uterine quiet, up, up into the heat and noise of the world.

She burst from the pool, clawing in a long, desperate breath. She kicked at the water, reaching for the rim and not quite finding it. She plunged under, those hands grabbing her again, trying to haul her below.

Then a hand on her wrist, pulling her up. She let it, flopping out of the water and over the lip of the pool onto the beautiful, solid ground.

Mammon was there, his face a boy's face and yet also a hundred different faces, like his flesh couldn't hold him. He held on to her for a moment more—and in his touch she saw his story in a heartbeat, a child who lived inside the Engine, whose brothers and sisters played among the moving parts; a child who was betrayed by one of his own, and who now wanted to *destroy* the Engines, always to destroy them—then he let go, holding his fingers like he'd been burned.

"You know," he said.

"Oh God," she groaned. She coughed black water from her

lungs, the droplets squirming across the stone as they tried to make their way back to the pool. "Oh God, you were telling the truth."

The awful, unbelievable, soul-ending truth that her life was a lie.

She would have cried if she could remember how.

The world trembled again with the force of another explosion. She sat up, grimacing. What's done was done. She had to think straight.

"That's Charlie out there, right?" she said, using the lip of the pool to get herself to her feet. "What's he doing?"

Mammon wasn't looking at the Engine, though, he was looking up, and he was looking scared.

"Too soon," he said, shaking his head. "Too soon."

Noises were rippling through the open vault door, distant screams. There was another dull crunch overhead, like a giant was jumping on the floor up there. Rocks pattered down around her, some bouncing off the liquid surface of the pool and clattering to the stone. A section of the wall high above them bulged and cracked.

The elevator shaft, she thought. Something was on its way down.

Something big.

Mammon turned to her, his eyes full of tears. He had opened his mouth to speak when a section of the Engine close to the platform burst into flames, so bright that Pan had to screw her eyes shut. When she looked again a mushroom cloud of smoke was billowing up, the mechanism beneath reduced to a collection of molten parts. Somebody was walking through the chaos, somebody crafted from fire. Around him the Engine whirred and roared, almost in a panic. She swore she could see parts of it withdrawing from the heat like a snail's eyes, pulling into itself.

"Pan," said Mammon. "I—"

The wall above the vault door split further, a booming howl rising even above the noise of the Engine and the roar of the fire. Mammon glanced over his shoulder.

"I thought we had more time," he said, then he turned back. "You have to get out of here, you have to survive."

"But—"

"I won't be able to hold him back, Pan," Mammon said. "You need to go, I will distract him as best I can. When you're clear—"

Another pillar of flames to the side, and more dull explosions from behind the wall. Pan felt like she was caught between a forest fire and a minefield. The concussive waves coming from both sides were enough to pulverize her. Mammon took her head in his hand, gently, and drew her back to him. He looked even younger than before, just a boy.

How had she gotten it so wrong?

"I got it wrong, too," he said, plucking the thought from her head. "I didn't see what he was doing. I thought I had outmaneuvered him. It was all part of his plan."

"But he's, he's just a *man*," said Pan, picturing Ostheim with his old clothes and his comb-over.

"It's a clever man who plays the fool," said Mammon. "A strong man who plays the coward. And only the very worst of us can pass as human."

"Wait, what?" said Pan.

A wave of blast furnace heat rolled over her, another section of the Engine melting into molten puddles. The figure on fire strode from it, followed by another. She could barely make out the second guy in the blazing light, but then he darted forward, clambering up the side of the platform.

"Marlow," she said, and it took everything she had not to run to him, if only because he was somebody familiar, an anchor to stop her flipping upside down with the rest of the world. He stood there, staring at her, then at Mammon. For a second she thought he was going to charge at him and she had her mouth open to tell him to wait when he spoke.

"I know," he said. "Charlie told me."

He turned, ducking onto one knee and offering his hand. Then Charlie was there, no longer on fire. He scooted onto the platform and Marlow pulled his hand free, yelping.

"Dude, you're *hot*."

He was also completely naked.

Something crunched from behind the vault door, a cloud of dust erupting through it.

"He is here," said Mammon. "Pan, do as I say. Get out. Ostheim will open the gates, but it doesn't mean the end. There is another way."

"Another way?" said Charlie as he and Marlow joined them by the pool.

"Find Meridiana," Mammon said. "She is the only one who can defeat Ostheim, the only one who can end this."

"Meridiana?" said Marlow. "The evil one?"

"Not evil," said Mammon. "Her mind has gone, but she is not evil, she was never evil. Find her."

"Where is she?" said Pan.

"Hiding," said Mammon. "She has been in hiding for years. Look for her in the spaces between, it's all I know. Look for her in yourselves. She's hiding in time, somewhere clever. Somewhere *he* could never find her."

"So how are we supposed to?" said Marlow.

"Because—"

The vault door spun off its hinges, flying out into the Engine like a cannonball. Something was moving in the darkness beyond. Mammon glanced up at it like a child waiting for a punch to land.

"Because she will feel the change," he said. "She will know that Ostheim has the Engines. She will want you to find her."

"And if she doesn't?" said Pan. Her heart was trying to crack her ribs on its way out, her whole body shaking.

"Then we are all worse than dead," said Mammon. "Go to Venice, to Castello, the old town. All I know is that the last we saw of her she had a shop, a mirror shop. You will find her there, somewhere, if she wants you to. It's our only hope. It's— *No!*"

Ostheim walked through the vault door and stood at the top of the steps. He looked exactly the same as he had that morning, drowning in baggy clothes, his lank hair falling over his face. Only his expression had changed. His eyes were bulging, his mouth twisted open into a rictus smile, one that seemed too big for his face. He looked out into the Engine and that smile split even further, a deep, unpleasant laugh spilling out.

"Go!" said Mammon. "And do not look back."

Ostheim heard him, his head twisting to look down the stairs. The smile fell away, replaced with a look of fury that was as far from human as anything Pan had ever seen. Something throbbed out of him, a pulse of evil that made her want to reach inside and pull out her soul, to trample it to dust.

"Go!" Mammon yelled.

No.

Her anger was demonic, was forged from fire, from all those years of blind loyalty. How many people had she killed for him? How many lives had she ruined for him? How many people were being torn to pieces in hell because of what she had done for him? She was going to murder him. She was going to end him.

She took a step forward and so did Ostheim.

And he *changed*.

His head flipped open like his jaw was hinged, his mouth a gaping black hole. Something pushed its way out of it, something oil black and too big. It might have been a lamprey eel, its tip ringed with teeth, its body slick and black. It kept coming, exploding up from Ostheim's maw—ten yards long, twenty, thirty, too long and too fat to have ever fit inside a human body.

Oh God.

It split into two, peeling from itself like a cheese string. Then again, and again, stretching into long, wet fingers. They all punched earthward, sliding down the steps so fast they were just a blur. Some cut to the side, feeling their way into the Engine.

The rest came right for them.

Pan ducked, feeling one of the huge black limbs thunder over her head. Another followed, the air growing dark and cold as their bulk blocked the firelight. They thumped into Mammon like charging bulls—two, three, six, ten of them now— one after the other, pounding him into the stone.

"Pan, we gotta go!" Marlow yelled, cutting between them, making for the stairs. Charlie was screaming Mammon's name, his body erupting into flames again. He stretched out his arms and released a plume of fire that cut across the platform, engulfing the squirming mass of shapes that hid Mammon.

Above them, Ostheim roared. His body was torn in a dozen places, dark, clotted blood splattering the stairs. Pieces of his flesh were dropping away like old clothes as more shapes forced their way from him, tapeworm-thin. They whipcracked through the air in a frenzy, one punching through the stone floor inches from Pan, showering her in shrapnel.

It is mine.

The voice was everywhere and nowhere, echoing around her skull like a cathedral bell had been rung in there. She felt a hand on her arm, Marlow dragging her across the platform. Some of the limbs had embedded themselves in the floor, stuck there like ivy as they grew over the edge of the platform. The Engine seemed to be welcoming them, grinding to a halt to let them in.

It is mine.

"No!"

The nest of snakes next to the pool blew like it was packed with explosives, showering the platform with rancid pieces of black flesh. Mammon rose from the carnage, his body shifting and glitching like it was trying to pull itself out of the universe. He opened his hands and a wave of black light burst from him, so impossibly dark that it seemed the world there had been erased.

Ostheim screamed again—although he no longer had a mouth to scream from. The last of his body split away, shedding muscle and bone. Beneath was a mess of sinew shot through with what looked like copper and bronze, an insane union of organic and mechanical parts. It moved, fast, scuttling onto the wall like a spider. Its countless limbs whirled through the air, a hurricane of impossible flesh. Then they darted down toward Mammon again, scorpion tails trying to punch their way through him.

Mammon vanished into thin air, appearing again almost immediately on the other side of the pool. He scooped a hand through the air and hurled another missile of nothing, an antimatter bomb that burned into the wall where Ostheim had been. The creature was already on the move, the stone splitting and dissolving where it was struck. More rocks fell from overhead, some as big as cars.

"Pan, come on!" Marlow was screaming at her.

She tore her eyes away from Mammon, focused on getting across the platform. They were at the stairs now, Marlow stumbling up them, Charlie behind her and pushing her forward on a wave of heat. A crunch from the platform and Pan couldn't not look. It was like her head was on a string, somebody else tugging at it.

Ostheim propelled himself from the wall, his immense insect bulk landing on Mammon. Those limbs rose up as one, then stabbed down—so hard that the platform groaned, cracking away from the wall. One side tipped, water slopping out of the pool and hissing as it poured into the fires that raged there. Mammon fought back, waves of negative light pouring off him, each one ripping away some of Ostheim's skin, gouging out chunks of flesh, sending limbs flying.

But for everything that Mammon cut away, something else grew. Things were pouring out of Ostheim now, liquid-quick but as solid as obsidian. The limbs pounded the rock with industrial speed—so fast that Pan couldn't bear to look at them. The noise of them was like a thousand pneumatic drills at once, a cloud of smoke pouring from them, smoke and *blood*, misting into the ruptured air.

"No!" Charlie raged, burning so fiercely that the stairs were melting around him. He fired out another jet of molten heat, right into Ostheim's back, but he didn't even seem to feel it. The noise of it, of Ostheim's attack, of the howling Engine, was too much. Pan felt deaf from it.

And yet something still rose from the madness, a voice whisper-weak and haunting.

Go, Pan. And find her. You do not have long.

"Come on!" yelled Marlow from the top of the stairs. Pan turned, tripped, sprawling. She climbed the rest on all fours because she couldn't trust her legs to hold her. Marlow grabbed her, helping her up. He ducked through the door but she couldn't bring herself to follow, not yet. She looked down, the view from here like the boxes in a theater, everything perfectly clear.

Ostheim was a hulking mass, the body of a vast spider but at least thirty limbs snaking from him. Only a couple were still pounding at the ground, because there was nothing left to pound. Mammon was a scattered mess of parts, a butcher's waste bag scattered over the ruined platform. Pan could make out half a skull, a flap of face still attached, one eye roving madly. It seemed to see her, or maybe she just imagined it.

Find her.

Then a pincer-like limb skewered it and the skull shattered like glass. Ostheim lumbered off the remains of Mammon, each of his limbs darting over the edge of the platform and plunging into the smoking mess of the Engine.

"No!" Charlie yelled, a voice made of heat and fire. He loosed another strike, one that melted rock, that made the air burn bright. Ostheim's head—just a tumorous lump on the bulk of his body, the vague shape of a face there—twisted up, the flames washing over it like they were nothing but water. He dismissed Charlie with a snort, then crawled over the edge of the platform, the Engine opening up and welcoming him like a mother bear welcomes a cub.

Charlie looked up at Pan, and even though he was an inferno she could see the emotion there, the grief pouring off him.

"There's nothing we can do," she said. "Come on."

For a moment he burned even more fiercely, the metal staircase squealing in the heat. Then the flames snapped off and he ran up the last few steps, the heat ebbing from him. Together they took one last look at the platform, at the remains of Mammon, at the shape that scuttled into the Engine, that stretched out its limbs into the smoking chaos and began to mend it.

Then Marlow called to them and Pan turned away, Mammon's voice still echoing inside her head.

Find her.

LET'S GET THE HELL
OUT OF HERE

They crossed the room in a heartbeat, piling into the elevator. Marlow jabbed a hand on the button, waiting for one of those limbs to snake through the door, to wrap itself around his throat. He pressed the button again, and again.

"Come on, you piece of garbage."

The doors rumbled shut and the elevator started to rise, whining in protest. Marlow slid down the elevator wall. It was too much. Something was rising inside him, something huge— surely too big, too powerful. It felt like a tsunami, and even with all the power of the world inside him he could not hold it back. He curled his legs up, pushed his face into his knees so that nobody would see the tears. But there was nothing he could do to hide the sobs that racked him, making his whole body shake. It was too much, too much.

He felt somebody sit down next to him. Somebody else sat on the other side, kicking off so much heat he might have been leaning against a radiator. Hands wrapped themselves around him from both sides, tight. No words, they just held him until the ocean calmed.

Of all the things Charlie and Pan had done for him, Marlow thought, this was the one that truly saved his life.

He scrubbed the tears away on his pants, blinked up at Pan. She was crying, too, her eyes red-rimmed with exhaustion and confusion. Sniffing, she gave him one last squeeze and let go. Marlow felt weirdly naked without the weight of her arms on his shoulders, like she had taken a piece of him with her.

Charlie *was* naked, and when he leaned in for another hug Marlow pushed him away.

"Dude, not until you've got pants on."

And the thought of it—of sitting next to his naked best friend in the elevator from hell—made something else rush up his throat, a bark of lunatic laughter that exploded wetly from his nose.

"Gross," said Pan, getting unsteadily to her feet. Her mouth was a thin gray line. Marlow didn't want to know what she was going through right now, the horror of finding out she was one of the bad guys. He turned back to Charlie.

"Why *were* you prancing around in the altogether, though?"

Charlie sniffed, his tears evaporating from his skin. He looked down at himself as if truly noticing for the first time.

"I was wearing clothes," he said. "They must have burned off."

"Any excuse," said Marlow as Charlie got to his feet, everything hanging out. "You got no shame?"

Charlie shrugged his skinny shoulders, his grin lighting up the elevator.

"Hey, it's what God gave me."

"He didn't give you much," said Pan.

"Hey!" Charlie said, finally slapping a hand to his crotch. His cheeks were glowing so much, Marlow thought he was about to burst into flames again.

The elevator rattled upward ridiculously slowly, grinding against the walls. How could it be taking so long?

"You think Ostheim's coming after us?" Marlow asked.

Pan shook her head. "You saw him, all he cares about is the Engine. *Christ.* How could I have been so *stupid?*"

"It wasn't your fault," said Charlie. "He's been doing this for so long. He's fooled so many people."

She shot him a look that could have blasted him out the side of the elevator shaft.

"I . . ." She swallowed, the fury leaving her face, leaving her with nothing. She put her head against the wall, her fists clenching and unclenching, over and over. "I was so sure. I never even thought to question him."

"I don't get it," Marlow said. "We saw him, like a few hours ago. He was just this old dude. He had a comb-over, for God's sake."

"You must have felt him, though," said Charlie. "Mammon always said that something as evil as Ostheim can be hidden from the eye, but never from the soul."

Marlow thought back to that morning—it felt like a million years ago. When they'd arrived at the church in Prague he'd felt like his insides were being minced. But that had been the Red Door, hadn't it?

"He used it to mask himself," said Pan, slapping herself on the forehead. "That's why he arranged to meet us there, so the stench of the door would hide him. Dammit, the door wasn't even there anymore, why didn't we just *think?*"

The elevator rattled so hard that Marlow thought it was going to come loose and drop them all to their deaths. Then the gears whined and it shuddered to a halt. Pan wrenched open the gates. Through them was the bullpen, drenched in darkness and silence. Marlow had been so caught up in the fight downstairs that he'd completely forgotten about the others. He shared a look with Pan, then watched her stick her head through the opening.

"Herc?" she said quietly. "You out—"

A gunshot, ricocheting off the outside of the elevator. Pan staggered in, a spark tearing itself from her fingers and zigzagging from ceiling to floor. Past the crack of thunder Marlow could hear somebody shouting inside the bullpen.

"Sorry, sorry, my bad!" Herc yelled.

Then his ugly face was there, peering inside. He offered them something that was probably a smile.

"Wasn't expecting to see you all alive," he said. "Thought it was *him*. I thought it was . . . Ostheim." Marlow saw his face crumple under the weight of the truth.

"Then it's a good job you're an awful shot," said Pan, barging past him. Marlow pushed himself up the wall and followed her. It was so dark in the bullpen that he could barely see, the light from the elevator a copper penny in an ocean of ink. It wasn't a bad thing, though. The air was heavy with the stench of gunpowder and blood, and he could make out collections of broken parts scattered in the black. Whatever had happened up here, it had been bad.

"I'm sorry, Pan," said Herc. "I couldn't—"

Pan snapped around, jabbing a finger at him.

"Did you know?" she said, baring her teeth like a feral animal. "Did you know?"

"No!" said Herc, shaking his head, making sure to look her right in the eye. "I didn't know, Pan. Ostheim showed up here and I thought . . . I thought he was here to help us, but he just . . . Christ, he just killed them all. Us, them. He didn't care, he just mowed right through us on his way to the elevator. I'm sorry. I'm so sorry."

She swallowed, then scrubbed the back of a hand over her face.

"Holy guacamole," said Truck, lumbering from the shadows. He scooped Pan up in a bear hug, putting her down again only when she started slapping him on the shoulders in protest. "Man, I didn't think I'd ever see you again. What happened?"

"Ostheim," spat Pan. "That asshole. I can't . . . I just can't . . ."

"Hey, kiddo, don't go there," said Herc. "None of us saw it coming."

"But why?" she said, toe-to-toe with the big guy. "Why did nobody question it? Why didn't *you* question it, Herc? You were supposed to be watching out for us. They died, Herc. All of them. And for *what*?"

Herc turned away, blinking. For all the gristle and all the scars, he looked about twelve years old in the half-light.

"Hey," said Truck. He rested a hand on her shoulder and she shook it away. He tried again, more forcefully this time. "Hey, Pan. We can talk about this later. Right now, we got to go."

He was right. The room was trembling, like the beginning of an earthquake. Marlow could barely feel it, but it was there, tickling the soles of his feet.

"He's right," said a voice, another person emerging from the dark. A girl dressed in black, a shock of red hair. "Ostheim will already be opening the gates."

"You," Pan said, jabbing a finger. The redhead stood firm.

"I *what*? You better watch the next thing that comes out of your mouth. *You* brought him here, *you* did this."

Pan's face crumpled, her shoulders sagging under a hundred tons of truth. She didn't reply. How could she? The redhead was right. Pan had done this, and Marlow, and Herc and Truck. They might as well have opened the gates to hell themselves.

"Where is Mammon?" the redhead said. Nobody answered, and she put her hands to her face, groaning into them. "No, no, no."

"Come on," Herc said gently. "I don't know how long we've got, but it isn't much."

"I took out some of it," said Charlie. "I burned some of that bastard machine into dust."

"Yeah?" said Herc.

Charlie nodded. "Not much, though. There was no time."

"It might slow him down," said Herc, dropping onto his knees and rummaging in his duffel bag. "I've got something else here that will help as well."

"Where's Taupe?" Pan said, staring into the dark with an expression that Marlow instantly hated—like she was *longing* for him. He'd almost managed to forget about the French guy. He was probably abseiling down the elevator shaft, about to single-handedly wrestle Ostheim into submission before carrying Pan off in those big arms of his.

Herc sighed, shaking his head.

"Caught a stray bullet," he said, tapping his temple. "Right here. Never even knew about it."

Oh. Marlow swallowed the guilt back down his throat. Pan's face was made of stone again, her jaw clenched so tightly it might shatter.

"He would have been happy to know he'd died fighting," Herc said. "If it makes you feel better."

Not really, Marlow thought. *Not at all.* He'd died fighting for the wrong side.

Herc went back to whatever he had in his bag, a series of clicks and beeps from it echoing around the hall.

"What is that?" Charlie asked. Herc glanced at him, then

performed a perfect double take when he noticed Charlie wasn't wearing anything.

"Don't ask," said Marlow.

"Fair enough," said Herc. "This, my friends, is a Mark-54 Special Atomic Demolition Munition."

"A what?" said Marlow.

"A nuke," Charlie replied. "Right?"

"A tactical nuclear weapon," Herc confirmed. "Six kilotons of pure trouble for Ostheim."

"It'll take out the Engine?" Marlow said.

"It won't even dent it," Herc said, his knees popping as he groaned to his feet. "But it might bury that asshole for a while. Come on, we've got twenty minutes."

He jogged back to the elevator, squeezing through the doors. Nobody followed him, the cloud of exhaustion that hung over them so heavy it was almost a physical thing. Marlow wasn't sure he could move even if he wanted to. Herc looked out at them.

"I should add that this particular nuke was built in the 1960s," he said. "And I can't vouch for its reliability."

That did the trick, everyone scuttling away from the clicking bag like there was a demon inside it ready to clamber out. Pan went in first, Marlow and Charlie almost wedging themselves as they fought to get through the gap. The redhead was next, standing in a corner and looking nervously at Pan.

"Room for a little one?" said Truck, barely able to haul his capacious frame inside. Herc thumped the button, the elevator wobbling up a few feet then falling still.

"Don't you dare," said Pan, so much violence in her voice that the elevator shuddered into life again, reeling them back to the surface. Nobody spoke, everyone thinking the same thing.

Keep moving, please don't stop. Marlow could picture it, the day overhead. The craving he felt for sunlight was overwhelming, an addict's need.

The elevator ground to a halt again and Marlow almost ripped the gates off completely as he clattered out into the corridor. Even here the ground didn't feel particularly solid, the Engine a gaping maw directly below him. He flinched when he saw the girl up ahead. Claire was hunkered down, blinking at them through big, frightened eyes. She almost smiled, then leaned over and retched. A string of black bile hung from her lips.

"Told you we'd come back," Marlow said, doing his best to find a smile. She got to her feet and wiped her mouth, her weak grin the next best thing to daylight.

"It is over?" she said, rubbing her stomach.

"Not even close," said Herc as he walked past them.

"They led Ostheim right here," said the redhead. "Did you see him?"

Claire looked at the floor, her eyelids blinking hard as if trying to scrub the sight of him from her corneas.

"He walked right past me, Jaime," she said. She shivered, wiping away a tear. "I don't think he even saw me."

"He's in the Engine," said the redhead, Jaime. "He's won, Mammon's dead."

"He hasn't won," said Marlow. "Not yet."

"How'd you figure that?" Herc said.

"I'll tell you on the way."

They reached the Red Door, still hanging open. Beyond was the cathedral of candlelit rock, those fires roaring. They walked out together, Herc pulling the door shut behind them. The sound it made when it locked could have been a depth charge going off beneath the ocean. He didn't waste a second, bolting between the columns and shouting over his shoulder.

"Hey, Red, you know the path out? I don't feel like crawling through the Liminal again."

"Left," she yelled, and they jogged together. Marlow was running on fumes but the sickening waves of bad energy pouring out of the Engine were a powerful tailwind, propelling him around corner after corner, through seemingly endless corridors forged from bone. It took him a while to notice that the ground was sloping upward, slightly at first, then steeper.

"This one," said Jaime. She had stopped next to an alcove in the wall, barely big enough to let one person through. They'd passed hundreds of them on the way.

"You sure?" asked Herc.

"With Ostheim behind us, not to mention an atomic bomb, I'd better be," she replied, disappearing.

Herc grumbled something and followed her, and Marlow was next, almost tripping on the stairs. It was another spiral staircase, decorated with the dead.

"We came down this way," said Marlow.

"No, you didn't," Jaime replied from up ahead, her voice echoing off the walls. "This place is a warren. Only a couple of paths actually lead to the Engine, the rest are traps. Get stuck in one, and you'll be there forever."

"Unless you punch through the wall," said Truck.

They climbed in silence, their breaths ragged and desperate. Marlow lost count of how many stairs there were after two hundred, but there had to have been as many again. At one point he swore he could hear Truck sobbing.

Then they were out, squeezing from a narrow doorway into a tunnel. They were still underground, but Marlow could feel the change in pressure—no longer a mile of rock overhead. The cry of the Engine was still in his veins but it was quieter now. There was a sign on the wall that said something in French, a picture of an electric bolt. Pipes ran the length of the corridor. Beautiful, human pipes that carried electricity or water or gas to a world he'd been sure was lost to him.

And he was smiling before he remembered that the world wouldn't be there for much longer. Not once Ostheim had opened the gates.

Marlow wasn't sure how any of them made it up the last few flights of steps, but they did. Jaime reached a huge cast-iron door and tugged on it until it squealed open. A torrent of sunlight poured through, a river of it, wrapping Marlow in fingers of gold and pulling him out into the day. He dropped to his knees, pushing his face into the glorious heat, crying again.

"Hey, Marlow," Pan said, grabbing his T-shirt, helping him up. "Nuke. About to explode."

They were on a street next to the river, Paris laid out before them in shades of white and gold. Smoke rose from five or six places, the sound of sirens filling the air like birdsong as the Engine continued to pollute the air.

"Now what?" said Pan.

"Now we find transport," said Herc. "Something big."

"On it," said Truck, wobbling up the street.

"Herc," said Charlie. He stood naked as the day he was born, shivering despite the heat. "Won't a nuke, you know, like, destroy the whole city?"

"No," said Herc. "Too small, too deep. We probably won't even feel it up here." He checked his watch again. "Ten seconds."

They counted down together, silently.

"That was almost disappointing," said Marlow. "Did it go off?"

"It better have," Herc grumbled. "Paid a goddamned fortune for it. Should be—"

The entire street bucked beneath Marlow's feet, almost knocking him over. In front of them, the river surged up the sides of the banks, foaming in a frenzy as it crashed back down. The city beyond it looked as if it had hiccuped, everything bouncing once. Half a dozen buildings crumpled into themselves, sagging like they were made of cardboard. A cloud of dust rose, filtering the sunlight and turning the whole area red. Herc, though, had paled considerably.

"Whoops," he said. "That wasn't supposed to happen."

"Least that asshole Ostheim will be picking rocks from his hair for a while," said Jaime.

Marlow heard the sound of an engine, the crunch of gears. He looked back to see an ice cream truck making its way toward them. The street was a patchwork of shattered asphalt, a busted fire hydrant spraying rainbows. Truck leaned out the window and flicked on the siren, a blast of "Pop Goes the Weasel" filling the air over the sound of a thousand alarms. He already had a cone in his fist, and he was grinning.

"Seriously?" said Herc.

"Best I could find," he yelled through a mouthful of ice cream.

"It'll do," said Herc. "Everyone on board. Marlow, I need to know everything that Mammon told you."

Marlow nodded, opening the side door and hopping up the steps into the back of the van. He sat on a box of cones and Pan squeezed in next to him, neither of them saying anything but both of them thinking the same thing.

There was still hope.

"We're Hellraisers," Herc said from the broken street. "It ain't over yet."

The old guy watched as they all clambered in. Charlie was last, and Herc's face creased in disgust as he watched him climb the steps.

"First thing first, though," Herc said, hauling himself up and slamming the door shut behind him. "We find Charlie some goddamned pants."

PART III
ANNIHILATION

CONTRACTS

After so long stuck inside the festering anus of hell, a shower felt like heaven.

Pan pushed her head into the spray, the powerful water massaging her scalp. It was so hot it was almost scalding, a hundred cuts and scrapes and bruises protesting. But the heat was good, scouring her skin, scrubbing her clean of every last trace of the Engine.

A torrent of black water spiraled around the plug—smoke and dirt and dust and blood. She wished that the shower could cleanse her inside as well, carry away all of the hate and the grief and the guilt. Her soul was blacker now than it had ever been.

It didn't make any sense. The day was a blur of disbelief, her mind doing its best to push the truth away. All this time she thought she was fighting for what was right, fighting to save the world. Not a hero, *never* a hero—she had killed too many people to ever be called that—and certainly not a saint. But the things she'd done, she'd done them for the right reason.

Take one life and save a billion, she'd always told herself. But she'd been taking the wrong lives, and put billions more in harm's way.

She gripped her hair in her hands, pulling until it hurt. More dirt ran from her, as thick and dark as oil—so much it seemed like it was pouring from inside her, like she was rotten in there. And that was true, wasn't it? She'd been doing the devil's work, and what did that make her if not something truly evil?

It's not your fault. You didn't know.

But she didn't *ask*, either. She didn't question it. She'd taken Ostheim's words for granted, she'd obeyed him mindlessly. After everything that had happened with Christoph, after she'd almost knocked his head clean off in that apartment in Queens, she'd needed something good. She'd needed a way to redeem herself. When Herc had marched into her cell all those years ago he'd given her exactly that.

You did a bad thing, kiddo, but you know what, it doesn't have to be the end. He'd smiled at her—so much younger, all his teeth still where they were supposed to be, so hard but so kind—and he'd said it. *Take one life, save a billion. Pick door number one and I'll show you how.*

She'd been so relieved that she'd said yes and never looked back.

Letting go of her hair, she cranked the temperature up even further. She wrapped her hands around herself, shivering despite the heat. It was too bright in here and she closed her eyes, but all she saw there were the enemy Engineers she had slaughtered. Dozens of them. All those kids in Paris, thrown into a war they couldn't possibly understand, all the ones before that.

Not to mention Patrick, and his sister Brianna. Pan's stomach cramped at the memory. She hadn't killed Brianna but she'd captured her, and let her die in the worst possible way. Patrick, too, his body fused with the concrete of Rockefeller Plaza, screaming as he held the bloated body of his sister. *Oh God, what did I do to them?* It was unimaginable, it was unbearable. Why hadn't they just said something to her? Why hadn't they told her the truth?

They had, she realized. How many times had they told her she was fighting for the wrong side? *They told you the truth, but you wouldn't hear it.*

She pounded her head against the wall, again and again, harder each time until a wave of vertigo grabbed her, trying to haul her into darkness. The exhaustion had completely emptied her, left barely enough inside to keep her standing. Her left leg was actually twitching as her muscles struggled. But there was something else there, too, something not entirely unpleasant in the way her body felt. It was as if a cloud had been lifted from her soul.

It wasn't just fatigue, she realized. Stretching her fingers out in front of her, she willed up a charge—just a small one.

Nothing happened.

Again, drawing it up from deep inside, snapping her fingers like she was sparking a lighter.

Her contract had been canceled.

She didn't know whether to scream with fear or howl with laughter. She saw Ostheim—the thing that had posed as Ostheim—stretch its spider limbs into the Engine, could picture them probing the machine, flicking those infernal switches and ending her deal as easily as programming a washing machine. If Ostheim was anywhere near as powerful as Mammon said he was, if he knew as much about the Engine as Pan feared, then why wouldn't he cancel her contract, leave her defenseless?

Hey, at least you don't have to vacation in hell, right?

Except sooner or later, once Ostheim had opened the gates, hell would be right here, walking the streets. The whole world would burn.

Suddenly the slap of the water on her shoulders was too much, too hot. She turned off the shower, her whole body trembling, steam rising off her. She just stood there in silence, trying not to feel anything much at all. Right then, one more thought, one more emotion, would be enough to scatter her cells in a million different directions.

Eventually, she wasn't sure how much later it was, the cold started to creep back in. She stepped from the cubicle and shivered her way across the bathroom, grabbing a plush dressing gown from the back of the door. Truck had driven them south, through the mountains and well into the night, and now they were in a luxury hotel somewhere in northern Italy. Her room was huge but it still wasn't large enough for all of her ghosts. Her dead—the ones she had killed, the ones she had let die— crowded on the bed, on the carpet, on the desk, in the shadowed corners, all of them watching her. Patrick and Brianna were there, too, their twin faces gaunt, their dark eyes accusing.

"I didn't know," she whispered to them. "I didn't know."

None of them replied, their eyes bulging from cracked sockets, their flyblown lips speaking soundlessly, their withered fingers reaching for her. She couldn't bear it so she ran to the door, escaping into the silent, deserted corridor beyond. She slammed it behind her, trapping the dead inside.

Where the hell was everyone else?

They were scattered through the hotel, but she'd seen Marlow enter his room, almost directly opposite her own. She ran to it, pounding on the door loud enough to wake everybody on the floor. Everything ached but at least some of the tiredness had gone, some of that endless ache the Engine pushed inside you, like your body was made up of lead and concrete and corrugated iron. She pressed her ear to the wood, hearing nothing.

"Marlow, open the door, goddammit," she yelled, thumping again.

A groan, footsteps, the click of the lock, then the door swung open to reveal Marlow's face. He blinked at her, his mouth hanging open like he'd just woken from a hundred-year sleep. He was wearing nothing but jockey shorts, his lean body a patchwork of scars and bruises. He smelled of the same luxury-brand shampoo as she did. It seemed to take him a while to recognize her.

"Pan?" he said after a moment. He yawned.

"No, you idiot, it's Santa Claus." She pushed past him into a room lit solely by a table lamp. The bed was ruffled, and she perched on the end of it, drawing cotton threads from her dressing gown and rolling them into balls. Marlow closed the door and traipsed over, clambering back under the covers. His eyelids looked like they were holding sash weights and he squinted at her through them.

"Can't sleep?" he said, yawning again.

"Just didn't want to be . . ." *What? In a room full of ghosts? On your own?* "Just thought I heard something. Wanted to check."

Marlow nodded. "I'm cool," he said. "Well, you know, not cool exactly. Not after today. You okay?"

"Yeah, sure," Pan shot back. The anxiety was a lump of stone right in the middle of her, heavy enough to pull her down through the floor, through the ground, to drown her in the dark. She opened her mouth and the air refused to come. It took a desperate gulp and a bolt of adrenaline to kick-start her lungs. "Contract has been canceled."

"Yeah?" said Marlow. "That's good, right?"

"Great," she said. "When Ostheim comes after us, not having a contract is gonna be real helpful."

227

Marlow sighed, chewing at his knuckles in the infuriating way he always did. She rubbed at her chest, over that lump of stone where her heart should be. All she could feel right now was pent-up rage, like there was a live grenade in there, too, pin pulled.

"Right," she said, getting to her feet. "Well, this was fun."

"Hey, you came to my door, Pan," said Marlow.

She spun around to face him and for a second she thought the grenade had blown, the world burning white for a second. The anger was boiling up her throat but she choked it back down, just standing there. Her fists were balled so tightly her finger bones could snap. Why had she come here?

Marlow didn't speak, just lifted the sheet and tilted his head to invite her in.

Yeah, right, she thought and almost said. She didn't move, her feet glued to the carpet. It was Marlow, the guy who'd ruined everything, who'd let Charlie into the Nest, who'd led Ostheim right to the Engines. *Not his fault any more than yours. Ostheim had you all fooled.* And when she looked at him again he was just a guy, just a teenage boy, caught up in the same crapstorm as her. They were both puppets in a show that neither of them really understood. And the sudden tide of exhaustion that swept through her was enough to carry her to the side of the bed, to climb in beside him.

Smiling gently, he lowered the sheet down over her. His hand lingered for a moment then landed on hers, as delicate and hesitant as a butterfly. They lay there, face-to-face in the twilight. Pan tongued the gap where she'd lost a tooth, her heart drumming faster now than it had back at the Engine.

What on earth was going on?

Marlow pulled her close and she didn't resist, putting her arms around him, her cheek against the smooth skin of his chest. She could hear the thump of his pulse, the soft wheeze of his lungs. He was so warm. He held her tightly and she let him. She didn't even know why, other than it was quiet here, in his room. Being here with him, it kept the ghosts away.

And she kind of loved him for it.

She moved her head, her lips brushing his neck, then his jaw. Her heart was hummingbird-fast, no longer made of rock but hollow-boned and light enough to lift right out of her. A smile danced on her lips and she was suddenly sure, so sure.

"We made a deal," she said, her fingers tracing patterns on the bare skin of his arm. "I owe you a kiss."

Marlow murmured and she pressed her lips to his before he could say anything stupid. She held them there, everything quiet, everything beautifully peaceful, everything perfect.

Marlow opened his lips and started to snore.

Pan pulled back in surprise. Marlow was fast asleep, his mouth hanging open, his nose flaring. She gave him a gentle nudge, then a firmer one, but he didn't so much as stir. She wasn't sure whether to be angry or humiliated, but in the end she laughed, returning her face to his chest. His breaths were like the soft whisper of ocean waves and when she closed her eyes that's what she saw—sunlight and surf, golden sands in every direction and the gulls wheeling overhead. She lay there, in the warmth, in the quiet. She just lay there next to him, and she slept.

BREATHLESS

The first thing Marlow noticed when he woke was that he wasn't alone.

There was somebody else in the bed, somebody warm, somebody practically *naked*. Pan lay on her back next to him, almost drowning in the downy piles of soft sheets and duvets and pillows. She was wearing a dressing gown and it had untangled in her sleep to reveal a glimpse of stomach, curving up. It rose and fell gently, and Marlow might have stared a little longer if he hadn't become aware of the second thing.

He couldn't breathe.

He tried to inhale, and nothing happened. The panic of it made him sit bolt upright, his fingers clawing at his chest, his neck. He tried again, sounding like a kazoo as he wrenched in a thimbleful of oxygen.

Pan was awake now, her eyes wide in alarm as she scrabbled from the bed. She spun around, surveying the room, her fists bunched and ready to fight. When she looked back at Marlow her dressing gown hung open.

He did his best not to look, then looked.

If his asthma had been bad before, it was *seriously* bad now.

"Marlow!" Pan yelled, following his eyes and pulling the gown closed. "What the hell?"

Can't. Breathe. He couldn't get the words out. Lurching onto his knees, he coughed as hard as he could, the blockage like industrial glue in his lungs.

"For God's sake." Pan jumped back onto the bed and slapped him on the back, hard enough to send him sprawling.

I'm not choking! he tried to say, rolling off the bed, winded now as well as wheezing. He made for the door, his accordion lungs turning him into a one-man band. Wrenching it open, he ran down the corridor and around the corner, jamming a hand on the elevator button.

"Marlow, where are you going?" Pan shouted as she followed, knotting her dressing gown cord. They entered the elevator together.

"In . . . ha . . . ler," Marlow stuttered, snatching in a breath between each syllable. He was awake enough now for it to have sunk in: Ostheim had canceled his contract.

"Oh," said Pan. "Hang on."

The journey down to the lobby seemed to take a hundred years. He didn't wait for the doors to open fully, just squeezed through them and ran for reception. There were two women and a man there and they all saw him coming, one of them reaching for a phone. Marlow slapped his hands on the desk, pointing to his chest.

Not that he needed to, he was pretty sure he was turning blue.

He hauled in a couple of shallow breaths and it was like trying to douse a house fire with a water pistol, the fear an inferno inside him. His vision was turning charcoal black at the edges. Nobody was moving.

"He needs help," said Pan. "Asthma. An inhaler."

The receptionists stared at one another, but still nobody budged. Pan leaped over the desk, scattering paper. Marlow tried to follow but he didn't have the energy for the jump. He ran around the side, ignoring the protests. Pan was already through the back door and he tailed her into an office. His legs were fast running out of steam and he crashed into a chair, each breath like there was a boulder on his chest.

Pan grabbed a green first-aid case off the wall, its contents flying as she opened it up. She dug among the Band-Aids and the painkillers, and it seemed like a million years later that she held up a small turquoise inhaler.

"This?" she said. He had no idea, but he nodded and she threw it at him.

He reached for it, missed, and it bounced off his face.

"Sorry," said Pan, picking it up and handing it over.

He put the end in his mouth and pressed, and again—*please please please*—until the pressure began to ease. He sucked in air, everything crackling like his respiratory system was made of popping candy.

By the time he'd calmed down, the receptionists were hovering in the doorway, yelling at them in Italian.

"Better?" Pan said, ignoring them.

He wasn't sure if he could speak yet so he nodded, wiping the foam from his lips.

"Good," she said, grabbing his hand and lifting him out of the seat. Together they walked back out into the hotel lobby. There was a small crowd of people there, all of them watching. One of them was Herc, sipping coffee from a china mug. He'd done his best to clean himself up but the old guy still looked like a bear that had wandered in from the forest. He did a double take when he spotted them.

"For the love of . . ." he started to say, putting the cup down and beckoning to them. He flashed an apologetic smile to the receptionists. "*Bambini*, eh? Kids today are always up to something."

He waited until Pan and Marlow were close enough before grabbing them each by the upper arm and steering them back toward the elevators. Only when they were safely inside did he let them go.

"You wanna tell me how that can be classed as keeping a low profile?" he said. "No fuss, no drama. I thought we'd agreed."

They had, on the agonizingly slow ice cream truck ride over. Paris had been nuked; it was all over the news. Nobody had the slightest idea who was behind it, but it didn't take much to get people talking.

"His contract was canceled," said Pan. "He woke up and he couldn't breathe. What was I supposed to do?"

"Use the phone, maybe?" he replied as the elevator dinged its way up. "Dammit. Charlie's contract's been canceled, too. Told me this . . . Wait, how did you know he woke up like that?"

Pan turned away, focusing on the wall like there was a TV screen. Herc looked at Marlow, one eyebrow conducting a lone foraging mission on his forehead.

"Uh . . ." was the only thing Marlow could think of to say.

"For the love of everything holy," Herc muttered. The elevator stopped and the door slid open. "We leave in fifteen minutes," he said, stepping out. "Meet me in the lobby. Don't be late. And, guys, put some clothes on? What is it with you young ones and running around naked?"

He threw them another look then disappeared. Marlow glanced down at himself, realizing he was wearing nothing but his jockey shorts. He covered himself up while Pan pressed the button for their floor.

She didn't so much as glance at him, her attention firmly fixed on the numbers as they flicked up. Marlow thought back, trying to remember anything from last night. He'd just been so exhausted. He could recall her knocking at the door, wak-ing him up, then climbing into bed with him.

Wait, she climbed into bed with me?

"What happened last night?" he said. "Did we . . . ?"

Pan spluttered a laugh. "You were upset, I couldn't face you blubbering all night. End of."

He could still feel her there, though, her body pressed against his. He had to angle himself against the wall, yelling, *Think of something else, think of something else.* But all he could picture was her, lying there beside him. And something else, too, her lips pressed against his as he drifted into sleep.

"Wait, you kissed me," he said, grinning. He put his fingers to his lips. "You totally kissed me."

"What? No way, Marlow. You must have dreamed it."

But she still hadn't turned to face him. He could just about feel the heat radiating from her cheeks.

"You did!" he said. "Last night, you kissed me."

"Whatever," she said.

The elevator slowed to a halt, the doors sliding open. Pan walked out so quickly she bumped her arm on the way, lurch-ing into the corridor.

"You kissed me," he shouted after her, the grin making his face feel like it was being stretched on the rack. She didn't look back, just stuck up her middle finger.

"Thirteen minutes, Marlow!" she yelled.

He gave her a head start then walked back to his room, let-ting himself in. He must have slept nine hours straight but all he wanted to do was throw himself back beneath the covers, back into the sweet shampoo smell of her. After yesterday he could have been unconscious for a week solid and still woken up tired.

But the thought of Herc dragging him from his bed in twelve minutes was enough to keep him standing.

He used the restroom and slung on the clothes he'd bought from a gas station somewhere in the Alps—Truck had stopped the truck after a few hours and declared that the smell was so bad he couldn't focus on the road. They weren't exactly fashionable—a pair of green combat pants and a black T-shirt that claimed SKI YOU AGAIN SOON!—but at least they didn't reek of violence and death.

He pocketed the inhaler, giving it a shake first to gauge how much was left. Enough, he thought. Although if the world really was about to end then it might be wise to stock up. Nothing was guaranteed to bring on an asthma attack like a demon chasing you down the street.

The thought brought him home, to where he kept his spares. The memory was so vivid it had the effect of a punch to the solar plexus, and he had to sit on the bed before another attack came on. He could see the cupboard beside his bed, always buried beneath soda bottles and candy wrappers and the glasses of water he took to bed each night. His bed, too, never made unless his mom was having a good day and she did it for him. He lay back and closed his eyes and for a moment, for a blissful moment, he was right back there on Staten Island, horns blaring outside and the smell of the city drifting in through the open window, about to head to school or go hang out with Charlie.

For those few seconds he was *right there*.

And it broke his heart.

He snapped his eyes open, reality rushing back—all the more powerful for having been momentarily forgotten. It seemed utterly ridiculous. No, it seemed *impossible*, that just one day ago he had been waging a war beneath the streets of Paris, fighting in a battle that would decide the fate of the planet. He laughed at the absurdity of it, but the laughter was hollow, and it ended in a sob.

He sat up, knuckling his eyes, everything flashing white. He thought about the last time he'd seen his mom, her chasing him from the house, the dog trying to chew his face off. She hadn't even recognized him. She'd have no idea where he was, no idea if he was even alive.

There was a monitor on the desk in his room, the hotel logo spinning lazily on the screen. A keyboard sat next to it and Marlow walked over, prodding the mouse to wake it up. It took him a moment to work out how to access the Web browser, then another five minutes to remember the password for his Gmail before it finally loaded.

Twelve pages of junk, insurance claims, injury compensation, online degrees, a notification that his X-Box Gold membership was about to expire—sadly nothing about dealing with demons. He found an old e-mail from his mom—*Hey Marlow I got my phone working can u tell me if u get this momx*—and clicked REPLY.

Hey Mom, he typed, popping his lips, the cursor blinking impatiently at him. *Sorry I haven't been in touch, been real busy. Got a new job, was a mad rush. Nothing bad, don't worry. All legit. You could even say I was saving the world.*

Saving it? He'd pretty much single-handedly destroyed it.

So, yeah, he typed as he thought. *Things are cool. But Mom, I think something bad might be coming. Something really bad.*

Hell is coming, he thought, clamping his mouth shut so he wouldn't spew all over the keyboard.

Just make sure you stay safe, promise? Lock the doors, get some bottled water and flashlight batteries.

Yeah, that would really help.

I love you, he wrote, his eyes burning, the type suddenly blurry. *I really do. I'll be back soon, okay? Just don't worry.*

He read it back, touching the cold screen with the tips of

his fingers as if he could send a thought alongside it, send something of himself.

"I'll be back soon," he said, as if by speaking the lie aloud he would somehow make it true. Then he clicked SEND.

There was nothing else for him to pack.

Logging out of the computer, he left his room and slogged back down to the lobby. There was nobody else there, but when he looked through the big glass doors he saw them all in front of the hotel, basking in the sunlight. Herc, Pan, Truck, and Charlie stood to one side, Claire and Jaime on the other.

They all looked over at him, and their collective grins seemed brighter than the shimmering white walls of the hotel.

All except for Pan, who looked like she'd just swallowed a cheese grater.

"Morning, lover boy!" said Truck, his laughter like the distant rumble of a storm.

Oh God.

"I warned you!" Pan said, jabbing a finger at Truck.

"Sorry," Truck said, holding up his hands. "Just hate to see you fight. Can't you kiss and make up?"

Pan stormed at him, ready to swing. Herc stepped between them like a boxing referee, pushing her away.

"Cool it, Pan," he said.

She turned away, glaring at Marlow like it was all his fault.

"Okay," said Herc. "You guys had enough? Let's go."

He walked off the forecourt, heading around the side of the hotel and into a parking lot. It was sweltering even though it wasn't quite seven in the morning. The concrete swam in a heat haze and Marlow half expected to see demons dragging themselves from the molten earth. Charlie cleared his throat.

"So, like I was saying, Mammon told me that's what it meant, Circulus Inferni. Not the Circle of Hell, like a group of devil worshippers or something. More *circle* like, I don't know, like a wall, like a prison. That's what they meant, they wanted to lock hell inside a circle, to stop the bad things getting out."

"Bit late to be finding that out," muttered Herc.

"And the Fist," Charlie went on. "It's not so much a fist that strikes hell but one that strikes with the *force* of hell."

"Who the hell thought these names up?" said Truck. "And in Latin, too. Why didn't they just have the Good Guys and the Evil Mothers? Would have saved us a bit of heartache."

"It doesn't matter," said Herc, leading them past the parked cars. "Fist, Circle, none of that means anything anymore. You just have to know one thing: we're Hellraisers. Raising hell to save the world. That's us. Okay?"

Nobody replied, and Herc tutted loudly as he led them toward a minibus with British license plates.

"Saint Agatha's Convent of the Sacred Heart?" Charlie said, reading the elaborate script on the side of the bus.

"Let's just say Saint Agatha doesn't want us riding in the cab of an ice cream truck anymore," Herc said, sliding open the door.

"You're stealing a bus that belongs to a bunch of nuns, aren't you?" Marlow asked.

"They're lending it," he said. "Without knowledge or consent. Not like I ain't going to hell already. Hang on."

He held out a hand to stop Charlie from entering the bus.

"Look, I'm not gonna lie to you," he said, squinting into the sun. He sighed, rubbing a hand over his gray stubble. "Ostheim has taken the Engines. I don't know how long it will take him, but he will find a way of bringing them together and opening the gates. Of that, there is absolutely no doubt. An hour, a day, a week, a month, then this, all of this, becomes a wasteland, a feeding ground for hell's worst."

Marlow looked across the parking lot, seeing a couple strolling from their car, the mom carrying a wide-eyed toddler. Past them, an old couple, the man in a wheelchair, in the shade of the hotel awning waiting for a taxi. Past them, a valley town, buildings glittering, looking like they carried the mountains on their shoulders. How many people there? How many in this country? This continent? Seven billion people on the planet, and none of them could do a damn thing about what was about to happen.

"I honestly don't know if there's anything we can do to stop it," Herc said. "We've got no powers, no contracts, no weapons. We only—" He swallowed, something dark boiling in his eyes. "We only found out what side we were fighting on a day ago. We don't even know if this woman, Meridiana, can help us."

"Herc," said Pan, "you really need to work on your motivational speeches."

"Yeah, watch *Braveheart*, dude," said Truck. "'Freedom!'"

"All I'm saying," Herc continued, "is that I won't blame any of you if you decide you don't want to get on this bus. Some of you have family, friends, people you might want to . . . to say goodbye to. You turn around and walk away then I won't hate you for it. I'll even get you home. If the world's ending, then there's nothing wrong with wanting to see it out with the ones you love."

"Who the hell are you and what have you done with Herc?" said Pan.

"I'm not—"

"Are you going soft on us, old man?" Truck said.

"Maybe we should take him back inside," said Marlow, smiling. "I think the hotel has a babysitting service for toddlers."

"Hey—"

"Just get out of the way," said Charlie, nudging Herc to the side. "It's hot out here."

"Yeah," said Truck, rustling his pockets. "I got half my mini-bar in here and it's losing its cool."

"How you guys managed to evade Mammon so long, I have no idea," muttered Jaime, stomping up the steps. "Dictionary definition of *unprofessional.*"

Claire followed her, still rubbing her gut and looking like she'd eaten a pound of out-of-date shrimp. Pan put a hand on Herc's chest.

"Got nowhere else to go," she said. "And even if I did, I'm here for the ride." She started up the steps then dropped back down. "One more word about last night, though, and you're on your own."

She disappeared into the shade of the bus.

Marlow took one last look east, the sun hauling its liquid bulk up over the roof of the hotel. Then he turned the other way, west, toward home. That way was his mom, sure. But here, right here, was his family.

"Let's kick Ostheim out on his ass," he said to Herc. "New York City can wait. We're Hellraisers, like you say."

"Good man," said Herc, clapping him so hard on the shoulder he almost tripped up the steps. Herc slid the door shut, running around and clambering into the driver's seat. He started the engine, then turned to face them all.

"I . . ." he croaked, looking like he was trying to swallow a loaf of bread in one go. "I . . ."

"Yeah," said Marlow. "We love you, too. Now get us out of here before those nuns come back and catch us sinners red-handed."

MIRROR, MIRROR

Venice was as beautiful as Pan expected but it stank like a public bathroom.

The place was mobbed, too, tourists clogging the streets like artery-blocking sludge, their sweaty bodies rubbing against Pan every time she tried to squeeze past. Most of them were American, their shirts so bright and their chatter so loud she could have been back in Times Square or any other nightmarish tourist mecca in her hometown. One guy—who had to have been even larger than Truck—almost decapitated her while taking a video on his cell with a selfie stick and she'd flicked her fingers his way before she remembered she didn't have any electrostatic electricity left to Taser him with.

Just as well, really, because as they crossed yet another stone bridge a couple of *polizia* walked past, both of them eyeballing Herc. With his wounds, both old and new, he looked like the bad guy in a Bruce Willis movie. He was holding a map they'd bought from a vendor in Saint Mark's Square. Not that it had done them much good so far.

"You sure that's all he told you?" Herc growled as he pushed through the mob, scanning street names. He ducked into an alleyway between the rickety, jumbled buildings that crowded the saltwater lagoons. True to form, gondolas were idly cruising the waters, families and couples lazing on them and eating gelato. If any of them had so much as glimpsed what had gone down in Paris yesterday they would have scooped out their own brains and thrown them into the dirty water.

"That's all he said," Pan replied. A screaming toddler bounced off her knee and it took every ounce of willpower she had not to punt it into the water. "A shop, in the old town. A mirror shop."

"Why would one of the Pentarchy, with all the power in the world, work in a shop?" Charlie asked, popping gum.

"Not working," said Pan. "Hiding. Makes sense, to hide in plain sight, right?"

He shrugged. "None of this makes sense."

They exited the other side of the alleyway onto a cobbled walkway lined with houses that could have been built a thousand years ago. They were so crooked that she didn't know how they were still standing. Most had to be shops, their small, dark windows full of displays of soft toys, dolls, furniture, chocolates. Most of these looked untouched in just as long, lost beneath cobwebs as thick as sheets, drowning in dust. The doors were closed, some of them barricaded. There were no people here, not one. And it wasn't hard to work out why.

"Feel like I've just taken a sledgehammer to the family jewels," said Truck. "Anyone else getting that?"

Pan had no idea what that would feel like but she could sense there was something bad back here, no doubt about it.

"He ever speak about her?" Pan asked, sidling up to the redhead, Jaime. She'd not said much at all since leaving Paris but it was there in every look she threw at Pan, or Marlow, or Herc. *You did this.* There it was again, pure hate, her eyes burning.

"No," she said, spitting the word up like it was acid. "He told us she existed, and that she was best left alone. He told us she'd once been like him, fighting Ostheim and the Fist. Said she was injured so badly that she just ran, went into hiding. He hasn't . . . He *hadn't* seen her in, I don't know . . ."

"A hundred years," said Charlie. "More, maybe. He wasn't sure."

"He told *you*?" Marlow said, joining them.

"Told me everything," he said. "Was the only way he could make me believe he was on the right side. Meridiana was his sister, I think."

That made sense, Pan thought. She'd seen it herself, hadn't she? The truth, when she'd touched Mammon's hand.

"His *sister*?" said Jaime.

Charlie nodded.

"Far as I know, they were all brothers and sisters—Mammon, Meridiana, Ostheim, too. Then something happened, something bad. Ostheim turned against the others. They've been fighting for, I don't know, forever. The last time they met, Meridiana lost her mind. Mammon never saw her again."

"All that time, though," said Marlow. "How is that even possible?"

"All this, and you're asking how *that's* possible?" said Pan.

"The Engines," said Jaime. "Use them enough and they become part of you, they change you. Mammon, Meridiana, and Ostheim, too. That asshole was one of the Pentarchy and nobody even knew it."

Pan saw him now, his body erupting into darkness, those black limbs pouring out of him like a nest of snakes. She'd never seen anything like it, never seen anything so powerful. Even Mammon, with all his power, had lasted just seconds against him.

"So if she hasn't been seen in a hundred years, and she's crazy," said Marlow, "then why are we looking for her?"

It was a good-enough question, and she didn't have an answer other than "What else have we got?"

"Great," muttered Marlow.

They walked on, past more shops shut and shuttered. The rumble of the crowds was now a distant murmur, whisper-quiet, the group's footsteps on the cobbles the loudest thing in the world.

Pan felt something tickle the back of her neck and went to brush off a mosquito. It happened again, not an insect but something else, something *watching*. She could feel it as clearly as if their mad, bulging eyes were pressed against her skin. She didn't want to look back but she did anyway: just Marlow and Claire, both of them exhausted.

"We're close," she said with a shudder.

"Yeah," said Marlow, pointing a hand across the street. "Mirrors."

A building sat there, something out of a fairy tale—each floor jutting farther out over the street. The peeling white paint had to be the only thing holding it together. The leaded windows were dark and blind. There was a sign over the faded red door, almost illegible.

"Meridiana's," Pan read.

"So, she's been in hiding forever," said Charlie. "Nobody can find her. But she put her name on the front of her shop? Am I missing something here?"

Herc was already crossing the street, one hand stretched out for the door's brass handle.

"Wait!" yelled Pan. "Hang on, this doesn't feel right."

"What's new?" Herc said. He flashed her a grimace and then twisted the handle. The door resisted for a second, then groaned inward. Herc waved away a cloud of dust, peering into the gloom of the interior.

"Hello?" he yelled. "Anyone here? Meridiana?"

Nothing. Pan walked to the door, the cool current of air that blew from it refreshing in the muggy heat. Squinting, she could just about make out a room full of ghosts beyond—a dozen old white sheets draped over what could have been furniture and what could have been people.

"That's not creepy at all," she said.

"I'm not going first," said Marlow behind her.

She tutted, crossing the threshold. Her feet crunched on broken glass, so much of it on the floor that it could have been snow. It wasn't just cold inside, it was *freezing*, her skin breaking into goose bumps like the devil was breathing down her neck. She fought the urge to retreat, shivering into the room. It stank of age and time, the dust choking her, as though she had pressed her face into the funeral shroud of a long-dead corpse.

She took another crunching step, the sound of it echoing around the room. Ahead, one of the sheets rippled.

Pan spread her fingers.

Crap.

Then reached for her crossbow.

Double crap.

She bunched her fist. Whatever was under there, she could still pound its nose into its brain.

"Hello?" Herc's shout made her jump, a scream trying to rip its way out of her throat. Two more of the sheets billowed and a quiet, shrill cry rose up from the other side of the room— barely there. It was followed by a whisper, fast and low, tickling her ear like a fly's wings. She couldn't catch what it said.

"Keep moving," Herc said to her. It wasn't like she had a choice, everybody was tiptoeing through the door behind her, pushing her into the shop. The room was small, a rectangle of darkness at the far end where a passageway led deeper.

Herc gave her another shove and her fingers brushed against one of the sheets. It was clammy, and it moved against her like it was trying to take her hand. She recoiled with a groan, a tremor running through her.

That whine again, like a child's cry. And was that a choked sob that followed—the sound of a hanged man—or was it just the thunder of her pulse?

"Hello?" Herc said for a third time, his voice shaking.

The sheets rustled together, all of them flapping in a wind that Pan couldn't feel. The sound of it was like whispers in her ear, so clear that she could almost make out words.

. . . is he? Lost . . . where is my . . .

The sheet reached out for her again, actually curling around her hand—like seaweed wrapping itself around the limbs of a drowning woman. This time Pan grabbed it back and pulled, whipping it away. Tendrils of dust burrowed into her mouth, her eyes, and when the sheet fell lifelessly to the ground there was a mirror there.

It stood about six feet tall, a slab of dark glass mounted in a frame of long-dead flesh. It looked like something taken from a serial killer's apartment, something knitted together from dead skin and yellow bone. There was even a face, Pan saw, at the very top of the frame—so old and withered and desiccated that it didn't look like it could ever have been human. The shrunken head stared back at her with beady black eyes, a doll's eyes, alive but dead at the same time.

"What the . . ." said Marlow, appearing next to her in the mirror and taking a puff on his inhaler. Charlie joined on the other side, pulling an expression of disgust. The glass was dark, stained at the edges with something that might have been black rust. It was warped, Pan's skin mottled and distorted. But no amount of damage to the glass could explain what was going on in the mirror.

Right in front of Charlie was a reflection, but it wasn't his— it was Marlow's. In front of Marlow stood Charlie. When Pan lifted her right hand, her reflection in the glass did the same. It wasn't a mirror image, it was more like looking at the feed from a security camera. They weren't seeing a reflection, she understood, they were seeing what the *mirror* saw.

"Never seen you look so good, Marlow," said Charlie, but there was an edge to his voice. He stepped away from the mirror and so did Pan—*quickly.*

Jaime had tugged away another sheet, the mirror behind it wider and squatter, mounted on an old table. It, too, had a frame that belonged in a mortuary. This one had four faces on it, one to each corner. They were like death masks and they stared blindly back at her.

"Who would make these?" said Jaime, brushing a shaking hand through her red hair.

Pan didn't answer. The second mirror was tilted so that she could see the reflection of the ceiling. Had something moved there, between the ornate painted carvings? She glanced up— *nothing*—but when she turned to the mirror again she could definitely make out movement snaking between the antique bosses.

"Cover it," she said quietly.

"Why?" Jaime replied. "It's just a—"

Something ran at them on the other side of the mirror, fast and hard. Pan could hear the thunder of hooves as if a bull was charging across the room. A shape hit the glass hard enough to shunt the table three feet across the room, a jagged crack splitting the mirror in two.

Jaime fell back, Herc trying to catch her and both of them

sprawling to the glass-covered floor. Inside the mirror was a creature the likes of which Pan had never seen before. It was a tumorous mass of sinew and muscle, like somebody had skinned a dog and thrown it into a wood chipper only to attempt to stitch it back together. It stood on four legs in the same way as a gorilla, its top half too big for its lower body.

The face, though, is what made Pan stagger away, what made her want to dive back into the day and stare at the sun until her eyes burned out.

It was made up of teeth, hundreds of them arranged in concentric rings and grinding like an industrial blender. It had no eyes, no nose—just row upon row of those jagged shark teeth.

It charged again, butting the glass with the ugly slab of its head. The crack widened, another one splintering in the top corner. The creature snorted from the red pit of its throat and a tongue extended, as wet and gray as old beef. It licked the mirror, probing it. It was making soft *uhk, uhk* sounds and she realized it was sniffing, even though it didn't have a nose. Something about that noise was so familiar, and when the creature reared again, every muscle bulging as it tried to slam those jaws down on the glass, she understood why.

"Oh my God," she said. "It's a *demon*."

It lunged again, trying to pound its way through. The glass cried out again, as if it were screaming for help. Any second now it was going to shatter.

"Move!" she shouted, running to where the sheet had fallen. She picked it up, shaking it like she was making her bed. It flopped over the mirror and she wrenched down the corners until the glass was covered.

More choking snorts, the shrill whine of cracking glass.

"I've never—"

"Shut up!" she hissed at Herc. "Nobody make a sound."

Nobody did, the room suddenly choked with quiet. Over the roar of her heart Pan listened to the sound of the demon sniffing, then the soft rumble of its feet as it galloped away. Even then she held her breath for as long as she could.

"I've never seen a demon like that," Herc said, picking himself up and helping Jaime to her feet. They both brushed broken glass from their clothes.

Neither had Pan. The demons could exist in this world only if they possessed inanimate matter—it's why they always burst from walls and floors and furniture and enormous bronze lion statues. This one looked like it had been made of flesh. It looked like a living, breathing thing.

Because it *was* a living, breathing thing.

"It's what they look like before they cross," she said as it suddenly clicked. "It's what they look like in hell."

And when Ostheim succeeded in opening the gates, she realized, that's what they would look like when they poured through. There would be no need for them to possess matter, they'd teem into this world like a plague of locusts.

"Anyone want to guess what they're doing inside that?" Marlow said, nodding at the mirror.

"Security," said Herc. "Gotta be. It's what Mammon must have meant, when he said she was hiding. She's in one of these."

"Crazy chick, hiding inside a mirror, guarded by demons. Why the hell not?" Marlow shook his head, biting at his knuckles.

"Which one?" said Charlie, nodding at the passageway. "There are loads. There might be more through there."

"And that," said Pan, "is how she has stayed hidden for so long." She blew out a sigh.

"Hey, Meridiana," she said. "Look, I don't know if you can even hear me, but we need your help. We work with Mammon."

Even saying it now, after everything she'd learned in the last day, felt utterly wrong. "He told us to come find you."

More whispers, but they were drowned out by a throbbing growl from the other side of the room, the sound of claws scratching at glass. Something was prowling there, inside a mirror. Something *big*.

Pan broke away from the group, weaving her way through the sheets until she reached the passageway. It was pitch black inside, but there was a shimmer of light at the other end. Feeling her way down the wall, she stepped into another room, this one twice as big and twice as full. Dozens of mirrors sat beneath their dustsheets, lit by a trickle of honey-colored light from the room's single shuttered window. Nothing moved, aside from the swirling clouds of dust.

It was hopeless. How were they supposed to find her?

Pan walked to the nearest mirror and lifted the sheet. It was the same deal—a macabre frame made from the dead, holding a plane of dark, warped glass. She could see herself there, and the shop behind her. But there was something wrong with the reflection again—the walls crumbling, a hole in the middle of the floor.

. . . have you done with him . . .

The words were louder now, coming not from here but from the corner of the room. Pan lowered the sheet, cocking her head to catch another line.

. . . no more, I cannot . . .

She checked over her shoulder to make sure the others were there—the six of them cowering in the passageway, watching her—then she made her way across the room. The sheets fluttered in her wake, whispering to one another.

"Be careful, Pan," Herc said.

Duh.

"Meridiana?" she said. "Is that you?"

More soft words, and a sound that made her think of a tiger padding through the woods—big feet keeping time with her. Something snorted again, testing the air. There were five mirrors clustered in the corner, separate from the others. The largest one stood before several of various smaller sizes. It made Pan think of a mother shielding her children from something terrible.

. . . do not, or I will . . .

There and gone again, a distant voice on the wind. Pan reached the large mirror—it had to be eight feet tall and half that in width—and lifted the sheet.

Another Pan peered back, the dark glass making her look even more exhausted than she felt. Again, the reflection didn't completely show the truth, the room behind her flickering. She leaned in, saw that inside the mirror the walls and floor were teeming with spiders—great big fat ones that swarmed over her reflection, pushing between her lips, into her eyes. The other her smiled, sticking out a too-long tongue and using it to scoop a giant, hairy spider into her mouth.

Pan let go of the sheet, hearing the crunch of her reflection's teeth, a wet swallow. Then laughter, a childish giggle.

. . . not, never was one for . . .

"Charlie," said Pan. "Did Mammon say anything else about his family? Brothers, sisters. Were there four of them?"

"Five," he said. "But one was Ostheim."

Pan walked behind the spider mirror and looked at the others. The smallest sat to the side, maybe four feet tall beneath its sheet. They got bigger from left to right, the largest standing a couple inches taller than her. She went to that one first, peeking beneath the cover.

Another Pan stared back, then burst into flames—a conflagration so powerful that it scorched the glass. Pan could feel the heat of it against her face. She staggered back, bumping into the tall mirror behind her hard enough to make it rock. In the glass she watched herself blacken and twist, her skin popping as the fat beneath exploded, her eyeballs hissing as the moisture in them boiled.

No, she didn't quite say, dropping the sheet and putting her hands to her ears until the sound of sizzling flesh ebbed away.

She reached for the next mirror, her fingers shaking so much she almost couldn't grab the covering. She didn't want to look, but she did. Her face here was bloated beyond all recognition, her eyes so cloudy they could have belonged to a fish, her skin peeling off in strips. There was a mark around her throat that she couldn't figure out—not until she saw the figures swinging from the ceiling behind her reflection, dozens of them, hanging there like flies on a sticky strip.

They're not really there, she thought, but she looked back anyway. No hanged men behind her, just Charlie and Marlow creeping across the room. Charlie squinted into the glass and put a hand to his mouth.

"Dude . . ." was all he said.

. . . show you, no matter . . .

"You hear that?" she asked them when the whisper had faded. They both nodded.

"Mammon told me about his brother," said Charlie. "Ostheim strung him up, hung him."

"And one of them burned, right?" said Pan. Charlie nodded, turning three shades paler.

"Alive," he said.

Pan let the sheet drop over her own dead face, turning to the second-smallest mirror.

"Was Meridiana older or younger than Mammon?" she asked.

"No idea," said Charlie.

She took a deep, shuddering breath and lifted the sheet in front of her. The movement provoked a reaction from the back of the room, that same growl as before—something stalking them, something *warning* them.

Her face. Or at least part of it, a chunk ripped away. She could see her brain, flecked with chips of shattered skull, and when she put her hand there a bolt of pain lanced through her. Grunting, she tried to focus on the churning darkness behind her reflection. Something was moving, something fast, something snakelike.

It almost looked like . . .

A black, sinewy limb darted toward the glass, whipcracking against her reflection. Her head split near enough in two, blood and brain exploding. She let go of the sheet, falling back into Marlow. He held her, and she held him until she could swallow her heart back down into her chest.

. . . nearly there, not long . . .

"That's what happened to Mammon," said Marlow when she had let go. "Looked like Ostheim behind him."

"So she had three brothers," Pan said. "Not including Ostheim, that is. One burned, one hanged, one pulled to pieces."

"And that leaves her," said Marlow.

The last mirror. Pan smeared her sweaty palms on her pants, wondering what horror she would find here. When she lifted the sheet, though, there was nobody there—not her, or Charlie, or Marlow, just the room, lying empty.

Almost empty.

One mirror stood alone in the reflection, in the opposite corner. It wasn't particularly big, or particularly small, concealed with a dust sheet. Pan looked over her shoulder, searching the packed room until she saw the mirror that was inside the mirror.

"Hey, Herc," she said. "Go take the sheet off that one over there."

Herc grumbled his way across the room, saying, "This one?" When she nodded, he grabbed the sheet and pulled it away, squinting. He ran a hand over his stubble.

"Nothing here, except a handsome guy who needs a shave," he said.

Pan turned to the little mirror again. The dustcover in the reflection had gone, too, revealing the same skeletal frame and dark-dappled glass.

"Think that's the one?" Marlow asked.

. . . *is it? Is it the one?*

The whispers echoed around the room, like they were mocking her. She was about to reply when she saw something moving inside the reflected mirror—just a tiny flicker to start with, growing bigger and faster.

"More importantly," Marlow said, "how do we get inside it?"

The thing inside the mirror that was inside the mirror barreled forward, the whole room starting to shake with the force of it. Pan spun around, looking at the actual mirror, and at Herc standing next to it. Dust rained from the ceiling onto him and he waved it away, coughing.

"What?" he said when he saw her expression.

"Get away!" she screamed.

Too late.

The mirror next to Herc exploded outward, something bursting through in a hail of glass. Herc didn't even have time to scream before a pair of jaws clamped around his stomach. In a flash of marbled flesh and muscle and bone-yellow teeth, he was hauled inside the broken glass.

He was gone.

LAST STAND

"Herc!"

Marlow ran, colliding with Pan. Somehow he managed to keep his feet, both of them skidding to a halt next to the shattered mirror.

There was no glass left in that twisted frame, but the view was identical—the same room, the same shrouded mirrors. Herc was nowhere to be seen, but Marlow could hear the old guy screaming, the crunch of something toppling, the muffled growl of a demon.

"Herc!" Pan screamed. She pressed her head through the gap and Marlow grabbed her shoulder. She turned, shoving him away. "Don't you dare," she said.

The frame was shaking, something pushing its way out of the inner edge. The face mounted on the top opened its mouth, its jaw twisting in agony, those dead eyes rolling in their puckered sockets. Glass was growing inward, the sound of it setting Marlow's teeth on edge.

It was *repairing* itself.

"We have to move *now*," Pan said, and she didn't wait for a reply before throwing herself through the shrinking gap.

Here we go again, Marlow said. He took a hit on the inhaler, coughing the dust and fear from his lungs. Then he stepped after her.

It was like walking into a freezer, so cold it burned. He chased a cloud of his breath into the room beyond, wrapping his hands around his torso. Pan was to the left, running toward a thrashing pile of limbs that could only be Herc and the demon. The creature had Herc in its jaws still, shaking him like a dog with a rabbit. The old guy's Desert Eagle was halfway across the room.

Marlow stopped, frozen by fear. What the hell was he supposed to do against a demon?

Demons.

There were howls coming from outside the room, like a pack of wolves was out there. Behind him, the mirror was sealing up fast. Charlie threw himself in, then the French girl, Claire, stumbled through, then Truck was there, trying to squeeze his bulk through the jagged edge. He was too big, the glass tearing through his clothes, blood running thick.

"No!" he yelled. The glass looked like it was growing *through* him. If he didn't move one way or the other he was going to be cut clean in half.

"We'll open it again," Marlow said. "Get back, we'll find another way through."

Truck was still pushing and Marlow ran at him, shouldering him out of the gap. Truck staggered back like a wounded bear, clutching the wounds in his flank.

"We'll find another way," said Marlow.

"I could have gotten through," Truck said, pounding on the glass, on the frame. "Dammit, Marlow."

Jaime was there, too, pulling something from her pocket. It glinted in the light when she threw it through the basketball-sized gap and it clattered on the floor.

A dagger, the one she'd conjured demons with.

She opened her mouth, yelling something, but the last of the glass had grown over the open wound. It sealed like an airlock door, the pressure making Marlow's ears hurt. Jaime's words were completely silent, Truck's fists not making the slightest sound as he pounded on the glass. Both of them were slowing down, their movements creeping almost to a halt as if Marlow were watching a slow-motion replay.

No time to think about it. He turned, seeing Herc on the floor, the demon still tearing into him. Pan was throwing punches at it, Charlie running for the gun. Marlow scooped up the dagger and ran across the room. He studied it as he went, the iron blade etched with symbols. It was heavier than it had any right to be. There was no doubt it was something from deep inside the Engine; it gave off that same bone-numbing hum.

"Get off!" Herc roared, punching the demon in the side of its head. It didn't even seem to feel it, those jaws snapping shut around his torso again.

Gunshots, Charlie holding the Desert Eagle and popping off rounds. Two missed, thudding into the walls. The third glanced off the demon's shoulder.

The beast reared up, roaring, and Charlie shot it again. The round punched into its chest, knocking it back.

Pan had her hands under Herc's armpits, hauling him across the floor. The old guy was clutching his ribs, his face bloodless and etched with pain. The demon shrieked again. Every inch of it glistened like it had no skin, only thick cords of muscle. Its eyeless face sniffed at the air, that raw red throat ready to swallow them all whole.

Charlie fired again, a bullet ripping off a chunk of the demon's cheek. The demon charged at him like a tiger, jaws churning at the air. With a crunch of its powerful legs it was airborne, Charlie swearing as he dived to the side. The demon missed him, its claws gouging canyons in the wooden floor as it turned. It charged again, Charlie rolling in a panic, too slow to get up.

Marlow put his head down and ran, the blade glinting in his fist. The demon sensed him coming, blasting out a cry that stank of charcoal. Then it was on the move, bouldering toward him.

What the hell are you doing?

He skidded to a halt, tried to turn around. The demon thumped into him like a car, knocking him across the room. He rolled onto his back. Everything hurt.

"Help," he croaked, but the only thing to answer was the demon as it pounced. It was like looking into a cement mixer lined with metal shards, that mouth big enough to swallow him whole.

Marlow felt metal in his fist, knew he still held the knife. He thrust it forward, holding it upright. The demon was midleap and it seemed to know the blade was there, its body twisting to one side, another cry halfway up its throat.

But even the spawn of hell had to obey gravity. It thumped down on top of Marlow, the blade sinking into the soft, gristly flesh of its stomach. There was a sound like a wing being pulled off a roasted chicken, then the creature exploded like a bomb in a butcher's shop The force of it slammed Marlow's head against the floor and he sank into something black and cold.

"Hey, Marlow."

It could have been a million years or five seconds later that the words dragged him up. He snatched in a crackling breath, barely any oxygen there. Pan was crouched over him, drenched in blood. It dripped from her onto him, as cold as lake water.

The room was decorated with demon guts. Charlie was doubled over and spitting chunks from his mouth.

"Little warning next time, maybe?" Pan said, shaking a chunk of something wet and black from her hair.

"Oh, sure," he said. "No worries. Next time I'll send an e-mail, make sure everyone has time to grab an umbrella."

He tried to get up, falling onto his backside. Then Charlie was there, grabbing his wrist and pulling him to his feet. The whole world seemed to be moving and it took him a moment to understand he wasn't imagining it. There was a pulse of sound running through the space, everything shaking for a few seconds then falling quiet, shaking then quiet, over and over. It was a sound he'd heard before.

The sound of the Engine.

"Everyone alive?" said Herc, staggering up. He winced, clutching his side.

"Just about," said Pan. "You?"

"Body armor took the worst of it," he said. "Couple ribs broken maybe, but hell, I got plenty more where they came from."

"What is this place?" said Charlie, walking to the mirror they'd entered through. Truck and Jaime were still there, but now they were frozen solid—as still as a photograph. He tapped on the glass and the sound boomed like a bass drum.

Before anyone could answer, something thumped into the wall on the other side of the room. Marlow heard the fluttering of leathery wings, the snap of teeth. Something else was growling, the sound so low that Marlow couldn't pinpoint it. He gripped the knife in a sweaty fist.

"We should go," said Herc, limping across the room toward the passageway that sat there—identical to the one on the other side of the mirror.

Whatever was outside was busy tearing its way through to

get to them. Another demon was screaming above, plaster dust raining down as it tried to claw in through the ceiling. Herc was almost at the passageway when a shape appeared in it, a hulking mass of twisted flesh that was even bigger than the one they'd just killed. Its head scraped against the top of the door as it lumbered through, its eyeless face taking them all in.

Marlow retreated to Pan's side, Charlie joining them. Claire was pounding on the mirror with her tiny fists, trying to smash her way back to the real world. It might as well have been armored Plexiglas.

"Well," said Charlie, the pistol rattling in his hands. "It was nice knowing you all. Apart from you, Herc. You can be a bit of a dick."

"*Please,*" Pan said. The demon stalked into the room on six legs that might once have been human arms, big, hairy hands flexing at the ends of them. Its face was a nightmare of moving parts, jagged rows of teeth leading toward the black hole of its throat.

"Somehow I don't think *please* is going to cut it," said Marlow.

"*Please*, Meridiana," Pan said, louder now. The wall coughed splinters as another demonic face pressed through. "We need you. We need help."

Nothing, just the throbbing snarls of the demons. The big one in the passageway hissed at the one in the wall, feigning an attack like a hyena squabbling for food. A chunk of timber crashed from the ceiling as the third tunneled its way down.

The knife in Marlow's hand felt like a cocktail stick. Herc took the gun from Charlie and checked the mag.

"*Please,*" Pan said again. "We knew Mammon. We knew your brother. We're here to fight Ostheim, but we can't do it by ourselves. We can't."

The big demon started to run, the floor trembling with the force of it. If Meridiana was anywhere here then she didn't care about them. And why would she? She was safe here, she was hidden. And she'd lost everyone now.

"We know how to save him!" The words were out of Marlow's mouth before he even knew it, before he even understood them. "We know how to bring Mammon back. We can bring him back to you."

The room shuddered, a subsonic noise that made Marlow's bones shake. The demon stopped in its tracks, looking back like a dog that has heard a whistle. It snarled, then turned, bounding out of the room. The one in the wall disappeared just as fast, a sickly light pouring in through the hole it had made. The noise from the ceiling stopped, hooves drumming across the roof like thunder before fading.

Pan threw a look at Marlow, one part *nice move* to three parts *what the hell do we do now?* She knew better than to say it out loud, though. Instead, she ran across the room to the passageway.

Marlow followed, gagging on the rotting-flesh stench the demons had left behind. They walked into the front room of the shop—no mirrors in this version, just the same door, wide open.

Marlow hesitated. He felt like he was on a carnival ride, one of the haunted house ones where you ride a cart through dark rooms, where people jump out at you and animatronics howl with recorded laughter. There was always some fresh horror around the corner, but you could never turn back, you could never retrace your footsteps. You could only let yourself be ratcheted forward and hope that the next scare, whatever it was, didn't make you crap your shorts.

Or, in this case, gut you, eat you, then crap *you* out into *its* shorts.

Nobody wanted to walk through the door, and in the end it was Claire who bit the bullet.

"I just want it to be over," she said, sniffing as she went, still rubbing her stomach like she was about to be sick. Marlow wanted to be a gentleman, wanted to stop her so that he could check it was safe, but the mechanisms inside him had jammed. They started moving again only when she had turned around and looked back through the door.

"There is nothing here," she said, scratching her wrist. "No monsters."

Herc limped after her, then Pan. Marlow let Charlie go in front of him then stepped through. There was no Venetian street here, no cobbled road and chocolate-box houses. They were in a vaulted brick cellar, the walls slick with algae, puddles of water pooling around the fat columns that held up the ceiling. Candles were mounted on the walls, fluttering in a nonexistent wind. The shop they'd come out of sat alone in the huge space, slumped into itself like the last dude at a party. There were archways in all four walls, each leading into darkness.

"Eenie, meenie?" said Charlie.

Something growled from the arch behind them, a demon padding into sight. It put its head down, ready to charge, but another deep, almost imperceptible blast of sound brought it to heel. It thrashed in protest, snarling at them. Another demon appeared from the archway to the right—smaller, but with that same nightmare face. It staggered on three legs, its fourth just a ragged stump protruding from its shoulder.

"They're herding us," said Herc as the first demon lumbered closer, baring its teeth. He was right, the demons pushing them toward the archway to their left.

"Miney, mo it is," said Charlie. He walked toward the arch,

his sneakers scuffing on the uneven floor. Marlow followed. They all did. It wasn't like they had any say in the matter. More demons were swarming from the archways like rats, fighting among one another. The weird call that seemed to vibrate in the air was the only thing holding them back.

The archway led into a corridor, as cold and damp as a sewer. Luckily it was short, ending with another arch up ahead. Through it seeped more firelight and that same pulse that seemed to resonate in Marlow's soul. It had to be the Engine up there. Nothing else could make that sound, could it?

"It can't have brought us back to the Nest," said Pan. "No way."

"I hope not," said Charlie. "If we're back at the Engine, then Ostheim will be here, too."

Claire shuddered, backing up against the wall.

"In all my time in the Nest, I never saw a tunnel like this," said Herc. "Not to mention a shop standing in the middle of the basement. No, this is someplace new."

Behind them the demons pressed closer, spittle spraying from their open jaws. Meridiana might have had some control over them, but even the best-trained dog in the world cut loose when it smelled a free meal.

"Well," said Marlow. "One way to find out."

He stepped through the arch.

MERIDIANA

It was an Engine.

But not one made of springs and cogs; not one made from nuts and bolts and iron and steel; not one made from anything mechanical at all.

It was an Engine made of flesh.

It filled a cavern easily as big as the one beneath the Pigeon's Nest, looking less like the surface of an ocean and more like a coral reef. Pieces of skin and bone and muscle and hair spawned from every crevice in the rock, covering hundreds of stalagmites and stalactites. They glistened in the guttering torchlight, and Pan saw the pump of blood through veins, the slick throb of exposed organs.

There were faces, too, she saw.

No, not faces. *One* face, repeated a thousand times. A *million* maybe.

A woman's face, old enough for wrinkles but at the same time strangely youthful, like a kid made up to look like an old woman. She had high cheekbones, sharp enough to chisel rock, a thin nose. Her hair hung in lank, white-blond streaks, moist bald patches peeking out between them. Her eyes were white marbles flecked with oxblood twists, and they flicked fast from side to side in their sockets like they were trying to escape. The sound of it, of a million wet eyes sliding back and forth, was like heavy rain.

The same face, everywhere she looked.

And they all twisted around to look right back.

Mammon, they said together. Individually they were whispers, but collectively it was a hurricane roar. Pan slapped her hands to her head before her eardrums burst, waiting for it to fade away. Even then the sound rolled around the cavern, echoing into infinity.

"Meridiana," she said.

It was, and yet it couldn't be. Each head was connected to a body that had been unraveled and unspooled. Blood vessels hung in the air like crimson cobwebs, nerves had tunneled into the stone, bones had been fragmented into minuscule parts that clicked and whirred like clockwork. Each of the cadavers was intertwined with those around it so that it was impossible to see where one ended and the next began.

Come to me, said the faces, another shock wave of sound that she could feel against her skin. It stank of death and decay, of things long buried.

The demons had entered the cavern behind them, whining like nervous dogs. They snapped at their heels, driving them on. There was no path here that Pan could see, so she hopscotched from one patch of exposed skin to the next, trying to avoid the tender flesh and nerve clusters and brain in between. The heads all watched her go, pink tongues poking from those bloodless lips, white eyes blinking.

The ground rose ahead, as high as a desert dune. Pan struggled up it, grabbing hold of bone and hair to haul herself toward the top. If the Meridiana Engine minded, it showed no sign of it. It was only when Pan slipped and planted her foot into a pulsing mess of organs that the cavern came to life again, every single head snatching in a pained breath.

"Sorry," Pan said. The horror was a nest of squirming things inside her, so unreal that all she wanted to do was howl with laughter. She bit back the urge, knowing that if she lost it now then she would never leave this palace of flesh. She would lie here until the Engine grew over her like so much ivy.

Struggling for breath, she crested the dune. The cavern stretched as far as she could see, but directly beneath her was an island in the madness. It held a pool of dark water, and next to it a wooden cabin that belonged inside a fairy tale.

"Oh God," said Marlow as he hauled himself onto the top of the living dune. "Oh God, this is . . ." He couldn't finish, just pumped a shot of his inhaler into his mouth. He was covered in old, sticky blood, scraps of skin. Pan glanced down at herself and saw that she was the same. Strands of yellow hair had wrapped themselves around her fingers and her skin squirmed as she tried to brush them loose on her pants.

The faces around her seemed to find it amusing, a laugh rippling from one end of the cavern to the next. The closest heads had to crane themselves up to look at her and she had the urge to kick one like a ball, see how far it went. Once again that tide of insane panic boiled up inside her. She had to close her eyes and count to five before finding herself again.

Descending the other side of the dune was just as hard, gravity tugging at her, trying to make her miss her step. Halfway down her boot sank into a rib cage, the bones grinding against her like she was a wrench caught inside a motor. When she pulled free she heard the mechanical flesh choke into life again, whirring like gears.

Careful, came that thunderous whisper again. *We work hard, we do not want to break.*

266

She took her time, hearing Marlow, Charlie, Herc, and Claire all curse as they followed her down into the valley. The closer she got, the more she saw. The shack wasn't made of wood at all. It had walls of bone and a roof of skin stretched taut. The pool, too, wasn't made of water but of blood. A wide stone bay surrounded the liquid, with a channel cut into it that was stained rust-red. It still looked like something from a fairy tale, but one of the old ones, one of the ones they told to scare kids.

And like so many of those, this story had a witch.

She had the same face as all the others, but her body hadn't been cut open and laid out for all to see. She stood beside the pool, stooped and shaking, a filthy rag draped over her shoulders. Her skin was pink—*bright* pink, like she'd spent her life wading inside a vat of grape juice. Her hair, too, was crimson and clotted.

Pan skittered down past the last few cadavers. She didn't think she'd ever been so relieved to touch solid ground. Marlow thumped into her back, apologizing as he tried to brush the residue of the not-quite-dead from his clothes. Charlie and Herc clattered down after him like train cars, followed by Claire. The old woman was thirty yards away and she paid them no attention. She was moving erratically, sweeping from side to side across the stone, her hands held out. She waltzed— that's what she was doing, Pan realized, dancing with an invisible partner—up to the edge of the pool and dunked a bare toe in the thick water. A peal of noise shuddered across the cavern as all of the old woman's heads sighed.

Pan swallowed, her throat like sandpaper.

"Um . . . Hello?" she said, the quiet words falling at her feet. The woman didn't hear them. She was holding a knife in her hand, Pan saw, a sliver of silver that flashed as she moved. Meridiana bowed, then glided back across the stone bay.

There was a second woman there, Pan saw, another Meridiana—identical in every way, except this one was naked. Her wrinkled flesh hung around her like loose cloth, her eyes watching her double as she pirouetted gracefully.

"I fell asleep," said Marlow. "Right? I dozed off somewhere back there. Because this . . . this is, like, pure nightmare."

And if it hadn't been before, it was now. The dancing Meridiana swept forward like a kingfisher diving for a fish, her blade a silver beak. It sank into the neck of her doppelganger without the slightest sound, a spurt of ruby-colored blood sluicing outward. It gushed down the channel then flowed into the pool, sending out a web of ripples.

We must keep it full. The words came from Meridiana and all her heads.

"Oh God," said Pan.

Meridiana held her twin until she stopped twitching, then she laid her gently onto the floor. She flicked the knife, running it over her rags and examining the blade.

Those myriad faces inside the Engine all snatched in a breath then spoke together—*we lose one, we gain one, we keep it full.*

Only when the echo of their voices stopped booming across the cavern did Pan step forward. The word didn't want to come up her throat, clinging to her insides like a stubborn child. But she coughed it up.

"Meridiana?"

The woman looked over her shoulder, right at her. Every head did the same and she could feel the force of their stares as a physical pressure. Meridiana's body trembled, but that knife was rock steady, and it looked sharp enough to cut the universe in two. Pan stepped forward, her hands held high.

"We need your help. *Mammon* needs your help." She glanced

at Marlow and he shrugged, nodding for her to keep going. "He sent us here, he told us—"

Mammon, the million faces said as one. *He is lost to us. The traitorous one took him. He took all of them. Just us left, just us, from one, yes?*

It didn't make much sense but Pan nodded, walking steadily across the stone floor of the cavern. Meridiana was fifteen yards away now, close enough for Pan to see that her skin was so thin it was almost translucent. She looked like she could have been a thousand years old.

More laughter, grinding like an earthquake.

Older than that, child. We are older than that. Time forgets us here, a hundred thousand years of hiding and time could not find us.

She ducked down, using the blade to open up the corpse of her double. For a few seconds she tugged and hacked at the body, seeming to lose herself in it. Then she looked up, her rheumy eyes blinking at Pan as though she'd forgotten who she was. She sniffed at the air, and her heads did, too.

We smell him on you, child. Our brother, we smell his blood. Where is he?

"Ostheim killed him," Marlow blurted out from her side.

The heads opened their mouths and wailed, a wall of sound that crushed Pan, that might have broken her. It was Meridiana, though, who slapped her hands to her ears, almost stabbing herself with the knife.

Do not speak his name. Do not speak any of his names. Not even that one.

The moaning went on and on until Pan thought she could not bear it, that it would end her. Then it ebbed gently into silence. Meridiana worked at the corpse again, drawing out a long, sticky strand of something red.

"What the hell is she doing?" Charlie asked.

We are building, came the reply. *We ran from him, all the life-times of the world ago. We ran here, and time forgot us. We had no Engine, we had nothing. So we built one of our own. We built one from all of us.*

Pan looked at the wall of flesh that grew all around them. How many moving parts here? There had to be billions, fueled by the channels of blood that ran through it. This thing was not made of metal, but there was no denying it was an Engine. Just staring at it she could feel the cry of whoever lay there, behind the countless Meridianas, behind the gears and cogs and still-beating hearts. She could hear that awful cry of the devil.

We did not know where to start, but we began with ourselves. Each body is an engine that holds its soul, and does that not make it the most powerful machine in the universe? Seven billion billion billion atoms, sixty elements, organics and inorganics. There is a world inside us, there is the power of the stars inside us. Everything you could ever ask for. We only needed to harvest it.

With a single stroke she cut open the skin of the corpse's chest, rummaging inside with blood-slicked fingers.

There are one million, eight hundred and seventy-nine thousand, four hundred and nineteen of us here, child. And this is just the beginning. We have lived here for a hundred thousand years, in our pocket of broken time. We will live here for a hundred thousand more.

"No," said Claire. "It cannot be."

Pan glanced at her, the girl still clutching her stomach like she'd been stabbed. Then she turned back to Meridiana.

"But how . . ." Pan said. "How did you know how to do it?"

Because the Engine is inside me, child. My brothers and I—even him—we were born to it. It lived inside our blood. We were its guardians. We kept it safe. Our circle was a thing of beauty, a thing of kindness. We were just children, younger than you. And there is no force more formidable than a child.

"Yeah, there is," muttered Marlow. "Try a pissed-off spider-snake dude with a comb-over."

He was one of us, once, one of the Five. But he let the Engine corrupt him. He let it fill him with darkness. He tried to take it, but no one entity could ever possess a thing so powerful as the Engine. We fought him, and time ruptured. The Engine split itself in two in order to protect itself. The same infernal machine, but existing inside two separate times.

"But time can't do that," said Marlow. "It's impossible."

Impossible to comprehend, perhaps. But not impossible. Impossible is a human word, it means nothing to us, it means nothing to the Engine. Time and space are what we make of them. The universes are ours to mold.

Meridiana grabbed hold of something and wrenched hard, a pistol crack echoing across the water as a rib snapped free.

"Universes?" Pan said. She felt as if she was sinking into a dark lake, like the truth was drowning her.

Did you think there was only one? Meridiana laughed again, all of them laughed. *Child, you should know better. The first of us believed we were the only living souls. The first of you believed that their tiny pocket of civilization was all there was. How long ago was it that we were certain this planet was the center of everything, and that the sun and the stars revolved around us? Not long, child, not long. There are many universes, many planes of reality, each identical but each unique, and each connected to its brothers. Where else would the Engine have thought of the idea of splitting itself in two? The universe has duplicated itself many times, again and again, in order that it might repair itself if something should happen.*

"Something like what?" said Pan.

Something like him. *Every universe has its dark side. Every universe spawns something bad. It is the very nature of existence that sooner or later the rot sets in. The things that should not be. The things that seek to eat worlds, and devour souls. The very worst of them. You will always find them, child.*

"I don't understand," said Pan, the understatement of the year. "All of it, all of this, it doesn't make sense."

"Yeah," said Herc from behind her.

Pan glanced at him and he, too, might have been the living dead. Beside him stood Charlie, rubbing his eyes as if he'd just woken up; then Claire, the girl wearing a thousand-yard stare that looked as if it would never leave her.

"None of it makes sense," Herc continued, "and none of it needs to. All we need to know is how we kill him. How do we kill that freaking—"

He cannot be killed, said Meridiana, cutting him off. *He is too old, and too powerful. Now he has full control of the Engine—the whole Engine, reunited—and he will use it. The Engine was only ever built for one purpose.*

"To open the gates to hell," said Marlow.

There was a sound like applause as all of the faces shook from side to side.

It is true that the Engine can open a path through the void. It can connect all of the universes the way the stitches of a book connect all of its pages. But this was not its purpose. The Engine was designed to be a prison. It was designed to keep the very worst of them at bay.

"The very worst of who?" said Pan.

"The devil, right?" Marlow added, taking another shot of his inhaler.

Just another meaningless human word, Meridiana replied. *These evils are worse than any name you could conjure for them. They are furies that devour worlds. They are strangers who make a mockery* of man's body and mind. *They are gods, old and terrible. The Engine is the door that keeps them quiet, that keeps them still.*

"And what happens when he opens it?" Pan asked.

It ends.

Those two words hit her like a double tap to the chest from a .45, the loudest sound in the world.

"But you're about to tell us how we can stop it," said Herc. "Because Mammon wouldn't have sent us here if you didn't have something."

We have this, Meridiana said, gesturing with the blade at the landscape of life-turned-machine. *In our hundred thousand years alone we built this.*

"Wait, how can it have been so long?" said Charlie. "I thought it was only a hundred years?"

We hid from time. We hid, and we built.

Pan remembered the way Truck and Jaime had frozen on the other side of the mirror, as if time had no hold here.

Our Engine is not perfect, we have only just begun. But it works.

"We can use it to make a contract?" said Marlow.

Only some. And it is not stable. I cannot guarantee that your contract will hold up. It can give you powers, though. This Engine is testament to that. We use it to clone ourselves, to keep building.

"Why don't the demons come for you?" Pan asked. And again, the heads laughed together.

The demons of which you speak, they are human souls twisted beyond recognition. Our father was the architect of this machine, we are its children. Those creatures serve us.

"Right," said Pan, breathing out a long, slow breath. She clutched her head, hard. It felt like the only way to stop it splitting open, to stop her brains slopping out. "So we can throw ourselves into that puddle of blood, hope that we don't drown, hope that this crazy old woman's machine works and we can somehow make a contract, then go find Ost—*him*—and hope that whatever powers we have are enough to kick his fat ass, before coming back here and hoping that this nutjob can crack our contracts before we get dragged to hell."

And the thought of it was prison-dark, a metal cage around her soul. It just seemed so much, so impossible. How had she gotten here? A girl from Queens who'd once dreamed of owning a cake shop in the city, of an apartment in Brooklyn and a cat. How many wrong turns had she made for her to be walking into hell like this, on her own two feet?

"Or we sit it out here for a hundred thousand years," said Marlow, chewing his blood-caked knuckles. "I bet she doesn't even have an Xbox."

"Call them choices?" muttered Herc with a weary smile. He clapped a big hand on her shoulder, drawing her close. "I'm sorry, Pan," he said softly. "I really am. I never should have come to you."

"What?" she said, resting her head on his shoulder for a moment. "And left the world-saving to Marlow and Charlie? Yeah, right."

She stood straight, and when the world stopped spinning she nodded.

"Okay," she said. "Tell us what we have to do."

She was answered not by Meridiana, but by a retching sound behind her. She looked to see Claire there, doubled over and holding her stomach. She was sobbing, bile dribbling from her lips.

"I am sorry," Claire said.

"No big deal, kiddo," said Herc. "Don't blame you for chucking your guts in a place like this."

"No," she said. "I am *sorry*."

She puked hard, her whole body convulsing with the force

of it. Something fat and black dropped from her lips, wriggling like a giant slug. And suddenly the cavern was a hurricane of noise, every face screaming. Meridiana pointed a finger at Claire, her withered face a Halloween mask of terror. She pointed, and she screamed.

You brought him here.

"I didn't have a choice," said Claire, staggering back, her words almost lost in the storm. "He made me."

"Ostheim," said Pan.

And the black slug thing exploded.

KNOCK KNOCK

The world went from nightmare to chaos in a heartbeat, leaving Marlow reeling.

Whatever had just fallen from Claire's mouth was swelling fast, sprouting dozens of beetle-black limbs. They erupted from its flesh in every direction, pushing their way into the Engine, into the eyes and mouths of the faces there, and erupting from the backs of heads.

You brought him here! Meridiana and her faces howled. *You have ended us!*

"He made me!" the French girl cried.

It had to have happened back in the Nest, Marlow realized, when they'd left her upstairs. Claire stumbled, backing away on all fours like a crab. She wasn't quick enough, though, those obsidian tendrils worming over her, covering her. "No! You promised me! You promised you'd—"

Then she was gone.

"Move!" yelled Herc, driving them across the stone toward the pool of blood.

Meridiana opened her mouth and howled, a cry so deep that it was almost subsonic. It was answered by a distant scream, then another one. Two demons appeared on the crest of the hill, pausing for a second, then bounding down it. More followed, an avalanche of twisted forms glistening in the torch-light.

Destroy him, Meridiana ordered.

The slug thing was now car-sized, its sides bulging. Thick black cords stretched from it like rancid intestines, pouring poison into the Engine. Even as Marlow watched the organic mechanisms began to darken, the faces closest to the pool withering and shrinking, falling still.

Snarling, the first of the demons pounced. The slug thing saw the attack coming, pushing out a razor-tipped spike that skewered the beast in midair. It screamed, thrashing. The next was luckier, thumping into the side of the abomination and sinking its teeth into the oil-slick flesh. The side of the slug burst like a wormbag, black steaming water pouring out of it. But it was still growing, as big as a van now, bloated and awful. It sounded like the whole universe was screaming.

Meridiana was on the move, too, running across the bay.

Marlow held up his hands in defense, waiting for the attack, waiting for that silver blade to puncture his skin. She loomed over him, maybe eight feet tall. She loomed over all of them. She was so close that this time when she spoke, Marlow could hear her voice above its earthshaking chorus.

"You must be quick," she said. "Use our Engine before it is destroyed."

Jump into that lake of oily blood? It didn't seem like the best idea in the world. Marlow looked back to where the slug thing seethed with demons, dozens of them writhing on its back and sides, opening wounds in its skin. Spikes sliced upward from it, piercing the demons, holding them upright as they shivered and fell still. It was like a forest of staked, flayed men.

Maybe the pool wasn't so bad after all.

"What do we trade for?" said Pan. "There's nothing. Nothing can beat *that*."

"You cannot overpower him," she said. "But you can outsmart him. Trade for the knowledge of how to pass in between."

"What?" said Marlow. The noise behind him was like a raging battle between two armies. The slug thing was now thirty feet tall and just as wide, a bloated, cancerous mass whose tendrils pushed out into the Engine. Everything around it was graying, dying. Only a handful of demons were still alive to fight. And when they were gone, Pan knew, it would come for them.

"Trade for the vision," Meridiana said. "Trade for the ability to step out of time, to step behind and between the physics of the universe. It will let you open up a pocket of time. Just go. It is our blood. It will show you what to do."

"Time travel," said Marlow, thinking back to his first time in the Engine. "But that contract can't be broken. It's impossible."

"That word again," said Meridiana. "So human. So meaningless. Go, child. Go *now*. But only one, or you will both die."

She whirled around, her rags fluttering as she charged toward the beast. Meridiana called out again, the Engine seeming to come to life—those countless heads tugging pathetically at the stone they were fixed to like they meant to roll to her aid.

"You get any of that?" Marlow said, turning to the pool. The surface of the water was pocked with ripples, as if there was something alive in there. This body of liquid, like the one in the Engine, gave off absolutely no reflection. Leaning over it, he could not see an inch of what lay below.

"No, did you?" Pan asked.

Marlow shook his head, looking at her, then at Herc and Charlie. Behind them the slug was building-sized, devouring the Engine like a white blood cell consuming a virus. Its bloated form was spilling out across the stone, maybe forty feet away and gaining fast. It had no face of any kind but Marlow could sense Ostheim there. The rancid, acidic stench of him clawed its way into his sinuses.

It was either that or the pool.

"Talk about being caught between a giant, world-ending slug and a hard place," he said.

"Who's going?" Herc yelled.

"Me," said Pan without hesitation.

"Hang on," said Marlow, but Pan was already stepping over the edge. He grabbed her arm, trying to wrestle her back. Gravity already had her, pulling her in. He let go, arms wheeling, but it was too late. "No!"

And for the second time in his life, he found himself falling into a pool of pure evil.

He hit it without sound or feeling, as if the liquid had yawned open beneath him. There was just silence, and darkness, then suddenly the sensation of thick, warm blood against his face. He held his breath for as long as he could but he'd breathed out just before he fell and his lungs were empty. They screamed inside him, feeling like they were attempting to crack open his chest. And when he could bear it no more he opened his mouth and took a breath.

The coppery roar of blood filled him, choking him. And it was as if Meridiana had ridden the wave into his soul. He saw her, just a child, her and her brothers. Five of them, playing inside the heart of the Engine as if it were a jungle gym. He saw through the Engine, too, to a world of darkness, a world where *they* lived. She had been right. These were not monsters, they were gods, long forgotten and full of fury. Marlow could feel the horror of them, and it promised to wring every last drop of goodness from his soul. He saw a man inside a storm, a beast who seemed to inhale whole cities through the tornado of his mouth. He saw a man inside what looked like an orchard whose face was a shifting illusion of forms, whose blood turned children into monsters. There were so many of them, countless unspeakable things, but *it* towered above them all—the creature he had already seen in the Engine, that mountain of madness that watched through the countless clustered rot holes of its face.

He closed his eyes but still he saw it, as if the sheer brute force of it had burned through his eyelids. He panicked, the blood gushing down his throat, as solid inside his windpipe as an iron bar.

What is it you desire? the creature said, a voice that resonated inside his skull.

Visions flashed before him, visions of the world drowning in blood and fire, demons stalking the streets, visions of Pan and Charlie and his mom screaming to him as they rotted away. Then, when it was too much, when it felt like he could scream himself into oblivion, they vanished—as quickly and absolutely as if somebody had flicked a switch.

He stood on Staten Island, on the waterfront. The old neighborhood was an oasis of calm, just the sputter of an accelerating car, a distant honk, the ceaseless chatter from the birds and the lull of the water. Across the bay lay Manhattan, sparkling in the sun. The ferry was pulling away from the terminal, a chopper shadowing it.

"You all right, man?" said Charlie beside him.

Marlow turned, gulping like a fish out of water. His friend smiled at him. "You zoned out for a minute there."

"What?" Marlow asked.

"You went AWOL," Charlie said, kicking a stone into the grass. "Anyway, come on, let's head back. Got homework to do and PewDiePie to binge on. You stopping at mine?"

Marlow shook his head, feeling the wind in his hair, the sun on his skin. A gull wheeled overhead, crying out. It was all real, it was *so real*. If he just kept walking then he'd get back to his house, he'd go in through the front door and his mom would wrap her skinny arms around him, would smother him with kisses. Donovan would try to wrestle them both to the floor, the old dog's tail thumping. All he had to do was wish it.

All he had to do was ask.

No, he said. *No, no, no*.

"Please," said Charlie. A bead of blood leaked from his eye, winding down his cheek. More dropped from his nose, pattering on the asphalt. His face was wilting, the meat sliding off the bone. "Please, Marlow. Just take us home, just take us back."

"No!" Marlow's scream bubbled out of him and the scene erupted, fading into blood.

Another shape floated where Charlie had stood, a dark outline growing closer. Then Pan was there, her face grim with determination as she churned through the pool. She reached for him and they grabbed each other, sinking fast.

What is it you desire?

What had Meridiana said?

No more than one, or you will both die.

It was a little too late to worry about that so he focused on what she'd asked them to wish for. The ability to travel through time? To travel behind and between. It didn't make any sense but he said it anyway, beaming the thought out toward the creature that sat there. He could see Pan doing the same, her lips working silently.

I want to travel through time, I want to travel in between. I want to travel through time. I want to travel in between. He said it again and again, pushing every other thought away.

It is done, said the voice. *And the price is your soul.*

He kicked upward, Pan doing the same. It was too far, he wouldn't make it, he wouldn't—

He exploded from the surface of the pool, clawing in a shrieking breath. Pan was there next to him and they hugged desperately, pulling each other beneath the surface again. Marlow reached, found the lip of the pool. He spat out a mouthful of hot, salty blood. Somebody grabbed his arm but he couldn't see who through the mucus over his eyes—everything bloodred and blurry. The noise inside the cavern was unbelievable, a million-strong orchestra of screams.

"Come on!" said Herc, hauling him up. "We gotta go."

Marlow wiped his face on his hands until the world came into focus. No time had passed while they were in the pool, Meridiana still charging into battle, the slug thing ballooning ever-outward. Herc heaved Pan up and she vomited a stomachful of blood all over him.

"You're alive, then," Herc said matter-of-factly.

And Marlow was surprised, too, because Meridiana had told them the pool would hold only one.

Herc threw Pan's arm over his shoulders, guiding her around the edge of the pool. "We'll have to flank it," he roared.

Marlow staggered after them, Charlie at his side. He kept looking back expecting to see the freak twist its behemoth body around, to flop and roll after them. But whatever this thing was, it was mindless. It was a weapon, programmed to destroy Meridiana's creation. She hurled herself at it, her glinting blade unleashing a torrent of black fluid. Then Marlow tripped and turned to face front, using everything he had left to put one foot in front of the other.

Only when the slug thing was a hundred feet behind them did they cut to the side, scaling the dune of screaming faces. Marlow scrambled upward, not caring where he put his hands and feet, grabbing hold of strands of hair, of wet, open jaws, of ribs and bones and ropy sinews. The faces simply screamed, capable of nothing more than watching as their creator fought.

Marlow closed his eyes, trying to find his new powers in the confusion. He reached out with his mind, grabbing hold of time. But nothing happened.

"Not working," he said, his lungs like bagpipes. He reached for his inhaler and took a shot only to find another gout of blood on his tongue. The monster he'd known since childhood had its hands around his throat again, squeezing hard.

Pan and Herc had reached the summit of the living dune, vanishing over the top. Charlie offered Marlow a hand, hauling him up the last few feet. They ran down the other side together, hand in hand, tripping and slipping on the wet, roiling, screaming ground. The end of the cavern was a patch of darkness in the trembling reef and they ran for it. Herc ushered Pan through, then turned, waving Marlow and Charlie on.

Marlow careered through the gap, skidding to a halt and looking back. The slug thing was so big now that it could be seen over the top of the hill, those black tendrils flailing. Whatever Meridiana was doing, it wasn't working. If it carried on growing like that then it would soon fill the entire cavern.

He felt a hand on his shoulder. Pan was there, drenched in clotted blood.

"You feel anything?" she asked.

He shook his head.

"Maybe it didn't work," he said. "I mean, she *was* crazy."

"Worked for her," said Pan. "She cloned herself a million times. I'm definitely under contract, I feel like crap."

So did he, now that she'd mentioned it—the same deep, sapping ache of the Engine. All he wanted to do was sleep.

Not with that thing still growing behind him, though.

Herc was on the move again, leading them up the short passageway and back into the vaulted room. The lonely shop sat where they had left it, its red door still open. They sloshed through the puddles and stopped outside. A booming cry rolled through from the cavern, loud enough to shake dust from the ceiling.

"The mirrors, right?" said Charlie. "That has to be what she was talking about. Stepping through mirrors. I mean, it brought us here."

It made sense. Marlow followed Herc inside, the walls doing nothing to mute the noise from the cavern. They passed through the empty front room into the back. The sole mirror still stood there, Truck and Jaime frozen inside it. Pan put her fingers to the glass. Nothing. She thumped her fist against it, shunting the frame back a couple of inches. Still nothing. Screaming in frustration, she kicked out at the mirror and it toppled, hitting the floor with a thud.

"Hey, cool your heels," said Herc.

"It should work," she shouted back. "I don't get it."

A tear wound its way through the blood on her face, her body shaking like she was holding in an explosion. When Marlow walked toward her, though, she fired him a look that was more terrifying than the slug thing in the next room.

He held his hands up in surrender. "If it's not the mirror, then what?" he said. There was nothing else in the room, nothing else in the building. The hopelessness crept into his marrow, building in his chest. If they didn't find the answer soon then he was going to lose it again, like back in the stairwell in Paris, start tearing through the walls and the floor. He chewed on a knuckle, the pain helping him focus.

"There were more archways in the room outside," said Herc. "Three of 'em. There has to be a way out there."

"Why wouldn't she just tell us?" Pan said. "Stupid, crazy bitch. Why didn't she just tell us how to do it?"

She doubled back, retreating out of the building. Herc thumped into the door in his haste and it slammed into the wall, rebounding and swinging shut. Marlow grabbed it before it could close and felt a rush of grief pass through him, the sensation of stepping out of the sun and into the cold, damp shade of a mausoleum. When he let go of the door the feeling passed, and he'd taken a few more steps out into the vaulted cellar before it struck him. He looked back.

The shop had a red door. Faded, yes, the handle green with verdigris. But definitely red.

"Hey, guys, wait up."

Marlow took hold of it again, ignoring the bad vibes that ebbed from it. He swung it to and fro, not the slightest noise coming from those old hinges. The door was heavier than it looked and it seemed to move in his grip, pulling like a dog on its leash.

"Holy crap," said Pan. "That's a Red Door."

"An old one," said Herc. "Think it still works?"

"I think it will now," said Marlow, flexing his fingers. "I think this is exactly what Meridiana meant by stepping in between."

Because that's what the Red Doors did, wasn't it? They were tunnels through space and time.

But only if you had the power to use them.

Marlow pulled the door shut and it closed with the sound of a muffled explosion.

Pan had walked to his side and she reached out, placing her fingers against the peeling wood. "Knock knock," she said.

Marlow grabbed the handle and closed his eyes. He thought about the Red Door that led into the Nest. He thought about the corridor, the elevator. He could see it, in his mind's eye, like he was standing right there. Pan pressed her shoulder against his and he could feel the heat of her, feel her fast, shallow breaths.

"Who's there?" he said.

He turned the handle and opened the door.

IN THE BLOOD

The Red Door swung open into another world.

In front of Pan was the corridor she knew so well, but it was almost unrecognizable. The featureless concrete walls had been scorched black. Parts of the ceiling were now on the floor, and parts of the floor embedded in the ceiling.

None of the lights here worked but that didn't matter because there had to have been a thousand sparks hanging in the air, glowing like frozen fireflies. Even though the damage was unbelievable, the sight of home after being in Meridiana's cavern so long made her weak with nostalgia. She collapsed against the door frame, holding back the sobs that battered the inside of her throat.

"Holy crap," said Herc, leaning past her. "It worked. Kind of."

Had it? Pan couldn't even remember asking for the power to pass behind or in between or whatever Meridiana had told her to do. It was all just a blur. But there was no denying that they had stopped time. Pan could see motes of dust suspended there in front of her, like she was staring into a photograph. Despite the devastation that Herc's nuke had caused, it was utterly, utterly peaceful.

"That all the damage there is?" said Charlie, leaning past her. "From a nuke?"

"Yeah, but this is the Engine we're talking about," said Herc. "It's clever. I don't know for sure, but it might have channeled the force of the blast out into the Liminal."

Out into the bone tunnels that ran for a thousand miles beneath the city, the foundations of Paris. No wonder it had done so much damage.

"It's a bunker, right?" Herc went on. "They're designed to cope with stuff like this. Besides, it would take more than a nuke to take out the Engine and the Red Door."

"What about radiation?" Marlow asked, holding his hands in front of his crotch like it might make a difference. "That stuff is bad for you."

At this, Herc just shrugged.

"Least of our—"

He was cut off by a roar from the cavern behind. It rode in on a shock wave powerful enough to shatter the windows of the shop, shards of glass raining down. Pan shook them from her hair, glancing back to make sure the slug thing wasn't oozing its way after them. Herc hurried into the corridor of the Nest, grunting as he crossed the invisible boundary, that shortcut through the Liminal. He looked back at them from a few feet—and a few thousand miles—away.

"Anytime you like," he said, scattering sparks with a wave of his hand. They still didn't fall, just sailed through the air like they were in zero G.

Pan didn't move. Something wasn't right here. Marlow must have felt it, too, because he was chewing on his knuckles again, wearing a frown like a Klingon's.

"What?" she said.

"How did you guys open the Red Door before?" he asked. "Like, back before Ostheim had the Engines?"

"We had to crack it from the inside," said Pan. "Radioed in, got the okay from Ostheim. Why?"

"So he was the one who opened it? He programmed where it would take you?"

Pan nodded. It was another thing she'd never questioned, she realized—how was Ostheim able to program the door? And why could nobody else do it?

"But *I* opened it," Marlow said. "Remember? Back when I ran away from the Nest. I just went up the elevator and grabbed the handle and opened it, right into Budapest."

"So did I," said Charlie. "When Mammon was there I opened it for him."

They all looked at one another, the answer as clear as if it were etched into their foreheads.

"He opened it for us," said Marlow, and she saw in his face that awful understanding that he'd been played. He looked at Charlie. "He needed me to find you and Patrick because he knew I'd get you into the Engine, and you'd let in Mammon."

"And he knew that if he let Mammon inside, the Engines would be united and he'd be able to find them," said Charlie, shaking his head. "Man, that guy . . ."

And Pan suddenly understood what was wrong, why she didn't want to step through that door. Because what if that's exactly what Ostheim wanted them to do? He'd been one step ahead of them all this time. Hell, he'd been a *hundred* steps ahead of them. Every single thing they'd done so far had been part of his plan—even now, bringing Claire with them into Meridiana's hiding place. How stupid could they be? She'd been sitting right here, in this corridor, all the time they were fighting down in the Engine. She'd even admitted to seeing Ostheim. And they'd believed her when she'd said he walked right past her? He'd opened her up and put something rotten right in the heart of her, turned her into a weapon.

"Christ," she said, pressing her fingers against her eyes until she saw fireworks.

They'd led Ostheim right to Meridiana the same way they'd led him to Mammon. Talk about serving him his enemies on a silver platter. What if this was what Ostheim wanted them to do next? What if by allowing them back into the Engine he was putting the last few pieces of his plan in place? She racked her brains trying to work out what he could be thinking, but there was nothing up there. She just wasn't smart enough to figure it out.

Unless he was simply waiting down there for them, waiting to end them once and for all. Then there would be nothing at all left between him and the end of the world.

But this was Meridiana's gift to them, wasn't it? Going through the Red Door was her plan, not Ostheim's.

Besides, what other options did they have?

Another howl from behind them, as if the slug thing was agreeing with her. The volume in the cavern was definitely quieting. Meridiana's screams were growing weaker. How many of her clones had Ostheim's obscene biological weapon already slaughtered?

Maybe it's just easier to stay right here, she thought, the exhaustion solid lead in her veins. *Just sit down and let it come for you. Better that than trying to fight Ostheim.*

Better *anything* than trying to fight him.

"Come on," said Herc. "If he's down there, at least we'll go out fighting."

"Yeah," said Marlow. "Because that's *way* better than going out at a hundred years old on a private island while drinking piña coladas and getting jiggy with a supermodel."

"Getting *jiggy*?" said Charlie, managing a weak smile. "Who are you, the Fresh Prince of Bel-Air?"

Marlow waved it away, taking a deep breath then stepping over the threshold. Charlie was next, actually taking a run and throwing himself through. Marlow caught him on the other side before he could trip on the rubble there.

Pan glanced back once more. *Sorry*, she said—to Meridiana, to Claire, to everyone else she'd dragged into this sorry mess—then she walked through the Red Door. She could feel it unknitting her and then reassembling her on the other side. She pushed the door closed behind her, listening to the hammer fall of the bolts.

"Open it again," said Marlow.

She did, too weary to ask why. The cold breeze nearly blew her off her feet, nothing out there but snow and a distant mountain. It was tempting to step out into it, to lose herself in the blizzard, to let the wind scatter her like so much snow. But she didn't. Of course she didn't.

It was still a relief to know that the slug thing was now a long, long way away.

"Did you do that?" she asked Marlow. "The snow? Because I didn't."

"Not me," he said.

She closed the door again, more confused than ever. Herc was already weaving his way past piles of debris and beneath sagging sections of ceiling toward the elevator. The Nest was quiet, like the whole place was cocooned in polystyrene chips. She could feel the Engine, though, calling to her the same way it always did.

"Well, we're not hitching a ride for sure," Herc said. She saw that the elevator shaft was a mess, the cable a hangman's noose. Herc had already made his way to the access door, wrenching it open. The stairs beyond were damaged, but not so much that they couldn't be used. Some of the lights still worked, thankfully. Herc started down them two at a time but she followed at a slower pace. She just didn't have it in her to run.

"So," said Marlow, out of breath by the first corner. "What did Meridiana say? That we can open a passage into a pocket of time?"

"Yeah," said Charlie. "But she was also dismembering a cloned version of herself so she could use its intestines to build a machine to talk with the devil. I'd take her advice with a pinch of salt."

There was something else here, Pan thought. Something she couldn't quite put her finger on. Just a *feeling*, an imperceptible juddering in the air. The only thing she could even remotely compare it to was being in a car when you needed to change down a gear, the sensation that everything is about to stall.

They twisted around another corner and she flexed her hands. Why hadn't she asked Meridiana's Engine for something else? For some proper powers? There was a good chance she was going into battle with Ostheim right now, armed with nothing more than the power to step between, and she still didn't have a clue what that really meant.

She wasn't sure how many flights they'd descended before they reached the first level—the bullpen. Herc was already there, opening the reinforced door. There was nothing beyond him, just a landscape of ruin that was end-of-the-world bad. There was no floor, only a pit that stretched down through the other levels, so dark it could have been bottomless. The ceiling, too, had been blown away, car-sized chunks of it frozen midfall. From here, in the dark, Pan could have been standing in the porthole of a spaceship staring out into the void.

"Jesus," she said beneath her breath.

"You think it might have taken out the Engine, too?" said Charlie with a hopeful smile.

"More chance of Ostheim walking up here, giving us a box of chocolates, and apologizing for being such a pain in the ass," said Herc. "Come on."

They tramped down in silence, all of them waiting to see one of Ostheim's serpent limbs curl around the stairwell, his grinning maw wide enough to swallow them all whole. Pan's legs were just about ready to fall off by the time they dropped into the cold, damp tomb that marked the end of the line. Herc did the honors again, pulling open the access door into the vault. It looked just as she remembered it, untouched by the explosion.

The huge metal door was still open.

They crossed the room in a huddle—the others the only thing keeping Pan upright. They reached the door and Pan peered through it. The Engine sat there in perfect stillness, nothing like the last time she had been here. A section of it was still on fire—or at least it would have been, if time was moving—the smoke frozen into a wall that looked as solid as stone. Other parts had been crushed by building-sized pieces of the ceiling, stalactites rammed into the infernal mechanisms like javelins. The black pool was a wreck from the battle that had raged here, only half full.

There was no sign of Ostheim.

"Looks like it's feeling pretty sorry for itself," said Marlow, his words fluttering out into the vast space where they were swallowed whole.

"That's good," said Herc.

"It's weak," Pan added. She could feel the Engine's call, but it swam quietly in her veins. She scratched at her arms, her nails catching on the scars and scrapes there, so many she could have been a patchwork doll. "It doesn't roar."

It doesn't roar? Where had that come from, the words pinging out of some subconscious part of her.

"Where's Ostheim?" asked Charlie.

Nobody had an answer, but again there were words in her head.

"He's here, but not here," she said, saying them out loud.

"He is caught outside of time," Marlow added with a shrug. "He doesn't know we're inside the Engine."

Herc was eyeing them both suspiciously. "You wanna tell me how you know that?"

"No," said Pan, barging past him and walking down the steps. The Engine seemed to watch her, seemed to recoil from her. And it was right to be afraid, because it *was* weak. The damage that Charlie had done with his fire, plus the power of the nuke, had put a pretty big dent in its capabilities. And it couldn't even repair itself because Ostheim had brought both of the Engines together.

A smile broke out across her face before she could stop it. This wasn't part of Ostheim's plan. No way. This broken moment of time, right here and right now, was where they pulled the machine to pieces. There was absolutely nothing that he could do about it.

"I'm going to kill you," she told it as she stumbled onto the wreckage that had made up the platform. There were droplets of black water here, skewered by time as they tried to wriggle their way back into the pool. She stamped on them, seeing them explode into pieces that bobbed through the air. "I'm going to take you apart piece by piece," she said to the ocean of parts that lay before her. "And I'm going to take my time, you asshole. Hear me? I'm going to make it hurt."

Because that's what Meridiana had given them, she understood. She'd given them time. Six hundred and sixty-six hours, nearly twenty-eight days before the demons came for her.

It was enough.

"Where do we even start?" said Marlow.

She saw it in her mind's eye, a section of the Engine where something dark pulsed—something huge and knotted and grotesque. Marlow put a hand to his head as if he were a secret service agent listening to something through an earpiece. He turned to her, a ghost of a smile dancing on his lips.

"The middle," they said together.

They were going to rip out the Engine's cold, dead heart.

Something bubbled up inside her, something that seemed so alien, so weird, that it took her a moment to work out what it was.

Laughter.

She slapped a hand to her mouth hard enough to make her lips sting, but it still came. Marlow cocked his head, looking at her like she was suddenly wearing clown makeup.

"Pan's finally lost it," he said, and it just made her laugh harder, her stomach cramping with it. She doubled over, her tears flying. It didn't seem possible that after all this time—all those years fighting and killing and running—they were finally on the last straight. The end was in sight. Not that her end would be a pleasant one, of course. But at least it would be over. At least they would have *won*.

She felt a hand on her back, straightened to find Marlow right next to her. He was laughing, too, like it was contagious. And it was, wasn't it? Hope. It had to be the most contagious thing in the world. He pulled her close and she let him, pushing her head into his neck. She could feel the laughter in his chest, something good living there inside him. She wrapped her arms around his waist and he tightened his over her shoulders.

For an instant—just one, over in a single, stuttering heartbeat—she wondered where she might have been now if she'd never left home that night, if she'd never gone to Christoph's apartment. No cops, no Herc, no Engine. Where would she be now, and who with? Marlow? The two of them could have easily crossed paths somewhere in the city, and would they have looked twice at each other? Well, Marlow would have checked her out, no doubt, but would she seriously have considered him? He was immature, and too young, and annoying—like, *really* annoying. But he had a good heart. There was no doubt about that. He had a good heart, and right now it was pumping out choked, nasal guffaws that seemed utterly ridiculous in this place.

Pull yourself together, Pan, she told herself. But she still didn't let go, and then Charlie was there, wrapping them both in his arms.

"Come on, Herc," he said. "Don't be a wallflower."

Herc scooped them all up in a bear hug, his stubbled cheek scratching her face, his arms so strong she felt her back creak. It was painful, but when he finally let go she didn't want him to, she felt too light, ready to just float away. Herc stood back, his eyes glistening.

"You really are a bunch of soppy losers," he said, almost choking on the words. "Now come on, we gonna do this or what?"

She wasn't even sure how she knew what to do, but she did. She vaulted down from the lopsided edge of the crumbling platform, the Engine a forest of metal parts before her. How many pieces were there? Billions upon billions of them. They, too, were stuck in time but she could feel their vibrations, a soft buzz as they struggled to pull free.

She walked into it, the parts on either side of her as big as trees. Branches tipped with blades and cogs and levers and springs and switches—each smaller than the one it was attached to until they were too tiny for her to see. She felt them against her skin as she pushed into the darkness, like insect bites.

"Know where you're going?" said Marlow behind her.

"Yeah," she said. "I think so."

She could see it in her mind's eye as if she'd known it all her life. Out there, in the very heart of the Engine—an *actual* heart. She'd never seen it. She'd never even heard about it, but it was still there.

"Meridiana," she said, looking over her shoulder. "We must have, I don't know, soaked some of her up in that pool."

"Makes sense," said Marlow. "I swallowed about a gallon of that blood. So gross."

There were more memories there, Pan realized. She could almost see them—five kids running around the Engine like they were at recess, playing hide-and-seek right here in this forest of metal death, darting between the trees as they chased one another, curling up at night against the huge trunks as if they were Hansel and Gretel. The Engine didn't just accommodate them, it *guarded* them—the mechanism grinding to a halt every time one of the children came near, starting up again only when they were safely out of the way.

It guarded them like a parent with children.

"Father," she heard herself say, and she knew that the word hadn't come from her but from the spirit that now flowed in her veins. She put a hand to her mouth but words still spilled out of her. "Father, it's me, it's Meridiana."

"What did you say?" asked Marlow.

"Nothing," she said, then she lost control of her mouth, the words tumbling out. "I'm sorry, but it's the only way. It's the only way we can all go home. It has been too long, we have all suffered too much."

The Engine seemed to pull harder at its binds of time, like a captive mummified in duct tape. And Pan saw more images, a thing that might have been a man, or something much worse, cradling five babies in arms that had too many joints, feeding them with fingers that had too many segments. She could feel the sadness flowing from it, the grief of some vast and unbearable loss.

"I know you did this to save us." Meridiana spoke again from Pan's mouth. "But now it is time to save us again. Let us do this, and let us go."

A click from somewhere out in the Engine, a soft whir as if part of it had managed to break free. She could feel the rest of it tugging, thrashing, pulling at the force that held it. Even time was struggling to hold it still.

"We should get a move on," said Herc from somewhere behind her. "I don't like this."

Pan broke into a clearing the size of a classroom. Meridiana was inside her head, clearer now, pointing her to a path through the mechanism.

"You ever hear of there being a heart in the Engine?" she said, looking at Herc as he stepped out.

"A heart?" he said, shaking his head. "Like a real one? No, nothing like that. But there are parts of this thing we haven't even gotten close to yet. Why a heart? And whose heart?"

She didn't know, not for sure. But she saw it again, something so old, and so sad, that its heartache had broken the universe.

Father.

"We need supplies," she said. "It might take us days to even reach it. Herc, can you go back up and see if there's anything left—"

More movement from somewhere nearby. This time it was

a spark, flashing between two sections of the machine—there and gone before she could really see it. Another one blasted out of the ground two dozen yards away, crackling upward and releasing a pulse of thunder.

"Uh-oh," said Charlie. "If this thing comes back to life then we're hamburger—literally."

But there was no sign of anything else moving, just two more whipcracks of lightning that snapped overhead. She ducked beneath them, clapping her hands to her ears as the air rumbled.

It should have been one, said a voice in her head, in her blood. *Only one.*

She screamed as two bolts of lightning discharged from the mechanism beside her, turning the whole world white.

"What?" she yelled. "I don't—"

But she did, she *did* understand. It couldn't have been any clearer, especially when the stench of sulfur rolled through the air, searing its way up her nostrils like mustard gas, especially when a grating shriek clattered down from the shadowed ceiling, especially when the heat of the ground began to creep up through the soles of her sneakers.

It was suddenly, awfully, utterly clear.

Hell is a place you walk to on your own two feet.

How could they have been so stupid?

"Only one," she said, turning to Marlow.

"Only one what?"

Only one of you can enter the pool, Meridiana had said. *Or you will both die.*

"Only one contract," she said.

And Marlow barely had time to say "Oh" before the first demon tore free from the ceiling and crashed down beside them.

TO HELL

It almost crushed him, a thrashing, dog-sized creature that hit the floor, spitting shrapnel. It was made of stone but he could see the demon inside it, the same feral force of nature that they'd come face-to-face with in Meridiana's cavern. This one wasn't here to herd them, though.

It was here to take their souls.

"No!" roared Herc, his Desert Eagle out. He squeezed off two shots that punched holes in the demon's face. Before he could fire off a third the demon was running, charging into the old guy like he wasn't even there. Herc flew one way, the gun flew another, the demon accelerating fast.

There was another thud, then the grating shriek of metal on stone as something tried to claw its way through the Engine to get to them. There was no time to worry about it, the first demon almost on them, leaping up on stunted legs.

Marlow moved fast, throwing himself into Pan and sending them both sprawling. He felt the ground shudder as the demon landed behind them, heard Charlie shouting something to distract it.

Shouting wouldn't work. Nothing would stop the demons from collecting what they were owed.

"No!" Pan said as they scrambled to their feet. "It's not fair, we—"

She ducked to one side and Marlow to the other, the demon skidding in between them. Then Herc was there, holding a baseball-bat-sized piece of steel he'd taken from the Engine. He brought it down like a sledgehammer, the demon's head exploding into dust. He hit it again, and again, until it stopped squirming.

"This is your fault!" Pan yelled, her finger pointing at Marlow. "Why the hell did you jump in, too? It was supposed to be me, I was supposed to do it. This is your fault!"

It was. The Engine couldn't make two full contracts so it had forged two broken ones. They were disintegrating as they spoke.

Footsteps, galloping through the Engine, a guttural growl from close by. The terror was poison in Marlow's veins, seizing him up, slowing him down. He couldn't think straight.

"I didn't want you to go alone," he said, the words drowned out by the crash of a third demon falling from the ceiling. This one landed on its back, squirming like a beetle. It flipped onto its long, ungainly legs then turned its eyeless face toward Pan, stone teeth grinding.

"Run!" yelled Herc.

Marlow staggered into action, the ground so hot that his sneakers were melting. He ran, but what was the point? They would keep coming. They would drag his soul down through the molten earth, where it would scream and scream and—

"Marlow!"

He couldn't even tell who'd shouted his name. Something drove into him and he was airborne. He landed hard, his arm snapping as it broke his fall. The pain was like another nuclear weapon detonating inside his wrist and he clamped it to his chest, his cries too big to fit up his throat. He turned onto his back, the ground griddle-pan hot. But he wanted to see it coming. He didn't want to die screaming into the dirt.

The demon reared above him, its forelegs clubs of stone that were bigger than Marlow's head. They would crush him into jelly. Its crude face was split in two, nothing but teeth and a gaping hole for a throat. It grunted, coughing out a cloud of warm, slaughterhouse stench. It sniffed like a bull, testing the air, trying to work out who he was.

Then it leaped right over him.

What?

It was charging across the clearing, its feet cracking the stone floor. Through its legs Marlow could see Pan stumbling back in horror.

No.

He pushed himself up, Charlie there to help him. Another demon crawled up from the floor, this one half stone, half metal. It ran right for Pan. They *all* ran for her.

No.

He ran, too, but Charlie held him back, the pain in Marlow's arm flaring in Charlie's grip. Herc was halfway across the clearing, yelling Pan's name as he reloaded the pistol. He fired, but it was no good—the bullets ricocheting off stone and pinging into the Engine. Bullets were no good. They needed *powers.*

The demons converged on Pan, and through their hulking forms Marlow saw the moment she resigned herself.

No.

She turned her eyes to him, that same expression of grim death as when he'd first seen her in the parking lot back on

Staten Island—like she was about to head-butt her way through a brick wall. Back then he'd thought she was the most beautiful girl he'd ever seen, and nothing had changed. He reached out to her as if there wasn't twenty yards of hell between them. She just looked back, her fists balled, her eyes burning like that first time. Back then she'd looked like she could take on the whole world single-handed, and nothing had changed.

"Finish this," she said. The noise of the demons as they closed in was too loud to make her out, but he read the words on her lips. "Just finish it for me."

"No!" Marlow yelled, the word burning out of him, full of fury.

And he could have been back there, in the smoke and horror of that first fight. Back then the demon had plunged its scorpion tail through her heart, and nothing had changed. One of the demons lunged with a shining talon and it sank into Pan's chest, flicking out the other side in a fountain of blood. She gritted her teeth. She didn't scream. She just mouthed those words again.

Finish this.

"No!" Marlow shouted again.

The demon's other talon slid into the soft flesh of Pan's neck and her eyes went out like somebody had flicked a switch. Then she was gone, hidden behind the thrashing forms of the demons as they clubbed and stabbed and bit and tore and shrieked with delight. The ground was glowing now, as bright as the sun. The heat blasting off it was furnace-hot and Marlow had to stagger away, hands up to protect his face.

Back then, in the parking lot, Pan had come back to life— the Engine stitching her back together, making her whole.

Not this time.

He could hear her. Even though she was no longer alive,

even though she no longer had lungs or a throat or a mouth, Marlow could still hear her scream.

She would be screaming until the end of time.

He collapsed to his knees, howling into his hands.

Take it back take it back take it back.

There had to be something he could do, there *had to be*. He could fight them, or rewind time, or pick up the broken pieces of her and put her back together. There *had to be something*. But all he could do was kneel there, rocking back and forth, Pan's endless, breathless cry echoing through his skull as she was dragged into hell.

OPEN YOUR EYES

He didn't want to look, but he forced himself to, smudging away the tears until the world came back into focus. There was nothing left of Pan but a steaming smear of blood on the molten stone. But the demons still fought over her, trying to devour every last piece. Her scream had fallen silent, her soul already dragged to wherever it was the demons took them. Marlow could still hear it, though. He would hear that sound until the day he died.

He gagged, trying to get to his feet and falling hard. There was nothing left in him.

Herc was trying to approach the demons but the heat was too much. He dropped to his knees in the flickering haze, howling her name, his hands clawing at his head as if he was trying to tear it open, rip out the memories of the last few seconds.

Charlie stood beside Marlow, quiet, his jaw clenched.

"We don't have long," he said.

"What?" was all Marlow could think of to say. Pan was dead. She was *worse* than dead. Hell had her now, and all it had to offer was an eternity of suffering. Charlie held out a hand to him, glancing at the chaos where Pan had died. The demons seemed to be slowing, which was weird. Why weren't they coming for him, too?

"Come on," Charlie said. "You might have more time. We might be able to do this."

"Let them take me," Marlow said. "It doesn't matter anymore."

"It matters to me," said Charlie. "It matters to everyone else on this planet. You're the only one who can go out there, who can find whatever it was Meridiana showed you. You're the only one who can destroy the Engine."

"It's my fault," he said, the hatred boiling inside him. "I never should have gone in the pool. I should have waited. She died because of *me*."

"And don't let it be for nothing," said Charlie. "You heard her. Finish this. Finish it for her."

One of the demons had frozen completely, the other two pawing weakly at the ground. It was glowing less fiercely now as the passage to hell closed up, sealing Pan down there. They still showed no interest in Marlow.

Herc limped over, his feet scuffing on the broken floor. His skin was glowing from the heat, his forehead blistered. But it was his eyes that burned most fiercely. He looked at Marlow and in that second Marlow saw a world's worth of rage. Then he blinked, swallowing it back down.

"Charlie's right," he croaked. "This is our only shot. We've got to get to work."

Marlow took a deep, wheezing breath. Reaching into his pocket, he fired off a hit of his inhaler, the blockage shifting. Then he grabbed Charlie's hand. Standing up was the single hardest thing he had ever had to do, but he managed it. Charlie clung on to him, the only thing stopping him from falling.

But then maybe falling wasn't such a bad thing? Maybe he'd fall right through the cooling stone, right into hell. After all, hell couldn't be that bad, could it? Not with Pan there.

"I have to—" He broke into a coughing fit, the monster trying to wrap its fingers around his throat. He used his inhaler again, watching the second demon freeze into a sculpture of itself. "I have to go get her."

"No, you don't," said Herc.

"I mean it," he said. "She's down there. I can find her."

And he could, couldn't he? It was hell, but they didn't even know what that meant. If he'd learned anything in the last few weeks it was that in this world, nothing was as it seemed.

"Marlow," said Herc, planting his hands on Marlow's shoulders. He fixed him with those tired gray eyes. "Pan is gone. But you're still here. We can still end this. Nobody has ever come back."

"I can—"

"Think of your mom, Marlow."

But he couldn't. All he could see was Pan. All he could feel was her face pushed into his neck, her lips against his, the unmistakable, unforgettable smell of her.

He looked past Herc and Charlie. The last demon seemed to be recovering, its movements growing faster. It looked up from the ground, its stone snout sniffing at the air, searching for him. His heart gave a sudden concussive thump, one that made his whole body rattle. And he didn't know whether it was fear he felt, or something else.

Excitement.

Because he knew, without a shadow of a doubt, what he had to do.

"You finish it," he said, not taking his eyes from the demon.

"We can't," Herc growled. "Not without a contract."

"Dude," said Charlie. "We need you. Come on. Don't you dare run from this."

The demon opened its muzzle and roared. Herc and

307

Charlie twisted around, the three of them watching as it tugged its feet free from the setting stone.

"No," said Charlie.

"I'll take it," said Herc, hefting the iron bar. "Charlie, get to the armory, there are shotguns in there. I'll hold them back."

Marlow pushed past him.

"No," he said. "You won't. Let them take me, and I'll find her."

"Please, Marlow," said Charlie, a tear winding its way down from his eye, instantly evaporating. "After everything we've been through, don't do this. Don't run. All those times you left me, man. All those times you thought you'd do better by yourself. This isn't one of them. We can fight them."

A spark of lightning from somewhere out in the Engine. More demons on their way.

"You guys do what you can," said Marlow. "I've got my mission."

"She'll hate you," said Herc. "I can promise you that. You give yourself to the demons like this, without a fight, and even if you manage to find her, even if you make it through the pits of hell and somehow find her, she'll know what you did."

But it was Pan.

It was *Pan*.

"Remember Brianna," said Herc. "Nobody comes back, 'cept as a wormbag. You do that to her and she'll hate you for the rest of time."

But this was different. He wasn't using the Engine to bring her back, he was going down there himself.

It would work.

He took another step toward the demon and it stared at him with that eyeless face. Its stone muscles flexed, its snout flaring as it searched him, as it tried to work out what he was doing.

The last few days were a blur of terror and violence but there was still a voice inside him—not his, but Meridiana's. She rode inside his blood and through her eyes he saw a place of ruin and fire, a place that looked so alien, but also so familiar.

Somebody has come back. Her words whispered against the inside of his skull, as soft as spider legs. *Hell is just a word.*

"Hell is just a word," he repeated.

Someone grabbed his arm but he tugged himself loose, taking another step.

"Marlow," said Charlie.

"I'm sorry," Marlow said, looking back, and the way his friend's face fell broke his heart. He turned to Herc, and he wasn't sure if the words he spoke belonged to him or to Meridiana. "Nothing is what it seems."

Nobody replied. Charlie turned away, staring out into the Engine. Herc just watched, shaking his head.

"You always run," said Charlie.

But this time he was running for the right reason.

He was running in the right direction.

Another bolt of lightning tore across the ceiling, thunder echoing around the Engine. For some reason Marlow found himself thinking of his brother, in Afghanistan, throwing himself onto a roadside bomb. He'd given his life for a war, and Marlow was doing the same thing.

Was it worth it? Was it worth dying for?

He would have said yes.

Pan was worth dying for. She was worth going to hell for.

"I'll find her," Marlow said.

He closed his eyes, tuned out a distant, demonic scream, tuned out the stench of sulfur and the roar of something pulling itself from the stone, tuned out Charlie's sobs, Herc's final pleas. He tuned it all out, and saw only her—Pan leaning in to kiss him, Pan lying next to him in a hotel bed, Pan throwing herself into battle, and Pan the first time he'd seen her, held above the ground by a demon.

Do your worst, she had said, not the slightest trace of fear in her voice. Incredibly, the thought of it—of *her*—made him smile. It gave him strength.

"Do your worst," he echoed, speaking to the demons, to Ostheim, to hell itself.

And with that, he threw himself at the demon.

It charged and he felt its heat, for an instant, the sudden blast of choking sulfur against his skin. A roar of delight as it opened its bear-trap jaws to claim him, then—

It was like being loaded into a slingshot, a reverse bungee jump.

Something wrenched him out of the world, out of his body, a cold, hard grip on his soul. He screamed, it was the only thing he could think to do.

He burned down, through the ground and the dirt and the mud and the stone, subway fast, everything a blur. Then he plunged into a tunnel of fire, the whole world roaring as he was pulled through it. There were faces in the flames, demons that ran alongside him like a pack of wolves, howling their fury into the inferno. His fear was mindless, and absolute. There was nothing else left of him but terror.

He fell, and he fell, spinning now, so fast that he could feel the very essence of himself being pulled apart by centrifugal force, unwinding. The tunnel burned brighter, as if he was a bullet fired into the sun, but there was no pain, just the endless rush and roar of the fall.

There was something down there. He couldn't see it so much as sense it—something big, something *bad*. It vacuumed him in like he was a mote of dust, the universe shuddering with the force of it. And he could see it now, too, just a glimpse of something vast and dark, there and gone, there and gone, there and gone as he spun in relentless circles. It grew, impossibly big, impossibly fast, a black hole in reality. It opened beneath him and he punched into it, into that awful, soul-ending darkness.

And then there was nothing.

Nothing.

No light. No sound. No feeling.

Marlow wasn't sure if he was standing up or lying down or just floating. He couldn't even tell if his eyes were open or closed. The quiet was utterly unbroken. He could not hear his own pulse, or the rattle of his breath. It was almost *peaceful.*

If this was hell, it wasn't anywhere near as bad as everyone said. Where were the demons? Where was the fire?

He tried to move but couldn't, a bright, hot flare of panic burning through him. He wasn't even sure if he had a body *to* move. What if this *was* hell? Just the void, just *nothing.* What if he was buried alive here, left to rot for a million million years? The thought of it, of being alone here, drove what was left of his mind right to the brink of madness. What if—

"Marlow?"

The word was a whisper, right into his ear. He tried to turn his head, reached out for it with arms he didn't have. He wanted to laugh, wanted to cry, wanted to speak, but he could do nothing but listen, willing the voice to speak again. An eternity seemed to pass before it did.

"Marlow?"

Not a whisper this time but a voice, *Pan's* voice.

And she sounded *pissed.*

"Marlow," she said again. "You *idiot.*"

Pan? he tried to say.

"Marlow, just open your eyes," said Pan. "You're not going to believe this."

Open your eyes. The easiest thing in the world, the hardest thing in the world. *Just open your eyes, Marlow,* he told himself.

And he did.